THE ANTONIDES LEGACY I

THE ANTONIDES LEGACY I

Charlotte Murphy

Thanks for the love x

CMurphy

2020

Copyright © 2020 by Charlotte Murphy.
All rights reserved.
First Printing: 2018
ISBN 979-866-387-1600

DEDICATION

This book is dedicated to the seventeen year old me who never thought she would finish it.

Contents

Mortania & The Known World ix
Prologue 1
One Of A Kind 9
Relationships 18
The Lady 31
Sins Of The Father 40
The Aftermath Of War 46
The Redeemer 55
A Helping Hand 62
Acceptance 69
Rites Of Passage 78
Surrounded By Enemies 85
The Prophecy 93
Ascension 98
Abuse Of Power 106
Heir To The Throne 117
Birthright 126
Follow Your Heart 134
Do What Must Be Done 141
Allegiances 153
Dreston City 164
The City Watch 178
Vigilantes 188
Rayne 198
A Mother's Love 208
Will And Control 214
To Do What Is Right 225
Hiding In Plain Sight 233
Thea's Point 244
The Final Gathering 256
Prisoner 265

Allies 277
Enemies 283
Final Destination 291
Pronunciation Guide 293

MORTANIA & THE KNOWN WORLD

PROLOGUE

MORTANIA
226 B.E.

The sky was an infinite sheet of star dotted darkness watching over the various creations below. So far from home and the lights of her village, Thea Antonides could wonder at the countless stars shining brightly above her. It was then she took her eyes away from their pervasive glow, and pondered exactly how far she was from home?

Then, as quickly as the thought had come, it left her completely.

She had no time to think about such trivial things

She had been walking for hours but the unwavering feeling to continue overwhelmed her; she knew what she sought was too important to give up.

Without further question, Thea Antonides looked ahead at the shining ball of light that waited patiently for her and marched forward.

The light had woken her, how long ago and how many times before she could no longer remember.

She had seen it countless times in her dreams but only on this night; the eve of her eighteenth birthday; had it appeared into her reality.

Where it was usually a constant light, shining steadily, it had suddenly begun to blink, sparking her curiosity.

So, obediently Thea got out of her bed, covered her nightdress with a woolen shawl and stepped out of her house into the dark of night.

Thea continued her walk across flat desolate ground before she realised with a certainty that she was heading toward The Forest.

Everyone within a thousand miles of her village knew they should never enter on pain of death.

The elders told stories of young men who had entered The Forest on foolish acts of bravery and never returned. It was said that fear made the trees grow strong there; that death kept them stronger, through old traditions she had yet to witness.

Somewhere, in the back of her mind she knew she should be afraid, but here, with her light guiding her she also knew she had to carry on; to enter The Forest.

Thea hesitated, everything simultaneously holding her back and pushing her forward, but the light brightened unexpectedly, revealing a small opening among the cluster of trees.

The light lingered there, commanding her to proceed and so, with a deep breath Thea obeyed.

As she entered The Forest, the light gathered speed and flew away from her, forcing her into a run to keep up.

She stumbled through the low hanging and overlapping branches, worried she would crash into one too heavy to push aside. She was suddenly very aware of her bare feet, broken twigs, fallen leaves and dirt squashed beneath them and cutting into her skin. Thea ran until her legs threatened to give way, until the light began to slow down and the distinct mouth of a cave reared into view.

Her cut and bruised feet momentarily forgotten Thea approached the mouth of the cave, desperate to get inside.

She walked forward without hesitation, her light guiding her unfailingly as the entrance was swallowed up by the impending abyss.

The Antonides Legacy I

She continued on, fearless of what was in the surrounding darkness until the light came to a stop.

For a few moments, nothing happened; the light simply hovered a few feet above the ground until it began to enlarge.

As it got larger, it rose into the air and got brighter, so bright she could no longer look directly at it.

Thea shielded her eyes from the glare and when the orange tint from the back of her eyelids began to dim, she opened her eyes.

The now enormous sphere of light had ascended so high; it was casting light over what she could now see was an immeasurable underground chamber.

Overwhelmed by the scale of the place, Thea finally noticed intricate markings on the surrounding walls. Taking a few steps to her right, she traced her fingers delicately over the fading markings and faint words seemed to seep into her mind:

The Great House will deliver a child,
To remake the world once more.
Lines of magic chosen,
For the truest power to be born.
To Make the strength needed,
To balance the world of Men.
Beasts of fire will soar the skies,
Purely once again.

***

When Thea finally emerged from inside the cave, the sun blazed high in the sky so she allowed her eyes to adjust to the sunlight. She heard birds chirping loudly through the surrounding trees, calling to their companions; singing their songs of the morning. She looked up to where even through the trees overhead, the warmth of the sun washed over her.

She turned her attention back to the cave, to find…nothing.

Nothing but The Forest for miles around her in every direction.

It was gone.

All evidence of what she had learned had just disappeared.

Thea's shoulders slumped but she turned once more and where The Forest had been only moments before, was now nothing but dry measureless dirt lands as far as the eye could see.

Her light, the cave; everything was gone and so was the knowledge she had discovered inside. Knowledge that she had to deliver and quickly.

Thea began to walk, to where, she didn't know but she had to find her way home; back to her village and her family.

In the second it had taken to think of her family, Thea felt a tug in her belly and closed her eyes against the nauseous feeling that followed. When she opened her eyes, her hand to her head, there in front of her was a river.

The Chylar River she realised, that ran along the edge of her seaside village, Tirnum.

Unsure of how she had got there, Thea approached the riverbank and looking upstream, saw a small cluster of what looked like people. Relieved, she hurried towards them. The Chylar meandered around the small coastal village but was not altogether wide or deep.

The closer she got, Thea could now see Tirnum. She spied a group of women washing clothes and talking amongst themselves on the other side of the riverbank. Little children frolicked in the water while their mothers worked, screeching in delight of the games they were playing.

The Antonides Legacy I

Thea smiled as she looked back to the river, and for the first time she noticed her reflection in the water.

Thea's eyes widened in surprise as she dropped to her knees and peered at herself in the water. Her hair, normally straight, was now a mass of intense black curls. Her skin seemed to glow golden, her eyebrows were perfectly arched and her eyes; although still the intense sea green they always were, now had a ring of blue... *flame?*

The water wasn't clear enough, but Thea could not mistake that there was *fire* circling her eyes.

She stretched her hands out in front of her, where instantly, they erupted into blue flame that while looked dangerous did not hurt her.

Thea fell back onto the bank of the river, astonished, trying to catch her breath but even as she tried to calm herself down, she knew she would be okay.

She took a long deep breath and listened to the voice inside her. The voice that had told her to follow the ball of light, to enter the cave and that the markings on the cave wall were her destiny.

She would not be afraid of this.

Thea watched as her feet were suddenly engulfed in flame and slowly crept up her body until she was entirely on fire.

She stood as the blue flames billowed around her and with a clear thought, they subsided. She held her hand out and once again, with only a thought, ignited it then extinguished it.

This was what she had been called for, this... *power.*

Her light had given her this she realised, this wonderful gift.

Thea looked to the riverbed in front of her and with a wave of her arm over the water, it began to part.

Fish suddenly out of water, flopped about her feet as she stepped into the now clear riverbed. As she passed the sea life at her feet, the water gathered behind her again, allowing them to swim away. She reached the opposite bank with her bare feet somehow dry and free of the mud from the riverbed.

When she touched the mossy ground on the other bank, the last of the water crashed together and the river was as it was.

Thea arrived in Tirnum in minutes and after passing wide eyed villagers, she finally came upon her mother.

Freya Antonides dropped the fruit basket she carried and fell to her knees, weeping with what seemed to be both relief and adulation.

Thea stepped towards her mother and reached out her hands but Freya would not take them,

"Mother...do not be afraid. Our family have been chosen."

Freya looked up into the blue flames embedded in her daughter's eyes as tears flowed down her aged cheeks.

"Chosen for what?" she whispered staring at her child.

"We have been chosen to return magic to the world."

***

THE WIDE, MORTANIA
1000 A.E.

"Mortania will never be like it once was Curian, you cannot win!"

"You are a fool Alexander, I've already won!"

Curian Greybold swung his broadsword high, his eyes never leaving the man who lay bleeding on the ground beneath him. He brought his sword crashing down into his throat and the superb Agmantian forged steel seared through his neck like silk.

The Antonides Legacy I

Curian watched as King Alexander XII – now the last Samai monarch – took his last choked breath, his blood gurgling against the metal lodged in his throat. The intense blue flames died from around his bright green eyes; leaving him staring out into the reaches of death.

With a heavy and laboured breath, Curian pulled his sword from Alexander's body but lost his grip almost instantly when the ground began to quake beneath him.

He looked around the battlefield at fallen soldiers from both royal and rebel armies. Lifeless mounds that were once great war horses lay scattered on the shaking and distressed ground.

The usurper surveyed his work then turned back to look down at Alexander's lifeless and wide staring eyes. Curian looked away, terrified of the emotion that suddenly crept up on him.

His eyes were forced open again though, when a bright light speared across his eyelids.

Curian watched in amazement as the king's body became aglow with a bright blue light. It gathered from all over his body into the centre of his chest, where his armour became transparent. The blue light was now visible where his heart lay in his chest and formed into a small white orb.

The light passed through Alexander's breast plate and hovered there before suddenly turning black.

It slammed into Curian's chest, right through his own breastplate, crashing him to the ground with his chest heaving before he blacked out.

Curian Greybold regained consciousness moments later, still laying on the battlefield with the beaten faces of his soldiers looking down at him.

"My lord, you're awake. He's awake!"

Curian looked to the different faces looking down at him before trying to stand up. As he got to his feet, he noticed with astonishment that he was engulfed in black flame.

He looked over his hands and legs, and down at his body as he cackled with sheer joy. This was more than he had bargained for.

"Yes," he said with a satisfied smile. "Your king is awake."

He allowed the flame to subside with only a thought and picked at the debris on his armour. The steel had served him better than Alexander at any rate.

"What of the Queen?" Curian asked quickly, "What of Rowan?"

Ignatius Rarno, his right hand stepped forward and cleared his throat before answering,

"There is no sign of Queen Rowan or the child lord. We have a hundred men still scouring the castle and the city." Curian swore viciously before rolling his eyes in obvious annoyance.

"Do you not think in the midst of a battle our dear Queen Rowan would not have *fled* the city?" Rarno said nothing. "Send our fastest men to all corners of the kingdom to find her and the child Rarno. I want her and Alexander's heir dead by morning."

ONE OF A KIND

REMORA, MORTANIA
1017 A.E.

Another nightmare shocked Trista Freitz out of her already restless sleep.

She sat up, breathing heavily and brought her knees up to her chest trying to calm the thunderous beating inside her chest.

Tendrils of dark hair clung to her forehead, her face slick with sweat. She rocked and shook her head trying to dislodge the recurring images from her mind.

It was the same thing over again; a clap of thunder rolled above her and a dark presence loomed in front of her. The woman, whose face she could never see, would go to attack her with a sword. Before the strike could connect; Trista's arm would rise and block the blow.

On connection, a flash of blinding white light would erupt, obscuring her vision and knocking her to the ground.

As her vision returned, she would look up and see the woman with the sword raised above her head, ready to drive into her. As the woman was about to take the deadly strike, she woke up.

While the nightmare played in her mind there was always a faint white light by her side.

It never did anything, but Trista could always see the small orb of light and for the few moments her eyes connected with it, she felt safe.

What troubled Trista most, despite the violence of her dream, there was something almost familiar about it.

She had given up trying to figure out why she felt as if she had been on that hillside before and more importantly, why she had an insatiable urge to go back.

There was something about her nightmare that called to her because no matter how she tried to deny it, Trista had always felt that some part of her was missing.

There was a constant yearning inside her that she couldn't shake, and the nightmare only made it worse.

It had got so intense she'd even questioned her parents about it, but nothing they said had put her mind at ease. Their answers were guarded somehow and she knew they were lying to her but about what or why, she didn't know.

Slowly she stopped rocking and looked towards her window where sunlight began to creep up from behind the curtain, pushing the shadows away.

When in darkness and now the dim light of dawn, Trista's room was cold. She uncurled her legs to reach for the shawl at the end of her bed, wrapped it around herself and left her room to head downstairs.

Trista's mother, Gwendolyn Freitz was always awake incredibly early, there never being a time Trista could remember being awake before her. She was a simple woman who found pleasure in looking after her small family in all the ways she was permitted.

"Good morning Mother," Trista greeted as Gwendolyn turned her attention from her cooking. She had a long braid of chestnut brown hair, streaked with a few grey hairs trailing down her back, ever the modest wife. Her brown wool, long sleeved and high necked dress fell to the floor, covering humble brown shoes; the standard attire for any respectable wife of Remora.

"Good morning Trista. Your bath is ready,"

The Antonides Legacy I

Trista could never understand why her mother chose to share this information with her when it was always the same. Gwendolyn rose early to heat water for Trista and her father's baths in the outside washhouse. While she left the water steaming, she would begin to cook breakfast.

Everything was always the same in their household.

Everything was always the same in their town.

Trista may not have been much of a traveller in her seventeen going on eighteen years, but she knew when a town like Remora was on the periphery of what remained to be acknowledged as fun.

"Where is Father?" she asked for something to say; knowing exactly where her father was. He was in the same place he always was, doing the exact same things he always did.

The predictability of their lives was stifling.

"He's at The Grange with Lord Remora this morning." Trista's eyebrows rose at the change in her father's routine. He should be at the Town Hall, not the home of their towns leader. She nodded before she grabbed a bar of soap from the pantry and turned to leave out the backdoor.

Out in the washroom, Trista undressed and stepped into the large metal drum of cooling water that was waiting for her and submerged herself up to her neck. The warmth felt wonderful against her skin as she fished the bar of soap out of the water and began to lather herself.

As an intoxicating scent of lavender and honey filled the air, Trista looked down at her skin wondering not for the first time, at its difference to everyone around her.

Growing up in such a small town, she had always known she was different. Although there were various races scattered throughout the kingdom and of course the native countries they hailed from; most of the Remoran townsmen and women were Man. Where the males and females of Man were pale with predominantly clear skin, Trista had skin like rich golden honey. She had never met anyone with the same complexion as her but then, she had never left Remora.

Travellers had entered their town on their way into the Remoran mountains beyond, and she had seen dark skinned men and pale men of different shapes and sizes, but no one ever like her.

Another obvious difference was Trista's hair, that was considerably different in length, texture and most importantly colour. Few people in Remora or any other person she had met passing through the town had hair that wasn't golden like the sun, deep rooted like tree bark or red like fire. Trista on the other hand had hair the colour of a starless night, long, thick and straight that streamed behind her in ebony glory. When the sun shone hard and bright in the summer, her skin tanned and glowed while the rest of the town flushed red.

Her eyes were a whole other case as Trista's were strikingly green, where everyone else's remained blue or brown. These differences in her appearance along with being quite tall for her age with full lips and long dark fan like eyelashes, had made her an outsider with the other children.

Trista smiled as the memory of one specific child came to mind. A child who would always include her in his games and never let her feel alone. Thorn; son of Fabias and Avriel; Lord and Lady of Remora had never made her feel left out. She couldn't help but wonder if it was because his mother had green eyes but hoped that maybe it was something more. She moved the thought from her mind with a smile and continued to get ready.

Finally washed and changed into a light cotton dress of dark blue, her long hair tied back in a messy ponytail, Trista walked back to the house. She had cropped the hem of most of her dresses to just above her ankles so she could have a little more freedom then the restrictive and downright ugly dresses her mother insist she wear. The dress fit comfortably against her shapely figure, accentuating her small waist and chest.

Trista opened the back door and sat at the kitchen table where her mother set out a bowl of thick steaming porridge with a slice of still warm bread on the side.

"You spend too much time in that tub Trista." Her mother scolded almost immediately. "There's too much to do around here without you wasting away in there all morning!"

"I thought cleanliness was next to Godsliness Mother?" Trista replied dipping some bread into her creamy porridge.

"So it is but laziness can be the root of most mishaps" Trista rolled her eyes as she laughed,

"You just made that up!" Gwendolyn ignored her as she finally sat down across from Trista with her own bowl of porridge. Her mother was like that, always looking after herself last.

"Have you thought about what you want for your birthday?" Trista sighed.

It was her eighteenth birthday in two-week's time and she had no clue what she wanted.

What she did know, was that her time as a bachelorette was running out. Once she turned eighteen her parents would expect her to get married. She knew it was already a disappointment that she hadn't at least been betrothed since she was fourteen but Trista was in no rush to marry. She believed wholeheartedly that love took time and in her situation, it just seemed to be taking longer than most.

"No…I haven't thought about it. I have to get to Selection."

Trista rushed down the rest of her food, not in the mood to follow that line of conversation and ran up the stairs back to her bedroom. Once there she picked up her thick shawl to drape over her shoulders and ran back downstairs, kissed her mother goodbye and out of the house.

Selection was one of the few things that the young women of Remora could do without the assistance or guard of a man that was not their father, brother, fiancé or husband. It was a concept arranged by Lady Avriel, as wife of the town leader, to get young women involved in certain aspects of running the town and playing their part in the production of the kingdom. Young women made clothes, cooked meals, made instruments and even weaponry in some cases. Women were entrusted to feather arrows and attach already shaped and sharpened arrowheads to arrows and blades to axes. For many of the girls that were confined to their homes within the domestic capacity, it was a rare occasion to group together for something more interesting than preparing the evening meal.

Trista hoped to be placed amongst the weaponry group this time as she had tried her hand at everything else. She wanted to try a lot of things that her parents were less then excited about, including her desire to get a more formal education.

She wanted to learn everything there was to learn, about the world around her and beyond. She wanted to learn about the different races she saw so few of and the lands they had come from; about the history of their own lands and the people who had shaped their kingdom.

She wanted to know more about the world than cooking, cleaning and raising babies. Her parents however, refused to understand that she just wanted more out of life. They continued to try and mould her into the dutiful daughter and wife-to-be for any one of the many pompous, self-righteous young men that viewed women as nothing more than their property. She refused to be a part of that mould and was desperate to find a way out.

Trista walked the narrow-weathered path from her small secluded home in the woods to the town square. At the far end stood the Town Hall where all the Councilman including her father and other high-ranking officials in town conducted their business and where Selection would be held.

As she emerged into the town square, passing the main tavern on the corner, that also housed the brothel if anyone was interested, she made her way toward the Town Hall.

The square and the surrounding streets were busy with market stalls and their vendors selling their wares. The familiar Remora fountain of their town's patriarch stood in the middle of the square with people and vehicle traffic bustling beneath him.

Despite its seclusion from the rest of the kingdom, Remora was as busy as any town or inner city. There was constant trade of the marble and wood from the Remoran Mountains as well as the spices and materials from throughout the kingdom that had to reach Remora. They saw few sailors of course, but travelling merchants were frequent as well as old women who claimed to have abilities that could help with any manner of ailments from infertility to curing blindness.

Trista smiled and nodded at the few people that showed her the courtesy but as she stepped into a crossing, a loud crash caught her attention.

Turning, Trista saw a horse galloping down one of the steep mountain trails that flowed through the forest that lead out of Remora.

The horse had a large cart harnessed to it but no rider and was heading directly into the square, having crashed into a stall of apples that lay splintered across the ground.

Trista saw the rider chasing after the horse frantically, screaming for someone to help. Stepping back to move to safety, Trista spotted a young child toddle into the path the horse was about to cross. Her eyes shot to the horse than back to the child in horror.

Just as the child stepped directly into the road, the mother who had been engaged in some apparently important conversation, turned and screamed out in panic as the horse continued toward them out of control.

Instinctively, Trista ran toward the child, stopped in front of it and held out her palm toward the oncoming horse,

"STOP!"

Trista closed her eyes as her chest jolted forward and her heartbeat slowed down, making her feel incredibly weak.

She opened her eyes and was startled as she stood inches from the flared nostrils of the feral horse. She jumped back, fearful that she would be crushed but realised that the horse was completely still. It stood immobilised in the position to continue its gallop.

"What in the world…?"

Trista, completely amazed looked around and saw that not only the horse was still but the entire town square.

Every single person was frozen in position; the mother of the baby was mid scream, children who hadn't noticed the commotion were playing on the side of the road, and merchants were captured in mid sale with customers.

Trista spun around in astonishment and fear when a realisation finally came to her: whatever this was could not possibly last forever and she was still in the way of the horse.

Quickly, Trista picked up the child that was inanimate behind her and rushed toward the mother. As soon as she reached the other side of the road and touched the mother, everything resumed itself. The woman stared at Trista wide eyed and confused,

"W-what did you…h-how did you?" Trista couldn't reply even if she wanted to. She had no idea what had just happened to her and she still felt weak. Trista handed the child to its mother and ran off as fast as she was able toward the Town Hall before the woman could ask her any more questions.

RELATIONSHIPS

On entering the Town Hall Trista went directly into the assembly room where a handful of girls her own age stood chatting. The slightly older women, mothers, grandmothers and other elders, were also gathered in their respective groups around the large room. Chairs were placed in neat rows but everyone remained to be seated until Lady Avriel arrived. Shaking off her nerves from her ordeal in the square and releasing a sigh, Trista stepped into the room and made her way to the group of girls.

As she approached them, she took a deep breath trying to steady her nerves,

"Morning!" she greeted as cheerfully as she could as the five girls turned to look at her. None of them said anything as they looked from her head to her toes and back again. The first to speak was the tavern owner's daughter, Adina. Adina was tall, blonde, beautiful and popular and made sure everyone knew it; especially Trista. She seemed to have made it her life's mission to make Trista's existence a leaving nightmare. She excluded her from the girl's gatherings; made a point of picking on her dark hair and general separation from the group.

"Oh...hello Trista"

Trista ignored her less than pleasant attitude and turned her attention to the rest of the group: Aviva the carpenter's daughter, Rachel and Mara the blacksmith's twins and Dana the tailor's daughter. Everyone either greeted her with weak reluctant smiles or blank stares except Dana who beamed at her.

"The weather's really nice, the sun is glorious this time of year, don't you think so Dana?"

Dana Black, the quiet one of the group smiled at being directly asked a question and nodded her agreement. While Dana was by no means stupid, she was usually the last to pick up on things; a simple and happy girl with short brown hair and deep brown eyes, flecked with gold. Most of the girls kept her in their groups because she had access to rare materials from her father's shop.

"I do Trista. How is you—"

"What do you want Trista?" Dana's question was cut short by Adina's interruption but Trista did her best to hide her anger and smiled politely.

"Nothing…sorry I interrupted" Trista left them and walked to the front of the assembly room to take her seat.

Despite having no real desire to be their best friends or anything of that nature, it was unfair Trista felt, that she had no real friends. Many of the girls in Remora distanced themselves from her because she was different and that she rarely played by the town rules. She was a rebel in their eyes and any affiliation with her would tarnish their own reputations.

Her lost desire to be the tool or trophy of the village patriarchy, made her a social pariah and even though she had tried countless times to fit in; she refused to change who she was inside.

She would rather be alone.

Having nothing better to do while she waited for Selection to begin, Trista's mind wandered to what had happened in the town square.

What troubled her was not so much what had happened but that she had somehow known what to do.

How had *she done it?*

Could she do it again?

Both obvious questions that she had no way of answering.

All Trista knew was that when she had stopped that horse, she had felt at peace somehow, like something had clicked into place and she needed to get that feeling back.

As she contemplated this in the light and airy space of the town hall's main room, Trista felt someone sit down beside her. She turned to see Dana Black, beaming at her with a sweet smile and smiled back.

"Are you sure you should be sitting with me?"

Dana smiled at Trista in a way that made her entire face light up.

She had a heart shaped face, slightly plump face and was one of those people in the world that was just genuinely nice. Dana was one of the few people in Remora that Trista liked and who seemingly liked her back,

"I can sit where I like," her sweet voice said with a giggle. "Just don't worry about Adina; she's just jealous of you"

"Jealous?"

"Yes, because you're pretty and fun!" Dana complimented but Trista had to snort at her remark.

"Fun I can do on a good day but pretty? I'm the town freak remember?" Dana shook her head,

"Thorn doesn't seem to think so."

Dana reached out and squeezed Trista's hand reassuringly before heading back to her friends.

What did Thorn Remora have to do with anything?

Trista chuckled to herself, pushed Thorn, Dana and the mean girls to the back of her mind and waited for the meeting to begin.

A few moments later, a bell rung and the women began taking their seats. As they filed into the aisles of chairs, Lady Avriel finally arrived but she was not alone. To the appreciation of every young woman in the room, she had brought Thorn with her.

Thorn Remora was a tall young man with thick black hair and startling blue eyes. He had a very polished look about him, nothing ever out of place but his eyes seemed to be ever mischievous and playful.

Thorn, having led his mother to her seat on the platform at the front of the hall, took the seat next to her and proceeded to listen patiently and Trista couldn't keep her eyes off him.

He was neither as dark as her nor as pale as the other Remoran residents and had the same dark hair as Trista. She liked him because even though he was a little different, he didn't seem to care. She continued staring at him when suddenly, he turned in her direction.

It was an eerie action as his entire head didn't move, only his eyes that fixed themselves onto her face. She acknowledged his gaze with a polite smile then looked back toward his mother. For some time after Trista felt his eyes on her but afraid of exposing her own desire to stare back, she faced forward.

"...and I'm very pleased at the outcome. Now, as you can see I've brought a guest with me today, Thorn?"

Thorn stood from his seat and walked to his mother's side looking every bit the leader he was destined to become.

Thorn's father Lord Fabias, along with the help of councilmen like Trista's father ran the town and communicated with larger villages and towns in the kingdom who then corresponded with the Barons and their cities. Thorn was due to inherit that responsibility and title when his father died.

He stood now in his dark blue doublet and trousers with long black leather boots and a sheathed sword at his side. Not that he would ever need or use it but his position of power had to demonstrated by something.

"…he will need the assistance of two young ladies for some administrative tasks at The Grange but he will also be recruiting help for the weaponry division as some of our gallant men are to proceed to the capital in three weeks. As usual we would ask the ladies to submit their names for the task or tasks they wish to be considered for and wait for Thorn, Mrs Bakerson and I to arrive at our decision."

Later, Trista submitted her name for weaponry along with some other girls and while they went through the names, she went outside to wait.

Trista left the square completely and strolled into the trees that lined the edges of Remora.

Growing up, Trista spent a lot of her time in the lush forests lining the town, alone. When the other children had shunned her for her dark hair or her strange coloured eyes, she had retreated into herself and found peace in her own company.

She walked far enough among the trees until she came to a small grassed clearing. She flopped onto the ground and looked up into the pale blue sky. Her ponytail lay fanned on the ground beside her as she lay with her hands on her chest and took deep breaths.

What had happened to her?

What did it mean?

She knew there were people who possessed unknown magic, people from faraway places. The elders mentioned other races who could do special things but nothing like that had ever happened in Remora. She had heard that the king had special abilities but no one she knew had ever witnessed it so where would this have come from?

She lay there for a long while speculating, when the crunching of leaves diverted her attention and she sat up to see what was there.

Trista was surprised and embarrassed to see Thorn standing there looking over at her.

He smiled as he stepped toward her, while she got to her feet, dusting herself off.

"What are you doing?" he questioned softly. Trista quickly placed her hands in front of her, looking down as she did so, suddenly nervous.

"Nothing…do you make a habit of sneaking up on people?"

"Only if there's something worth watching," was his reply and Trista had to laugh at his honesty.

She finally looked up toward him, catching the gaze of his eyes that she knew would be there.

He advanced until he was directly in front of her, enough for her to smell him but not enough for her to touch him.

For a few moments, they stood staring at each other until Thorn reached out and gently pushed a stray strand of hair away from her face. His eyes bore into her own so intently, she had to look away, pretending to be engrossed in the activities of a bee, before eventually he spoke.

"We haven't spoken much since the Harvest Fête…was that my fault?"

Trista looked back at him in confusion. Thorn had invited her to the Harvest Fete almost a month ago and she had had a wonderful time. It was one of the best nights of her life if she was honest. He had made her feel connected with the other people her age and because he had invited her, they had been decent to her. She had finally felt like one of them, even special as Thorn Remora's date.

"No, why would you think that?"

"I guess I had assumed or rather… hoped that something would have come from our time together"

"Something like what?"

"Maybe a friendship…a relationship?" he confessed.

His face flushed red but seemingly in a case of decisiveness, Thorn gently took hold of Trista's hands.

"Thorn I…I don't know what to say. I am flattered…"

"But," he let go of her hands and stepped back, upset. "My feelings aren't reciprocated?"

Trista quickly took hold of them again, realising that she liked the feeling of his skin on hers, skin that was so much like her own but yet so different.

Trista looked up into Thorn's handsome face and conjured the best smile she could, trying to tell him in that look how she really felt about him. Even now, staring into his mystically azure eyes she knew she could love him, if she did not already.

"No Thorn, they are reciprocated, I just…don't know if I'm ready for what it would mean if I said yes to…being with you."

Thorn nodded slowly,

"I understand that,"

"Can I think about this for a while?"

A smile grew on his face before he leant forward and placed a soft kiss on the middle of her forehead before answering,

"I will wait until you're ready Lady Trista, for as my companion, a Lady you will be among men."

Thorn and Trista embraced each other warmly then separated, looking at each other with shy smiles on their faces. The late morning sun shone down on the young people, their dark hair and light eyes so similar in ways they were yet to understand.

Thorn reached down to take hold of her hand and led them out of the clearing and back to the town square. As they approached the edge of the town, Thorn released her hand and they stepped out side by side.

As they emerged into the road however, they bumped into a group of their peers deep in conversation.

Adina was in the middle of a conversation with Maron, Rachel and Mara's older brother but was the first to approach them with accusing eyes for Trista and adoring ones for Thorn.

"Why Master Thorn there you are!" Her voice was high pitched and completely unnatural, it made Trista cringe. "I've been worried sick about you!"

Her overtly dramatic response sent a ripple of giggles through the teenagers but Trista said nothing. Along with her earlier group of friends, Adina was joined by her own younger brother Alaric, the baker's boys Richard and Henry and Taran, Thorn' best friend and eldest son of a local councilman like Trista's father and of course, Maron.

"It seems you're playing second fiddle again Maron," Richard teased him as Adina completely dropped their conversation to take notice of Thorn. Maron elbowed him in the ribs but Richard just laughed at the anger on his face.

"Your mother has been looking for you; it is time to go back inside. May I escort you?" Adina continued, ignoring Richard's comment and extending her arm towards Thorn.

Thorn stepped away from Trista as though to take Adina's hand but bowed courteously instead and replied,

"As wonderful as that might be Adina, I have known the location of the town hall for quite some time and can find my way there unassisted. Trista," he bowed to her personally then once to the other women that stood with Adina, "Ladies." then left toward the hall.

From a slight nod of Thorn' head in his direction, Taran followed in his footsteps after bowing quickly to the other girls.

"I'd hate to be his little lap dog," Maron spat viciously as the rest of the group followed in Thorn's footsteps toward the town hall.

"He's not his lap dog," Aviva said. "Taran and Thorn have been best friends since they were babies, you're just jealous!"

"Jealous of *him*, you've got to be joking?"

All the teens just shook their heads in disappointment knowing full well that Maron had been jealous of Thorn for as long as they could all remember. Being the son of a blacksmith was reputable enough but it would never beat being the town leader's son.

Although they had all grown up together, when they became adults and ultimately ran the town themselves, there was going to be a clear divide. Maron however was the only one who seemed to have a problem with the dynamic.

Trista walked with them saying nothing while Adina ran back to Maron after recovering from her earlier embarrassment. Everyone knew that Adina wanted nothing better than to be Thorn's bride but she still kept Maron on a short leash in case that plan fell through and he continued to let her. He was besotted with her and no matter how many times she dropped him like a sack of potatoes to run to Thorn, he kept taking her back.

"You're the only one joking Maron, pretending not to be jealous when we all know you want Adina for yourself," Rachel laughed at him and the others joined in.

"When are you going to learn that you'll always be second best with her?" Henry said slapping him on the back but Maron shrugged him off.

"That's not true!" Adina protested but when they all turned to face her with un-amused looks on their faces, she didn't protest any further.

As they arrived at the town hall, the other boys began to fall back in their steps.

"Well, this is where we leave you little ladies to have your taste of freedom," Richard teased. "Don't get too many ideas, when you get married freedom will be all but a dream." The other boys laughed with him as he mocked them.

"Please be quiet Richard. You're boring me." Mara rolled her eyes.

"Don't worry Mara, I'm sure Richard will be a liberal husband." Henry laughed alongside Richard while Mara blushed furiously.

"Mara will never marry you!" Rachel came to her sister's defence immediately who still said nothing.

"Not if your father has anything to say about it," he continued to tease them as the girls just rolled their eyes and walked away from them into the town hall.

Trista watched as the rest of girls followed Rachel and Mara and the boys laughed themselves into the market, neither group saying anything to her.

As she stepped into the hall and closed the large oak door behind her, she told herself over and over that she didn't mind she didn't have any true friends.

Once all the women were seated again, the allocated names were called out and when and where their assistance would be needed.

By the end of the list, they still did not know who was helping Thorn and since their talk in the forest, Trista now regretted that she could not have used that time to be with him.

She had however been given the weaponry post like she wanted and was eager to get started. She proceeded to the front of the room where the weaponry team had gathered but when she got there she realised, to her disappointment that Adina was on the same team although Dana was too.

It was then that Lady Avriel and Thorn came over to the group.

Trista smiled at Thorn shyly who returned the gesture but in a way, that would not incriminate his advances. Tearing her eyes away from him, Trista looked at his mother who had begun talking again and admired the woman's demeanour.

She was every bit the lady Trista had hoped to be for her mother's sake but could never manage to achieve. Avriel exuded power and status and responsibility. She was always smartly dressed and poised and Trista admired everything about her. The way she brought the townswomen together on ventures like Selection and was always someone to look up to. As she admired Avriel, Thorn suddenly appeared by her side and Trista stole a glance at him to find him doing the same. Adina seemed to detect the exchange of glances and took the other position beside Thorn.

At that moment, Trista had never despised anyone more in her entire life.

"Thorn, have you decided who you'd like to help you?" Avriel suddenly questioned him and his eyes immediately turned to look down at Trista then back to his mother.

"I would hate to take any of these ladies away from their already allocated position," he threw the comment out there with an air of confidence that made one assume he knew any of the girls would be willing to drop the most appealing of tasks for him. "I have however decided that I would greatly appreciate the assistance of Trista Frietz...if she'll accept?" Trista looked up at him with the same air of adoration that the rest of the girls were showing him but felt better for it because she knew the feeling was mutual.

"I'd be delighted to help" Trista answered but as she looked at Avriel, this seemed to both please and upset her.

Thorn turned to leave with Trista when Adina spoke up,

"Did Master Thorn not say that he needed *two* assistants?" she inquired looking directly at Thorn and he indicated his forgetfulness with a nod.

"Ah yes, so I did Mother. I wonder…"

As Thorn spoke, it seemed to Trista that his words disappeared into the very air even though she was looking directly at him.

Again, she felt a sense of weakness take over her and even swayed slightly. While trying to compose herself, a voice crept into her head, a voice that was unmistakably Thorn's.

Trista looked up at him and saw that he wasn't speaking but she could hear him as clearly as though he were talking directly to her.

It was happening again.

"… do I really want Adina with Trista and me? Maybe Thrya or Murrin or even …"

She could hear Thorn's thoughts!

Thinking quickly, she knew she had to tell Thorn she didn't want Adina to join them…but how?

Dana

It was just a thought but as it happened, Thorn turned his head in her direction with a quizzical look on his face and Trista knew that he had heard her.

Her eyes widened then narrowed as she repeated herself, *Dana. Pick Dana.*

Thorn looked away from her and instantly sound returned to her.

"Very well, Dana it is." His mother was saying and went off with the other elders toward another group. Dana passed a tight faced Adina and took hold of Trista's hand firmly,

"I never thought he'd pick me!" she giggled.

He didn't

Trista smiled to herself before looking towards Thorn, who looked back with a puzzled look.

He asked both girls to thread their arms through his own and led them to the lunch that had been prepared for everyone in the dining hall.

THE LADY

When Trista finally arrived home that evening, her mother was in the kitchen as usual and her father she was told was in his study.

She did not see or speak with him until dinner when he was seated at the head of the table, her mother on his right and she was descending the stairs from her bedroom.

After their prayers were said, Trista and her family ate in silence as was the norm. As luck would have it, at this meal, Trista's father spoke.

"I heard some talk today."

Trista looked to her father eagerly, thankful for some sound other than cutlery hitting against plates. Her father, Matthias Freitz was a serious and educated man. He was tall and thin, with greying hair and a look about him that made it look like he was judging everyone all the time.

He was an efficient man who praised order and liked everything to run accordingly, which usually meant the way that he wanted.

"Talk about you Trista…and Master Thorn."

At that moment Gwendolyn seemed to have lost the use of her limbs and clumsily dropped her fork onto her plate. Matthias ignored her and kept his focus on Trista. Trista cleared her throat before speaking,

"What about Master Thorn and me?" Matthias lowered his knife and fork to look over at his daughter,

"That you were seen coming out of the forest earlier this morning and that it looked as though you were up to something that would be less then honourable."

Trista repressed her need to defend herself viciously against what she knew were lies concocted by Adina and decided to play her father at his own game.

"I have behaved in no less than a respectable manner whilst in Master Thorn's company and will continue to do so."

Her father's eyebrows rose questionably as he placed his wine goblet down to look discriminatingly at Trista. He dabbed at his mouth with his napkin and placed it onto his near finished plate,

"Continue?"

"Yes Father, continue. Dana Black and I were selected to assist Master Thorn in organising and cataloguing the studies and libraries at The Grange. Lady Avriel wishes to open a school of some sort."

Even as she relayed the details to her father, Trista was slightly disappointed that she was no longer in the weaponry group. Still, she would be with Thorn and that would be all the more exciting.

"And you…must do this?" he questioned.

"Would you have me deny the request of the town leader's son?" his response was a grunt as he picked up his goblet again.

Appearances were everything to Matthias Frietz. As Lead Councilman, he had an image to maintain and there was no way he would be seen to disrespect the town leader or his only son. Looking over at her mother, Trista saw that Gwendolyn had a slight grin on her face, which she returned. It was only then that her mother spoke but Trista would have appreciated it if she hadn't.

"Who knows Matthias; if things were to work out Trista may end up betrothed before her eighteenth birthday."

Trista wanted to crawl into a hole and die. She knew it troubled her parents, her mother mostly that she had not been courted yet but she was in no rush to marry. For women like her mother who had been betrothed since they were children, to be seventeen and single was an unspeakable abomination. Despite half her meal still on the plate, Trista pushed it aside.

"May I be excused?" Matthias nodded giving Trista leave to place her plate in the washbasin and escape to her room.

The following morning, Trista was woken again by her dream, still with the unseen face and that ever-present light.

Pushing aside the usual unanswered questions, she got dressed for her time at The Grange.

She was washed and changed and sat at the kitchen table with her parents an hour later eating breakfast when the door knocked. Trista rose from her seat, went to answer it and to her surprise and delight, Thorn was standing there.

"Good Morning Miss, is your father home?" she smiled at him with the obstruction of the door averting her father's prying eyes,

"Yes he is, please come in."

Thorn walked into the house in doublet and trousers of light grey. The detail on the threads were a darker grey with black boots and he looked incredibly handsome. Matthias was there to meet him almost at once and as he and Thorn exchanged words, Trista remained quiet.

"Good morning Councilman Frietz. I've come to escort Trista to The Grange."

Trista had been planning to walk the long road to The Grange, Thorn's home that sat on the highest hill in Remora.

Trista watched as her father eyed Thorn suspiciously and wished she could say something to get them out of the house faster.

"I do not think it would be honourable for my daughter to spend the duration of the trip alone with you Master Thorn,"

Thorn nodded his agreement and Trista smiled to herself knowing what Thorn had in store.

"A chaperone has been brought along Sir. She is waiting right outside." Trista had seen the young woman in the carriage when she'd opened the door.

Thorn gestured toward the window so that her father could see for his self that there was indeed a young woman outside. Before her father could protest anything further, Trista spoke firmly

"Goodbye Father, Mother. I'll be back later."

Without giving her father the chance to speak again, she left the house with Thorn following behind her.

He helped her into the carriage and Trista smiled politely at the young lady that was already seated there. It was only after Thorn had climbed in alongside them, drove them into and then through the town square, that the young woman spoke,

"Will you need me for anything else Master Thorn?"

Thorn shook his head as he brought the carriage to a halt just outside the square on the path that led to The Grange.

"No thank you Lysa, just to meet us back here at six,"

"Yes Sir," and after a polite nod to Trista, Lysa made her way back into the town.

It was not until they were on the winding path that led up to Thorn's home, did he take one of his hands from the reigns and place it on her own. Trista squeezed his hand back with a shy smile,

"I'm glad we have this time to get to know one another Trista."

"Me too,"

The couple arrived at The Grange a few minutes later, and once again Trista was in awe.

Thorn's family had lived there for countless generations and to be invited there was a great honour. Many parties and other events had been held there, hosted by Fabias and Avriel, which unlike the rest of the dwellings of Remora was able to occupy near half the population of the village.

One major difference about The Grange was that it was the only building within Remora that was made entirely of stone. The colossal mansion reached to four levels, two above the usual with countless rooms and studies and other entertaining rooms.

Trista and her mother had been extended an invitation twice before and she had enjoyed herself on both occasions. Though her mother had been slightly disconcerted by the extravagance of the estate, Gwendolyn had managed to enjoy herself too.

Thorn stopped the carriage just outside the large front doorway where a stable hand emerged from what seemed nowhere and took the reins from him. Thorn jumped down from his seat and helped Trista out to lead her into his home.

The Grange, despite being made of stone was neither cold nor dark.

There were various candles and sizeable fireplaces situated throughout and the plentiful, yet superbly placed furniture created a feeling of warmth and security that resonated throughout the house.

On the walls were portraits of Thorn's paternal ancestors as well as others, not directly connected to the family but of some great importance. Leading her through the foyer and reception room, past the drawing room and into the first study, Thorn talked frantically about all the work they were going to do for his mother's new project.

Over the years his family had accumulated a lot of documents, books and materials that contained invaluable knowledge of Remora and the surrounding kingdom. Information on the Age of Man before The Fall and the change from SAmai rule to that of Man with the current king, Curian.

Avriel had left it to him to organise these priceless documents to keep them organised as well as safe and be of use during her new educational venture.

The ground floor study they entered, where the school was to be held, was large and Trista marvelled at the daunting task ahead.

Draped down the stone walls, were crimson and gold embroidered tapestries hanging perfectly in line with each glassed window. They were framed in mahogany with wooden candle fixtures lining all the walls for use when the curtains were drawn.

In the centre of the room were two great mahogany tables with intricate designs carved into the legs and along the sides. At either end of the two tables were two chairs of the darkest red leather that Trista had ever seen.

There was paper and writing material scattered on the tables together with books and scrolls. On the far wall and anywhere that was not taken up by decoration or candlesticks, were endless rows of bookshelves.

Trista walked over to one of the built-in shelves and ran her fingers along the spines, feeling every dent and crevice. She was entranced with the fact that knowledge and understanding were at her fingertips within those slender pages.

"This is the first of two studies and an extensive library that need to be organised and catalogued. My mother wants to start a finishing school eventually and so needs these rooms in a particular order to conduct her lessons." Thorn explained their task as Trista just nodded and gazed around in awe.

"Where is Dana, shouldn't she be here?" her eyes still transfixed on the books in front of her as she absentmindedly brushed dust from her fingertips.

"She will be. I've arranged for a carriage to have her picked up from her house. She will be here at nine." Trista smiled as she finally turned to look at him, her eyes twinkling with mischief.

"So, what made you come and get me personally?" she asked walking up to him in the middle of the large room.

"I wanted to be with you without the intrusion of prying eyes." Thorn admitted and Trista stretched out her hands for him to take hold. They stood holding hands, gazing into each other's eyes when the door to the study suddenly swung open, Lady Avriel entered and they quickly sprang apart.

Avriel Remora was draped in a dress of the deepest crimson with gold thread stitched along the hem and bodice. Trista stared at the beauty before her and admired for a moment how much Avriel reminded her of herself. Not in a conceited way but in the shape of their eyes that were set in what seemed to be an angled position rather than directly across their faces and the fact that they were also green.

Avriel walked elegantly toward them, holding out her hands that Thorn took hold of and kissed lovingly.

"Mother you know Trista; daughter of Matthias Freitz. She kindly agreed to help me organise the studies."

"Ah yes Trista," Avriel looked at Trista from the tips of her plain shoes to the top of her dark head. There was something eerie about the look that made Trista feel nervous, the hairs on her arms standing on end. "I have heard much about you." Trista rearranged her footing nervously,

"I hope, my lady that you haven't taken much notice of what you've heard. I'm not normally the subject of positive conversation."

Avriel did not reply but smiled enigmatically instead, leaving Trista feeling uneasy and even a little ashamed. Avriel scanned the room briefly with a slight turn of her head then addressed Trista once more.

"I gather that my son has much more exciting things he would occupy your time with, but I do hope you will get these studies done?" Thorn looked away embarrassed, but amused.

"I will help Thorn as best I can," Avriel smiled at that, then unexpectedly reached out to take hold of Trista's hands.

"Thorn…will you excuse us?"

"Mother I was just…"

"It will only take a minute dear." Her tone offered no further argument and so Thorn nodded his head and left the room.

Avriel, still holding Trista's hand led her to one of the two seat leather couches that lined the perimeter of the room. When they were seated, Avriel stared into Trista's eyes so intently she thought the older woman could see into her heart.

She smiled reservedly before reaching out and taking a stray lock of Trista's hair between her fingers and releasing it again.

It was then Trista realised that she had never seen Avriel's hair. It was always expertly wrapped in a headdress that concealed all her hair and framed her exotic looking face.

As Avriel continued to analyse her, Trista became aware that she was feeling the same sensation that she had when she had stopped the horse and heard Thorn's thoughts.

She closed her eyes trying to block out the dizziness and when she opened them, it was gone.

"You know that you're different?"

"Excuse me?" the question was unexpected to say the least.

"Do you know that you are different Trista, quite different to all the other young ladies in Remora?"

"I don't know what you mean,"

"Yes, you do, you're just too afraid to admit it." Trista said nothing. "There is nothing wrong with being different Trista…special even." She spoke wistfully as though she were somewhere else. While she was looking at Trista, it was as though she were looking *through* her at the same time.

Avriel shaped the edges of Trista's face with her finger and as she did so uttered words that Trista neither clearly heard or understood. Then suddenly she was upright,

"It's a shame," Avriel said softly. "You could have been great."

Confused, Trista went to ask what she meant but the door knocked, and Thorn re-entered, clearly impatient to get back to Trista. Avriel stood up and looked down at Trista,

"Have fun…there is a lot of work to be done." Avriel gave her son a kiss on his cheek before exiting the room as elegantly as she had entered.

Charlotte Murphy

SINS OF THE FATHER

Curian paced the battlements of Tirnum Castle staring attentively into the night, as though he could see through the blackened void.

His mind raced with plans, schemes, anything he could devise in order to prevent the coming dangers. He couldn't physically see it right now in the darkness, but he was watching his country crumble around him. The petty battles amongst the barons and lords in each corner of the land, the droughts, landslides and increasingly bad weather, were all signs confirming what he already knew: Mortania was dying and it was his fault.

He didn't want to accept it but he knew what the Prophecy had predicted; what he had put into motion, but he was determined to stop it, whatever the cost.

He knew the time had come, that his throne could be taken away at any moment, but when?

He had always known his reign over Mortania would not last forever, but he had hoped at least for a son to succeed him. A son who would help cement their family name in its rightful place.

As fate, would have it, he had no son but a daughter, barely seventeen who was the thorn in his side. The girl was rude, spoiled and had no respect for the life that her father had provided for her. If only she had witnessed the battle and sacrifice that had allowed her to be a princess, then maybe she would appreciate her status.

The Battle at the Wide had been no laughing matter; the fate of Man had rested on the outcome of that battle but still his daughter had no respect for the position it had given her. He realised then that he despised his daughter because he had never been that way as a child, choosing instead to dote on his father's every word.

It was his father, Magnus Greybold that had told him the history of Men and the Samai. It was his father who had educated him on the origins of Mortania, once known as Kymaen and how, before an event known as The Fall, the gods forsaken Samai had usurped the rightful rulers of their land and stolen the Everlasting.

Of course, Magnus had not been alive in the very beginning, but the stories and the golden age of The Fall when Samai had been pushed to extinction, had been passed down through their family for generations. Curian had made sure that his father saw him take the throne before he died, his one gift to him, allowing him to die at peace rather than in war.

Now, a generation later Curian's own life and reign was threatened not only by the disobedience and disrespect of his young daughter but the coming of a prophesized warrior.

Curian and his armies had ransacked villages and murdered countless women and children in search of this warrior, so their own rebellion could never rise. Still, it loomed over him like a night sky; dark and seemingly never ending.

They were still out there, taunting him unknowingly, letting him know that he hadn't succeeded in destroying them.

His daughter knew the same stories, knew the possible outcome and still she remained selfish and cruel. She revelled in the fact that despite the prophesised warrior, *she* had not been foreseen.

Born on the same night that he had slain the Samaian King Alexander, she viewed herself as the saviour that would rise to claim victory for Man despite the Samaian legend.

Trained in combat since the tender age of four, there was no one in Mortania that could best her.

Many a warrior had tried, men and women alike, but it remained truth: Princess Briseis, daughter of Curian the Conqueror, heir to the throne of Mortania was the greatest warrior Man had ever seen and in these questionable times, she was the only thing standing between Curian and eternal victory.

His daughter aside, there were still parts of his past he could not face since he had slain Alexander Antonides almost seventeen years ago.

Those large green eyes still haunted him, watching him; knowing what he had done and that he would one day pay the ultimate price for it.

Over and over he told himself that he had done what was necessary by killing Alexander, that the Samai were fraudsters hiding behind their power that they used to control the kingdom and its people. Every day, he told himself that he was not a murderer but a saviour who had taken Mortania out of the hands of the corrupted and delivered it from evil.

The destruction of all that he had acquired, continued to prove his theory wrong. If he had been just in his actions, why was the country dying?

Why had he been burdened with a daughter who knew no mercy and thrived on death and devastation?

How dare Alexander make him feel this way? How dare he make him feel he had not done what was right by his own people?

Curian felt the anger boil up inside of him and unable to contain it any longer, yelled out at the top of his lungs, erupting his mental torment into a piercing scream.

His entire body was suddenly engulfed in black flame that streamed up into the sky, like a beacon piercing it with a distinct crack. Lightening flashed as Curian yelled his frustration into the night.

He collapsed to the floor, the fire extinguishing as he held his head in his hands and began to rock with despair.

The door leading back into the castle burst open and three of his Kings Guard came rushing through, swords unsheathed,

"Your Majesty, are you alright?"

Curian's best friend and commanding general of his army, Ignatius Rarno stepped toward him, but Curian recoiled. "My king, speak to me!"

"Get away from me!" Rarno said nothing about the retort but looked to his fellow guardsman then back at his king.

Curian was dishevelled; his crown by his feet, discarded while his doublet was torn at the throat and he reeked of alcohol.

"My king you shou—"

"I must do *nothing*!"

Their twenty plus years together had taught Rarno to recognise when Curian was serious. He took a step back from his king and motioned for the other two guards to go back inside.

He sheathed his sword as the wooden door closed behind them and took off his helmet, his tussled greying locks of hair falling into his face which he quickly pushed aside. He placed the priceless Agmantian headgear on the floor, beside Curian's crown and made a slow step towards him.

The king was silent, but his body was shaking,

"It only gets like this when you are truly troubled...what was it this time?" There was an impenetrable silence for an age before Curian spoke.

He looked Rarno directly in the eye and smiled shakily,

"You presume to know me well Rarno," Curian said, straightening up from the ground and readjusting himself. Rarno said nothing, "You presume correctly old friend."

Curian reached back down to pick up his crown along with Rarno's helmet. Looking down at them both intently in each hand, he chuckled,

"Perhaps you should wear the crown…and I the helmet," Rarno was obviously offended,

"I would never wish to take your place majesty."

"Why not? You'd be a far better king than I!" Curian was angry Rarno knew but why remained unclear.

"You are a great leader,"

"Yes…I am. I led you into this once great city nearly twenty years ago and I led you into battle. Then, I led you to victory. I *am* a great leader Rarno…but I am no king." Curian turned away from him to look back into the sky.

"Every day I pray to find purpose for my rule and every day I fail!"

"You rid us of a great evil, an evil that threatened to destroy us all"

"And what of my own destruction?" Curian blew up at Rarno, turning to face him again. "What of the evil I have brought down on this kingdom?"

Rarno said nothing, he knew what was happening to the country…they all did.

"Look around you Rarno; it cannot be ignored any longer. The Barons all want my blood, the people are starving, and the land is dying; crumbling beneath us and that is *my* doing. Where is my salvation from *that* truth?" Rarno stepped toward Curian and grabbed him by the shoulders,

"You are a great man, a man that did what was necessary to deliver your people from slavery. Lives were lost but that is the truth of war, no one can change that, not even a king as mighty as you. You must not blame yourself for doing what had to be done!" Curian shook his head,

The Antonides Legacy I

"I am no king!" Curian roared at his friend. "The true king died on the battlefield seventeen years ago and took my soul with him. I deserve what is happening to Mortania but Mortania does not deserve it. *That* is where my sorrow lives Rarno; in the knowledge that what I did to save my people is destroying them." Rarno looked on in disbelief.

"If you don't believe in your cause then, why should we? We fought and died for you. Would you like me to think it was all in vain?"

Curian pushed away from Rarno,

"No, that is exactly why this torments me so! I had hoped a son would fix my mistakes, right my wrongs and possibly save my soul but in that…I am cursed."

Even Rarno had no answer for him. Everyone who had ever met her knew that the princess was no gift. That one person could be so innately cruel was beyond their comprehension.

"The princess is…" Curian laughed dismissively,

"The princess is my punishment Rarno, it's as plain as that. Briseis is the price I pay for what I have allowed to happen to Mortania."

Rarno knew Curian was right and that they would have to deal with Briseis when the time came. He only hoped that it wouldn't be any time soon.

Bending, Rarno picked up the crown and helmet before leading his king steadily back into the castle.

THE AFTERMATH OF WAR

Dreston Castle was a cold place even though it was based in the middle of the desert city it was named after. It was the ancestral home of the Dreston family and housed a large work force and sizeable court that still were not able to add warmth to a place that bred greed and contempt.

In the years since Curian's rebellion against Samaian rule, the castle had played host to many secret meetings with guests carefully selected for their distaste for the current ruling family. This was in addition to creating a sense of unity in the now breaking kingdom. The tension of these meetings and circulating plots, hung in the air like a bad smell. The high-born residents of the cosmopolitan city ignored it, choosing instead to indulge in their decadence with no thought to what destruction and poverty went on outside the city walls.

It was known all over the kingdom that crops were failing, and natural disasters were erupting; devastating large towns and small cities everywhere. They were in the middle of the summer and the south had been getting considerably colder for months it seemed. For the wealthy residents of Dreston, a city surrounded by the sands of The Plains, and connected to a water source that flowed beneath them from the Alzo Sea; were rarely affected by outsiders.

Still, as he lounged in his banquet hall amongst other wealthy inhabitants from around the kingdom and surrounding lands, Baron Lyon Dreston knew that their safety was about to be disturbed. He had waited too long to get what was owed to him and it was time for his lesser peers to take their heads out from the ground and face the coming storm.

The Antonides Legacy I

He sat atop the platform at the far end of the banquet hall, in his adorned chair watching them all. He wore a black leather doublet and trousers with sturdy black leather boots. His family arms were embroidered on the front right breast in red and gold thread. The red flame shooting from the jaw of a mighty gold dragon against a black night sky was a symbol many had cause to fear.

His clothes only sort to accentuate the lightness of his blonde hair, caught in a ponytail at the nape of his neck, thin beard and his piercing amber eyes. Although the colour was warm, what exuded from them was cold, cruel and calculating.

As his guests spoke amongst themselves of frivolous things, Lyon made a mental note of the men he believed he could bring into his confidence.

Despite being the richest man in the kingdom, he still needed men of influence, men who had the king's ear. He had been declared a favourite of the king due to his efforts during the war, but his own audiences with Curian had been less then successful and he needed results. Considering that Curian's rebellion had been predominantly funded by himself, Baron Dreston felt simply, that he was owed.

On the three occasions, he had travelled to the capital and confronted the king about this directly, he had been cast aside with promises of riches and titles.

Riches and titles, he had, he wanted power; true and absolute power that no Man or Samai could contest.

Curian had had the right idea by overthrowing the Samaian king but had only done so with the help of lesser men looking for status from around Mortania. Lyon had personally sent ten thousand men to aid Curian at The Battle at the Wide and he knew that the current Baron of Thelm; Baron Erik had sent at least five thousand.

Erik had been a lesser lord of some insignificant place in the kingdom and had sacrificed his own social standing in the hope of backing the winning side.

Lyon in comparison had sacrificed his men, money and even his position if the Samai had won; and received no more than what was considered a simple thank you.

Curian sat, high on his marble throne watching the destruction of Mortania below him but did nothing. True, Lyon was also doing nothing, but he did not care for bushes and dirt. He wanted to be king, to have the power of the king and he knew that power came from the Everlasting. The power source that had once fuelled the Samaian king Alexander and the natural world around them, now powered Curian and allowed him free reign over the country.

Since the rebellion, a few had dared to oppose Curian, even seeking the fabled Free Magic that could make them credible contenders against him. The power that had streamed from Curian however was more than any could have imagined, if not witnessed.

King Curian the Conqueror was seemingly unstoppable, but Lyon was determined to prove that theory wrong

Lyon's attention was brought back to his guests when a loud crash echoed from the corner of the room.

"You *stupid* fool! Do you have any idea how much this cost!" the shriek came from Lady Clara, wife of Lord Tyus of Priya and carried to the front of the hall where Lyon sat.

"What on earth is going on?"

A young boy dressed in a simple long crimson tunic with a black belt around the middle was immediately by his side,

"Lady Clara lord, has had her drink spilt."

"By whom?" the boy's eyes darted away for a fraction of a second before looking down again.

"I did not see lord." Lyon looked at the boy intently,

"Have this one hanged," Lyon rose from his large velvet clad seat as two of his guards rushed forward to drag the boy away.

"No, no please lord I beg you *please*!"

"Liars have no place in my household," came his curt reply as he stepped down from the small platform and made his way to Lady Clara.

The guards swiftly assembled a rope from one of the rafters and were now fastening the noose around the young man's neck.

"Please lord! *Please*!"

By the time Lyon had reached the far corner of the hall, the guests were silent. All that could be heard were the gargled chokes of the young boy until finally, nothing. The shackles around his ankles were barely visible but could be heard, like a wind chime in a soft breeze as he swayed slowly from the rafter beam.

Lyon stopped in front of the Lady Clara as her eyes stayed focused on the young man swaying from the roof,

"What seems to be the problem here?" Lady Clara turned her attention to him and immediately beamed with joy as she curtseyed, the hanging man forgotten.

"Lord Dreston, how kind of you to enquire about me!"

"What happened dear lady?" Clara made a big show of being seen talking to the baron and displayed her dress to him. Her light blonde hair gleamed in the afternoon sun that streamed through the windows all around them. The bright blue of her dress a perfect complement to her hair and eyes, wasn't lost in the see of darker hues that all the other attendants were wearing.

"One of your imprudent servants knocked my goblet out of my hand and completely ruined my dress!"

"Dear lady, you have my deepest apologies for my deplorable excuse for help. Come, join me and I shall refill your glass."

"Why thank you lord, you are most kind."

Lady Clara was always one for a show as she gathered her skirts as elegantly as she had undoubtedly been taught, before threading her hand through Lyon's. As they walked through the crowd of guests, various individuals nodded their greetings and raised their goblets in respect to the Baron.

Lyon talked with the lady, marvelling at her attempts at wit until they had left the party completely. Clara hadn't noticed there was not another soul around until her ushered her into a room and closed the door firmly behind him.

"My sincerest apologies once again lady, can you ever forgive me?"

Clara turned to him with a blush creeping up her neck,

"There is nothing to forgive lord, it was not your doing."

"Yes, but the culprits were in my service and so a reflection of me."

"On the contrary, only something or someone quite grand could reflect you."

Her flattery did not go unnoticed as Lyon smiled and stalked his way towards her. He watched as Clara's breath caught in her chest, but she didn't turn her eyes from his own.

So, a feisty one, he thought to himself.

Lyon watched her watching him as he observed the rise and fall of her chest with every shallow quick breath she took. It accentuated the smooth mounds of her breasts, peeping from the top of her bodice

"Let me make it up to you?" Clara's eyes widened in shock. Whether it was genuine or not, Lyon couldn't tell this time.

"My lord husband…" she protested but Lyon cut her off.

"Lord Tyus can wait."

"Yes lord…as you wish."

Lyon looked over Clara's head to where one of his guards looked out at him. He nodded quickly and the guard disappeared into the shadows.

He led Clara into the midst of his private chambers and she finally remarked at her surroundings,

"You have many beautiful things lord," Lyon feigned indifference knowing that this room alone cost a small fortune. It had been his room his entire life, changing as he grew. His mother had died giving him life and his father had passed when he was only eight years old. He had been the Baron since then and his room had grown with him.

"I have no possession nearly as beautiful as you." Clara spun around to face him, making a strand of her hair fall from the chic yet tussled style that the high-born woman favoured these days.

"You should not say such things lord…I am married."

"And yet you are here"

"At your command," she said, though didn't protest. Lyon walked over to her, reached up and grabbed a hold of her hair to slowly tilt her head back and kissed her firmly.

Her arms flew up around his neck instantly as the kiss became more intense. He lowered his hands to pull at the strings of her bodice as he backed her over to his bed and lay Clara down.

***

"What in the Gods' name is going on here!"

The door to Lyon's chambers banged open, making Clara scream, roll off Lyon where she had been expertly making love to him. She dragged the silk sheets with her as she frantically tried to cover herself but exposed Lyon in the process.

"Lord Priya, how good of you to join us"

Lyon lay on his bed, unashamed as Lord Tyus marched towards them with his sword drawn. Clara scrambled over on the bed; the sheet bundled around her slender naked frame.

"My lord please, this was not my doing!" Lord Tyus reached out with his free hand and back handed her, knocking her off the bed and onto the ground. She didn't bother to get up as she lay there sobbing.

"Get your clothes on!" he barked at her, and she scrambled to do so.

Tyus turned his attention back to Lyon, where he placed the tip of his sword to his throat, but the Baron did not move an inch.

Lord Priya was twenty years his senior, was slightly round in the gut area and losing his hair. He offered no form of intimidation even with a sword in his hand. There were five guards posted expertly in and around this room that Tyus was completely unaware of.

"You dare to disrespect me!" Lyon smirked,

"I dare Tyus, but if you don't want the entire kingdom to know that your wife was bedded right under your nose, you'll do me a little favour. After all, what is a Lord without the respect of his peers?"

Lyon finally got up from his bed and draped a thick velvet robe around his lean frame that lay on a chair beside the bed.

"You son of a dog, have you no honour!" Lyon laughed,

"You don't know me at all, do you?" he walked towards Tyus with a wide smile. "Do something for me and I won't tell the kingdom that your very lovely, very young wife has been less than…honourable."

"You think I care for gossip?" Tyus turned to storm out of the room, sheathing his sword as he did so. "Come woman!" Lady Clara rushed to follow him; her head hung low.

"You may not care for gossip of this nature Tyus," Lyon called after him, making Tyus stop in his tracks. "But you may want to consider the very interesting news I received of your plans to assassinate Lord Balkin."

Lord Tyus turned to face him, rage and contempt evident in his eyes.

"I don't think his majesty would take kindly to knowing that someone was planning to gather more power in the kingdom. You know how he can get about rebellions, sensitive subject as it is."

Lord Balkin ran the provinces of Illiya and High Tower in southern Mortania. It was one of the neighbouring lands to Priya and if Tyus could gain control of it, he would have considerable wealth and advantage in the south.

"What do you want?" Tyus replied through gritted teeth as Lyon walked to stand directly in front of him.

"Your fealty. Swear your allegiance to me and I will not out you with the king or with this lovely ordeal." Lyon turned his eyes to Clara and blew her a kiss.

Tyus' face burned red, but he said nothing and turned again to leave.

"Come Clara!" he bellowed.

"I think Clara should stay with me a while longer." Lyon watched as Tyus' fists clenched by his side then one hand rose to clutch the hilt of his sword.

Suddenly, he released it and stormed out of the room.

Lyon held out his hands for Clara to take and helped her back to his bed.

THE REDEEMER

Princess Briseis of Mortania exited the luxurious fourth-floor library of Tirnum Castle and made her way towards the Great Hall.

Walking along the dimly lit corridors, she shuddered, hating the castle's stone walls, drab tapestries and furniture from an outdated time she didn't care to relate to. She vowed then, as she had too many times before, that when she was Queen, Tirnum Castle would be destroyed, and a new luxurious palace built in its place.

Descending a flight of winding steps, she arrived on the third floor and walked past a large mirror hung on the wall. Briseis stopped, took two steps back and surveyed herself in it.

She was dressed in a gown of the finest ivory silk, embroidered with silver thread in intricate floral patterns. She had the typically perfect figure of a seventeen-year-old, though firm muscles were visible on her strong frame. Despite her extensive combat skills, Briseis remained elegant in all that she did. The only thing that remained hard and discourteous was her attitude and her heart. Briseis was merciless and cruel and anyone who knew better was terrified of her.

While her father dealt with the political, financial and agricultural matters of the realm, Briseis had taken command of the Royal Sentry, the guards who monitored the city and she used them to rule the city and the lands immediately surrounding it, if not the entire country with an iron fist.

Her long golden tresses fell to the middle of her back in a cascade of curly light. Her intense dark grey eyes seemed to come alight when she was either extremely happy or ferociously angry, the latter being the more common.

Briseis continued to admire herself - vanity being one of her many traits - but as she watched the delicacies of her beautiful face, her eyebrows suddenly furrowed as the thought of her approaching task brushed her mind.

Why couldn't her ascension to the throne be a simple occasion? She thought with annoyance. *Why couldn't her coronation just be a normal day?*

Instead it was to be plagued by the impending and ominous arrival of a person she had yet to identify.

For the past six years or so, Briseis had been searching for who the Samaian history books, called The Redeemer. The Redeemer was a fabled saviour who after a usurpation would rise and claim the throne for themselves and return some great power back to the world.

From what Briseis had read, the Redeemer had to be Alexander's heir. The writings spoke of a fierce battle between a Samaian king – no king had been specified – and a usurper, in which the king would fall, and The Redeemer must take their place. The great power had not been mentioned.

What had not been foreseen however, Briseis thought smugly, was her arrival.

Briseis' mother Myrenda had gone into labour giving birth to Briseis on the same night that Alexander had been killed. Curian had claimed his crown on that fateful night and while he'd gained a daughter; he'd lost his wife almost a week later and Briseis; a mother she would never know. Something had happened that night, in the balancing of life and death and Briseis knew within herself that she was the unforeseen power that could defeat the Redeemer.

For six long years though she had been searching without victory.

She and her Sentry had reached nothing but dead ends in the search for the warrior…or Rowan.

The fallen Samaian Queen had not been seen for almost sixteen years since the death of her husband and Briseis needed both her and her child out of the way if she was to rule Mortania without contest. She knew that her father's men had hunted her all over the country in the early days of the new kingdom, but Rowan had managed to evade them.

Briseis had promised herself years ago, when she had first heard the prophecy, that if her father wasn't strong enough to have the woman and child found and killed, then she would.

"Princess!"

Briseis turned from the mirror to face the older woman approaching her in the corridor; Minerva the Castle Steward.

Minerva was probably the closest thing Briseis had to a mother. She organised the meals and the other servants and ran all other things domestic around the castle, she had done for many years, even during the Samaian rule. She had asked her father many times in the early years why he kept someone on who had worked for the enemy and he'd always said it was because Minerva herself, was not his enemy.

When Briseis was a little girl, Minerva had been the one to bathe and dress her and brush her hair before putting her to bed at night. She was a plump woman who always dressed in various shades of brown with her dull and greying hair caught in a tight bun on the top of her head. She had bright blue eyes that wrinkled at the edges when she laughed, which unfortunately wasn't too often. Now, they darted across Briseis' face in obvious distress.

"I've been looking for you everywhere," she cried hysterically. "Your father is waiting for you in the dining hall!"

"And?" Minerva was momentarily taken back,

"And well uh, he w-wants you there r-right away," the woman stuttered.

"My father wants a lot of things Minerva." Briseis replied not caring in the least whether she was late to meet her father.

"Princess?"

"Tell my father that I will not be joining him for dinner tonight."

Briseis smiled at the distressed look on Minerva's face. She had been on her way to meet her father but he had to learn that she did what she wanted, when she wanted and that that would never change.

"But your highness…"

"Now Minerva!" Briseis snapped at her and instantly her grey eyes ignited with grey flames ringing her irises. Her right hand clenched into a fist and a mist of grey fire instantly gathered around it. Minerva's eyes darted toward Briseis' fist then back up into her eyes with terror and Briseis laughed heartily as the flames subsided, she changed direction and headed to her room.

***

After dismissing her guards for the evening, Briseis entered her rooms and sat gracefully at the large wooden desk in her meeting chamber.

With a snap of her fingers the various unlit candles in the room came alight and with another flick of her wrist in the direction of the fireplace, the wood set alight and became a roaring fire. Her handmaidens would usually have her room ready for her but she was meant to be at dinner, they would not arrive just yet.

The Antonides Legacy I

Still, the nights were colder now; even in the midst of summer. Light snow had already begun to fall in the capital and further north in the Imperial Lands, it was full blown winter. Briseis ignored those anomalies, as she contemplated her next move.

She had her own small group of guards searching the kingdom for any trace of Rowan and her child but once she found them, what exactly would she do with them? It was easy enough to have them both killed but where would the fun be in that?

She took a seat by the desk in her meeting chamber, "Briseis!"

Briseis looked toward her chamber door, rolling her eyes in frustration as it flew open and her father stood there in blazing fury.

Curian was a large man, in width more than height with short light brown hair that flowed perfectly into a large beard and moustache. His hair was streaked with grey prematurely as the effects of ruling a decaying kingdom showed no mercy. He was not wearing his crown, but he was dressed in the finest materials. He stood in his daughter's doorway in black leathers with his house's sigil embroidered on his chest. Only the noble houses had sigils but when he took the throne, it was only right he had one of his own even if he had come from humble beginnings. So now, the black crow clutching a shining orb while in flight over a dark blue sky was his sigil; to remind the kingdom who had the power and how they had come by it.

"Briseis!" she turned away from him back to the journal that lay open on her desk.

"You bellowed Father?"

Curian looked at his daughter looking as graceful and delicate as any young woman could look. She reminded him so much of her mother, it broke his heart. He didn't let her beauty distract him for too long and growled out at her,

"Why must you aggravate me like this?"

"Aggravate you?"

"Don't be coy with me. Why didn't you come down to dinner?" Briseis stood up and finally faced her father,

"Do you really expect me to answer?" Curian narrowed his eyes at her with contempt,

"Your mother would never…"

"Don't start with that speech again. She's gone, get over it!" Curian's head shot back as though she had slapped him.

"How can you be this way? Perhaps if your mother were here…"

"Well she isn't, I think we covered that high point. What do you want father, besides to annoy me?" the disbelief was clear on his face.

"How can you be this cold Briseis?" she didn't answer and turned to look out of the window.

Her meeting chamber overlooked the training yard on one side while her bedchamber overlooked the sea on the other. She liked both views from time to time. She had never left Mortania, even though the sea held much allure for her. When she was queen and she knew, the kingdom was being run the way she saw fit, maybe she would see what lay beyond the Aquatic Ocean.

"I know you understand your importance, but I cannot let you get out of hand."

"Let me?" Curian's eyebrows furrowed and he unconsciously took a step back.

"Briseis…"

"Let me? You don't *let* me do anything!" she snapped at her father as she turned to him, her fists now engulfed in flame.

The Antonides Legacy I

"Briseis stop!"

"No! I won't stop until I get what I want!" as she screamed at him, the grey fire from her hands consumed her and suddenly streamed out of her, knocking her father clean across the room.

His back crashed against the adjacent wall as her power, manifested as flames beat against the shield, he had thrown up around himself.

"Stop abusing it Briseis. I didn't take it for this!" he yelled at her, covering his eyes from the glare of the flame and trying to keep his shield intact. He didn't use his powers often, there had been no need once he'd defeated his enemies and the kingdom was safe from Samaian tyranny. Now, he wished he'd maintained the training. Briseis continued to blaze,

"Maybe you should have taken it for this!"

Briseis stretched out her hand toward her father, opened then closed her fist then slowly lifting it into the air.

Curian began to choke while frantically clawing at his throat before Briseis threw her father clear across the room and out the chamber door that she had opened with her powers.

With a swipe of her hand she slammed the door behind him, the fire instantly subsided and when it did Briseis fell to the ground. She held her palm to her chest as she tried to calm her breathing. Gasping for air, she noticed blood on the floor and slowly placed her hand to her nose. The crimson liquid stained her shaking fingers; she had used too much. She knew the more she used the power, the more it drained out of her, but it was her best weapon against the Redeemer.

She would learn to master it she thought, even if it killed her.

Charlotte Murphy

A HELPING HAND

Truly knowing people was an exhausting talent.

Feeling their emotions, their every hope and fear was a burden she would rather not have when trying to sort through her own.

She had been taught of course how to drown out the noise, through years of training and mentoring but there were always those that got through, that were persistent in their quest to infiltrate her mind.

Still, it provided some distraction on evenings such as this when the world had gone to sleep and only a few people were around her.

The people in question were a man and a woman sat across from her in the bar of the inn she had selected for the night. They were clearly in love, that much anyone could see but what she felt from them was almost overwhelming. They were expecting something that both excited and frightened them and although their hushed voices didn't carry, she sensed they were coming to some kind of decision. She watched as the man leant closer to the woman to place a kiss on her now lowered head. With that, the man rose from the table, dropped two bronze coins onto it and left. She could see now that the woman was crying though she had felt that long before. The woman was clearly distraught, and she felt she had no choice but to go to her.

She was by the woman's side in seconds,

"May I?"

The large brown eyes that met her own were filled with thick tears that consequently streamed down her smooth dark brown face.

The Antonides Legacy I

"Can I help you?"

"No, but maybe I could help you?"

"What do you mean?" she took a seat by the crying woman and placed her hands gently over the woman's that were resting on the table top. The large sleeved cuffs of her navy-blue robe covered both their hands. She looked into the crying woman's eyes and smiled, it always worked best when she was closer.

"You're expecting a child."

The woman immediately looked terrified, her eyes shifting around the quiet and almost empty inn.

"H-how do you know that, who are you?" the tearful lady looked around frantically, clearly afraid that someone would hear them. She placed her hands onto the crying woman's forehead who was almost hysterical with worry and she instantly calmed down.

"My name is Lamya." Lamya said removing her hand

"Are you a witch?" Lamya laughed,

"No, I am not a witch."

"Then how do you know about my baby?"

Lamya closed her eyes and muttered a few words before opening her eyes again and looking at the other woman with a warm smile on her face.

"Do not get rid of your child, you will regret it if you do."

"But my parents...I am not yet married. I cannot go back home; they will cast me out!"

"Why does the father not claim you," Lamya had felt nothing else from him except the love he had for this woman and maybe some guilt. As the question left her lips, Lamya thought the woman would pass out right there in front of her; the pain radiating from her was almost unbearable.

"He is intended for another." The woman confessed

"I see."

The tears were now unstoppable as the woman lowered her head again in despair, causing her tightly twisted locks to fall in front of her face.

"You said you could help me," she mumbled. "What did you mean?"

Lamya placed her hand on the woman's back and sent some healing energy through her, a simple enough task when you knew how and as she did so the woman lifted her head and looked into her eyes, looking a lot calmer.

"I can help you but only if you want to help yourself," the woman nodded. "You must keep your baby."

"How can I…" she was cut off as Lamya placed her hand to the woman's forehead again and repeated,

"You must keep your baby. He will be a very special little boy, destined to do great things." The young woman's eyes widened,

"How could you possibly know that?"

"I just do."

Lamya didn't know where she would begin in explaining how she knew these things. It was a hereditary gift that allowed her to tap into people's emotions, even those of the unborn children they carried inside of them and see the paths their lives would take. She couldn't see the future, what was to be but she felt the positive or negative energy from someone that told her what they were meant for.

The young woman sat there for a moment staring at her before deciding to trust her. Lamya felt her anxiety and her anguish at the thought of being a single mother.

Still, in the far reaches of her heart she felt the love that this woman had for a child she didn't even know yet, a child she wanted to love.

"Where would I go? My family will not accept me."

The Antonides Legacy I

"Agmantia is a large country, you'll find somewhere. You do have gifts?" the young woman nodded.

"Ointments and other such things, my great grammy was Samaian."

"Is that so," she rose from the table. "Well, use your gifts to provide for the child. There are many travellers who would welcome your talents."

The woman nodded in understanding as Lamya made her way back up to her room without another word. Scattered across the small desk in the far corner of her rented room, were small leather bound books and various rolls of parchment. Ink pots and quills accompanied them as well as measuring instruments and other necessary tools that Lamya had needed and used on her expedition around the Known World.

Lamya Rubio was a skilled cartographer with extensive travel experience all over the world. From Agmantia, where she was in the east, the devastated lands of her native Lithania in the west, the mountainous continent of Coz in the north and even the Dyam Islands that were home to the Phyn in the deep south.

The five scattered islands that the sea people called home had the hottest known climate and so the inhabitants spent eighty per cent of their time in the surrounding water. Lamya had marvelled at this was until she journeyed there and discovered that like other sea creatures, the Phyn laid their eggs on the beaches of Dyam to hatch. The intense heat hardened the shell and the skin of the new born that when connected with water for the first time, almost crystallised the surface. Even Agmantian steel couldn't cut through the skin of a Phyn.

She had learned many things on her travels, as far east as Cotai and as far west as Yitesh, but none of that was important, at least not right now.

Lamya had been summoned by the elders of the Lithanian Council and she could only assume it was because her expertise would be of some use. She was a scholar, a learned woman of many different cultures with many talents, not just her racially inherited gifts so this must be of some use to the Council.

Taking a seat at the desk she rummaged through some papers until she found what she was after, a map of Mortania.

She had not been back there in many years, not since that wretched king had begun to rape the country of its natural resources.

She had been living in Thelm with the Council back then and when the Samaian king was slain. For a year after that fateful day, the country had begun to deteriorate before her very eyes and she couldn't bear to watch or feel it happen anymore.

She arranged with the Council to continue her studies away from Mortania and boarded the first available ship.

She hadn't been back since.

Now, the Council had summoned her back to come to the aid of the Samaian heir.

Liya, the sect of Lithanians who possessed her empathic powers had been friends of the Samai for many years. Give or take a few diplomatic discrepancies of course, it was in their best interests to have the Samai back in power. There was no corruption with a Samaian on the throne as they were the chosen people and for a people who thrived off feeling and emotion, to physically feel a country dying at the hands of its ruler, was not something they could stand for too long.

The journey to Mortania was going to be a long one she thought, but the country she had left was no doubt going to be extremely different to the country she was to return to.

She had been given simple instruction: Return to Mortania, find the Redeemer and accompany them to Thelm.

The Antonides Legacy I

Alexander and Rowan's heir had been missing for seventeen years and even if she found them, what more she was expected to do Lamya had no idea, but she knew she must obey. Although her people were not many, they were powerful in their abilities when united and even the Council knew that they must now take an active part in the continuation of the kingdom.

Lamya had always differed with the other council members in regard to their efforts in the war. She felt they should have played a bigger role, *any* role and they felt it was not their place. The Liya were a predominantly peaceful people who only fought when the need arose. Many of the elders still felt the pain of their own persecution and exile from Lithania and didn't want to be involved in anything like it again.

Their own Redeemer, an Everlasting Chosen had been defeated almost one hundred years ago. Their homeland could not survive and so Lithania was destroyed.

The Lithanians that could escape had left on ships as they watched their homes and cities crumble into the earth. They had taken refuge in Mortania but not as the mighty scholars and empaths that they had once been.

Lamya's argument that this very pain was exactly the reason they should be fighting, fell on deaf ears. The Liya preferred to stick to themselves, so much so that their people had become a myth.

Low born people who had never left their respective towns or villages found it easy to believe that the learned telekinetic people simply didn't exist. That their once great city of Yzna-Tum was a myth, along with other legends and history that had been housed there.

People no longer believed in Free Magic that once penetrated the land and its habitants or a land where dragons soared the skies.

Lamya was too young of course to have seen it herself, but she knew that it had been real and needed others to believe it too. On more than one occasion, Lamya had met people who refused to believe she was what she claimed and that all the Liya were extinct. The Council had hidden so well for so long; people couldn't see what was right in front of them. True, other than their abilities, the Liya looked much like everyone else except for their flaming red hair and hazel eyes; but that was no reason to deny their existence.

Even so, she had been summoned to Mortania and she would do as she was bid. She would find Alexander and Rowan Antonides' heir and help restore them to their throne. With their ascension, would be the dawn of a new age that would bring Mortania back from the brink of annihilation.

ACCEPTANCE

Trista and Dana had been helping Thorn tidy and catalogue his studies for just over a week and they still had not begun work on the second room.

Despite her earlier reservations about working at The Grange over being in the Weaponry division, Trista found herself enjoying herself. It also allowed her to spend more time with Thorn.

They spent their mornings together in the carriage talking about anything and everything. While working on the studies once Dana arrived, they would play and tease one another until the end of the day when he would accompany both girls back to their homes.

Trista had not wanted to admit to herself that she was falling for Thorn, but the more she spent time with him the more she couldn't deny it.

Not only had her relationship with Thorn changed in the last week, but since arriving at The Grange, her recurring nightmare had changed too.

It had been replaced by a new dream, a dream in which she was now following the white light. She would follow it endlessly, leading nowhere until she woke up in a cold sweat in her bed.

It was beginning to worry her but what could she do about it and who could she tell?

Later in the evening, Trista was in the study putting some books back onto the shelf when Dana walked in with a beaming smile.

"Trista; it's time to leave."

"Okay," she said. "Where is Thorn?" Trista slid the last book into place and Dana giggled and stepped further into the room to stand in front of Trista.

"He's talking with his mother; he told me to come and get you." Dana paused before adding, "Is there something going on between you two?" Trista was about to object when Dana cut, her eyes wide in shock as she fought not to blush.

"I'm not a spy for Adina or anything! I just thought, well…that we were friends now and that you could tell me…if you wanted to."

Trista was truly touched by Dana's words and smiled shyly in response,

"Thank you, that means a lot but right now…I don't know what my relationship is with Thorn"

"But there *is* a relationship?" Trista realised her mistake and instead of denying it, she admitted what she knew to be true in her heart. Dana couldn't contain her excitement and giggled, reaching out to hug Trista tightly.

The joy was evident on her sweet face when she straightened herself and looked into Trista's eyes.

"I do hope things work out for the two of you if not just for the look on Adina's face when you get married!"

"Marriage? Dana, slow down!" Trista laughed although she could not deny that the thought had crossed her mind.

Marrying Thorn and finally making her mother proud were things she had only dared to wish. Finally, being accepted into the town as a respectable married woman and earning her place amongst the townsfolk, even if that place would eventually be above them, she knew would make her mother so happy. Although she despised the idea of marriage and the imprisonment that it seemed to be, being married to Thorn didn't seem so bad.

The Antonides Legacy I

She knew he wouldn't stop her from being who she wanted to be. By marrying Thorn, she would belong to a family and eventually have a family of her own and there could never be anything wrong with that.

After dropping Dana home, Trista and Thorn made the short journey through town to Trista's house. They sat in companionable silence as they made their way up the narrow path to Trista's home. As the smoke from the chimney slowly came into view, Thorn turned to her,

"I hoped we could have spent a lot more time together then we have done Trista. My plans to come early in the morning to be with you haven't worked out quite as well as I'd hoped." Trista giggled,

"We have been pretty busy," she reached out and placed her hand over his that lay relaxed on the cushioned chair beneath them. "I did come to The Grange to help with the studies and that doesn't unfortunately include spending time alone with you." Thorn brightened up,

"So you do like spending time with me?" Trista looked at Lysa who always escorted them in the façade of a chaperone. Thorn indicated that she could be trusted, and Trista sighed placing her hand on his forearm this time.

"Of course, I do."

As Thorn brought the cart to a stop in front of her house, he helped her out and stood looking down at her. She knew he wanted to hug her, or even kiss her but they had learned that her father was never too far away and even her mother at times, once they heard their carriage approach.

If only they had more time...

Suddenly, Trista felt like her head was swimming and as she swayed, slightly losing her footing; Thorn reached out and caught her by the sides of her arms.

"Trista, are you okay?"

Trista looked behind Thorn and into the window of their kitchen. There, she could see her mother walking around, except she was wasn't. Her mother was in the process of walking but wasn't moving.

It had worked!

"I'm wonderful," she murmured as she quickly pulled Thorn into a hug. He was shocked at first, his hands jutting out awkwardly beside her before he wrapped them around her.

Trista took a deep breath and drew him in as she squeezed him.

"Goodnight Thorn," she pulled away from him, not sure how long this would last and quickly stepped toward her house.

"Goodnight," he called after her and when she turned to wave, she saw that Lysa was wrapping her shawl around her shoulders.

It was over

With a wave, she quickly stepped into the house.

Trista lay awake for a long time once she'd gone to bed thinking about what she had done. She had stopped time twice now and one had been completely on purpose.

She didn't know how this was possible, but something had happened to her and she had to find out what it was and what it meant.

When she finally fell asleep with a thousand questions, she was almost immediately woken by her new dream.

She woke up in the middle of the night, perspiration dripping down her face and her heart beating wildly. She tried desperately not to feed into the fear that was steadily beginning to overwhelm her, but she was terribly afraid.

Trista lay in her bed for hours afterwards wishing the fear and uncertainty would just go away. When the sun began to peek through her small bedroom window, she admitted defeat and went to get ready for the coming day. Even if she had wanted to consider what all of this meant, she told herself, there was no one she could really confide in; no one who could honestly understand what she was going through. Trista had always had no one, only now that she *needed* someone, did it really matter.

Trista went through the motions of getting ready for the day, washing and changing and having breakfast with her parents; her father seemingly needed in the mornings now that Thorn picked her up every morning.

When Thorn arrived, prompt as always, Trista escaped with a quick kiss on her mother's cheek. Once at The Grange, they finally got to work on the second study. Trista was organising various books and scrolls into piles while Thorn coded and catalogued them into a large leather book before placing them onto the shelves. It was still early so Dana had not yet arrived

"Trista?"

"Uh huh?" came her absent-minded reply as she tried to understand a rather faded scroll title.

"Will you marry me?"

She didn't look at him straight away.

Slowly and deliberately, Trista put the scroll to one side in an attempt to process what Thorn had just said.

When she finally lifted her head to look at him, his beautifully large blue eyes were wide with fear and apprehension.

"What did you say?" Thorn turned away from her before he spoke and continued to write into the huge leather-bound book

"Will you marry me?" He repeated.

"I heard that part Thorn but why would you want to marry me?" she demanded as he still refused to look at her.

"Because…I love you."

"Oh," Thorn laughed in amusement and only then did he turn to look back at her face.

"I tell you 'I love you' and all you have to say is 'oh'?"

Trista got up from her seat on one of the floor cushions and approached him, placing her hands on his chest. He looked down at her hand then back into her face with a shy smile.

"I didn't mean it like that it's just…how could you possibly love me enough to want to marry me?" Thorn took her delicate hands into his and held them up to his lips where he kissed the top of them,

"All that matters, is that I do. Will you be my wife, Trista?"

Trista stared into his striking azure eyes and knew her answer,

"Yes Thorn…of course I will."

Thorn slowly lowered his head, gently brushing her hair away from her face as he did so, going to kiss her.

As her eyelids begun to close, preparing for her very first kiss, the door swung open and Dana entered followed by an unexpected visitor.

"Adina?"

Adina's twinkling blue eyes surveyed the room with a satisfied smile,

"Surprised to see me, Master Thorn? Well, the pleasure is entirely mine!" she beamed at Thorn, barely noticing that anyone else was in the room.

Trista's fists clenched by her sides where her hands had fallen as she instinctively backed away from Thorn. Watching the other girl, Trista felt an intense heat begin to gather in the pit of her stomach. She clenched and unclenched her fists as the centre of her palms began to itch, feeling incredibly hot.

"Thorn she uh...Adina followed me in the carriage on my way here. She claimed Lady Avriel sent for her."

Dana was being uncharacteristically bold, but Trista had to admit she was just as confused. Adina noted the disdain in Dana's voice and gave her a piercing look before turning back to Thorn.

"I have completed my weaponry tasks earlier than anticipated and have been reassigned to aid you Master Thorn!" Trista wanted to kick the smug smile directly from her face but knew that she couldn't. Instead she cleared her throat rather pathetically which seemed to snap Thorn out of his bemusement.

"Oh uh...Adina, you haven't said hello to Trista...my fiancé."

It was at that precise moment that Trista's anger subsided and pure joy erupted inside her at the look of horror on Adina's face. Dana squealed excitedly and ran toward the couple, as Adina stood confounded.

"Your...*what?*" she repeated assuring herself she'd heard correctly.

"Yes," Trista replied with a smile spreading across her face and gently taking hold of Thorn's hand, "his fiancé. No congratulations Adina?"

Before Trista was able to delight in Adina's further humiliation, the door to the study opened once again and Thorn's parents entered the room.

Avriel was dressed in her usual long dress and elegant head wrap, this time the palest of blues with black thread embroidered along the hem, cuffs and bodice. Fabias wore black trousers and embroidered doublet that complimented his wife's attire.

"Good morning everyone. Adina, I trust you arrived here in good condition?" Avriel asked politely but all Adina was able to do was nod in her direction. Thorn stepped toward his parents still holding Trista's hand. Lord Fabias saw this and his eyebrows instantly raised in concern,

"Thorn, what is this?"

"Father, Mother...I have asked Trista to marry me and she has accepted."

From the distraught look on his face, the reaction Thorn received from his parents was not what he had expected.

There was an uncomfortable silence as Avriel and Fabias failed to respond and Dana and Trista stole a glance at each other.

Avriel and Fabias looked first at each other then Avriel to the floor and Fabias finally back to Thorn.

"Mother?" Thorn released Trista's hand and took a step toward his mother. For a split second, Trista had the odd feeling that she'd never hold his hand again.

"Mother please say something,"

"Congratulations," she replied looking up at him then over to Trista. "And to you Trista." Fabias finally found his voice as he patted his son on the back.

"Good heavens boy. It seems you're more of a man then I thought. What a lovely young woman you have chosen!" there was a slight disturbance from where Adina stood.

Lord Fabias approached Trista and kissed bother her cheeks, then suddenly proclaimed,

"We shall have a feast, a celebration to rival all celebrations. Thorn, son of Lord Fabias is to wed. The announcement shall be made as soon as I speak with Matthias!" Thorn cleared his throat,

"Father, may I speak with you?"

"Of course, come!"

Thorn, Fabias and a very quiet Avriel left the room leaving Trista, Dana and Adina alone.

"It doesn't seem as though you'll have mothers blessing does it Trista?" Adina sneered at her. Trista didn't warrant her with a reply but couldn't fight the insatiable feeling that Adina was right.

RITES OF PASSAGE

That night, Trista was hurtled through a thunderstorm.

On discovering that Thorn hadn't asked Matthias' permission for her hand before he'd asked Trista to marry him, Lord Fabias and his family went to Trista's house to discuss the formalities of the engagement.

After much discussion in which Trista and Thorn were present but not permitted to speak, the couple it was agreed could be married and the announcement would be made the following morning at the town hall.

It was only as she was leaving that Trista was able to speak to Avriel alone.

"My lady, could I speak with you please?"

"Of course, my dear, what about?"

Trista took a deep breath before she spoke, so nervous she didn't know what to do with herself. She had always admired Avriel, wanted to be like her but there was something about her now that was a little strange. She was mysterious and aloof at the best of times but since the announcement of their engagement, Trista couldn't help but feel that Avriel didn't seem to like her.

"Are you sure you're okay with Thorn and I getting married?"

"Do the three hours of negotiation not prove that?"

"Not really," she said quietly. "It only proves you're agreeing to it, but it doesn't look like you're happy about it." Avriel looked down at her, tilting her head slightly watching her making Trista want to squirm.

"Why do you wish to marry my son?" Trista noted how she avoided the question but had no choice but to reply.

"I love him,"

"People have been married for less than love Trista."

"I don't have anything else."

It was only then, that some remnant of a smile appeared on her face. Not happy just...pleased.

"No, you don't...but you will." she seemed to be speaking to herself rather than Trista. "Goodnight Trista."

Without another word, she left.

***

The following morning the town hall was completely full by the time Trista, Thorn and their parents arrived to formally announce their engagement to Remora.

As the town leader, seating was always reserved for Lord Fabias and his family and now Trista, Matthias and Gwendolyn were part of the entourage. To say that the new level of importance was overwhelming for Gwendolyn was an understatement. She was taken back by the congratulations and the adoration that followed the announcement. The other townswomen, who before had shunned her for her wayward daughter were now keen to speak to her and generally be in her company.

Once Fabias had given details of where and when the wedding was going to be held – a month later – Trista and Thorn were finally able to be together as they accepted the blessings of well-wishers.

Dana was immediately by their side,

"I am so happy for you Trista;" she squealed hugging her. "You are going to be so happy together!" Trista smiled at Dana's remark and looked up into Thorn's eyes,

"I do hope so," Thorn lowered his head to kiss her cheek, and Trista couldn't get over how good that felt.

"We will Trista, I promise. I need to speak with Taran for a moment, please excuse me," and he disappeared into the crowd.

Dana took Trista's hand and quickly led her out of the hall and onto the front steps where it was the quietest.

"Are you excited Trista?"

"I am," she replied. Dana looked compelled,

"Forgive me for saying so but why then do you look so unhappy?"

The whole morning, she had tried to hide her apprehension of now being in the public eye but it seemed she couldn't hide it from Dana. As much as she was happy about marrying Thorn, she was terrified about the responsibility that came with it.

"I am happy Dana; it's just…everything will change and…"

"Like what?" Trista sighed heavily; she didn't want to burden Dana with her issues.

"Nothing. Could you do me a really big favour?"

"Of course,"

"It would make me really happy if you'd be my Maid of Honour, Dana." Dana's face lit up.

"Really?" came her obviously excited and honoured reply as Trista nodded,

"Of course, I will!" Dana pulled her into a hug, that Trista gladly accepted as she giggled her troubles away.

***

That night Trista and her family joined the Remora family for dinner at The Grange. Gwendolyn had made sure that hey dressed in their most fetching attire and even arranged her hair. Trista had never seen her mother look so pretty and happy as she did the moment they stepped into The Grange as extended family. Her father was stoic and quiet as ever, but there was an air of happiness about him that even Trista couldn't deny.

She had done it; she had made her parents happy and proud of her and it felt good.

The meal was going well and now that their engagement had been announced, Trista and Thorn were able to be open with their affection for each other. They held hands when they made their way into the dining room and looked into each other's eyes when the conversation went into the realm of anything they didn't care about.

The merriment continued well into the evening with more talk about the wedding preparations and what would happen after they were married. Where they would live, what kind of work Trista would be involved in within her new position and when they would start having children.

"Children?" Trista's startled reply almost sent her cup of hot tea, flying across the room.

"Yes children; do you not want them?"

Lord Fabias asked looking directly at her while Lady Avriel, her parents and Thorn all did the same.

The room had become incredibly small and for the first time in her life, Trista wished that no one were paying her any attention.

"Of course, I want children but isn't it a bit too early…right now?" Fabias laughed to himself,

"Not at all. Once you get married, babies should arrive almost immediately. At least we all hope that you will get started as quickly as possible."

Trista's cheeks flushed with unremitting embarrassment, but she said nothing. There was no point making the situation any more embarrassing. She felt Thorn squeeze her leg reassuringly under the table as their parents continued their plans for her reproductive system.

It seemed that even though she had found the one man who she did care about enough to marry, she could never really escape the confinements and duties of town life.

As the night drew to a natural close, Matthias decided it was time for his family to make their way home. Servants were called and arrived with their cloaks in hand but just as they were saying their goodbyes in the large foyer, there was a flash of lighting.

Almost instantly, heavy rain fell from the sky drenching the front carriageway.

"You can't go home in this," Thorn called out as the rain pounded against the foyer windows.

"It is not far," Matthias countered but even Fabias shook his head,

"No, the path into town is notoriously unsafe when wet. Please, stay the night."

Her father could no sooner reject Fabias' invitation then he could not take his next breath and so, it was decided they would stay the night. The servants reappeared with a call from Lady Avriel to have two rooms made up for Trista and her parents. While they waited, everyone went back into the adjoining sitting room.

When the servants returned moments later to show them to their rooms, Thorn offered to escort Trista personally. She caught her father's disapproving glare but pretended not to, as she threaded her arm through Thorn's, and they headed up the large front staircase.

Once on the third floor, Thorn turned to her, his blue eyes twinkling in the low candlelight of the hallway. He looked incredibly handsome, Trista thought to herself as he smiled down at her

"My room is just up those stairs to the right if you need anything," he explained indicating a small stone opening that seemed to lead to winding steps.

"Don't hesitate to come up and just knock or…anything." Trista smiled up at him,

"I won't," without really thinking about it, Trista suddenly stepped forward and slowly placed a delicate kiss onto his lips. They stood there for a few moments, before she slowly stepped away and smiled sheepishly.

Thorn continued to look down at her before reaching out to grab her around the waist and pulled her into him, placing his mouth on hers as he did so.

It was perfect, as far as first kisses went. His lips were soft and warm and not too intrusive. They stood there, lips pressed lightly against each other's for a few moments before Thorn tightened his grip on her, causing Trista to rope her arms around his neck. Their kiss deepened, became more intense until Thorn' hands lowered to her behind, cupping it, making her jump,

"I'm sorry," Thorn was immediately apologetic.

"No, don't apologise," she said softly as she placed her fingers to her lips. They were hot and tender to touch but she liked the unusual feeling. She was ready to kiss Thorn of course but anything more than that, she wasn't sure she was ready for just yet.

Trista wondered then whether Thorn had been intimate with anyone else. Surely the entire town would know if he had, but there were brothels…

Trista ignored her negative thoughts and reached out to stroke his face before kissing him once more.

"Goodnight," she whispered as she pulled away and disappeared into her room.

SURROUNDED BY ENEMIES

She knew the Samai had once been extremely powerful but even they couldn't disappear off the face of the earth!

Briseis paced her large bedchamber, troubled that Rowan and her child, Alexander's heir; were still nowhere to be found.

Slowly she lost confidence that she would ever be able to find them and destroy them because it was taking much too long. They had been searching for years now and still nothing.

Her father was no help, having sent his own men to search the kingdom and had still uncovered nothing, seventeen years later.

Her father was weak where she was strong, of course and Briseis refused to fail the way he had. All she had to do was concentrate on what she did know, rather than what she didn't.

The Antonides heir would be eighteen years old, give or take a few months and was of course female, according to the history books anyway.

What she didn't know, was the child's name.

The Samaian archives had noted that the rebellion was well underway by the time the princess was born and so the royal family had been counselled not to disclose the child's name or to crown her until the initial threat was over.

As such, there were very few people in the kingdom who had ever met the child or knew her identity. Members of the royal family, both extended and immediate had been questioned if they were captured or not been killed in the war.

They had all refused to speak and had been executed to remove any threat or possible uprising against the new crown.

Many Samai had fled the country entirely, taking refuge in the surrounding lands under new names where possible but even some laws could stop kings. The Greybolds had no jurisdiction over Cotai or Agmantia and so anyone there, remained safe. It was very likely that Rowan and her child were in another country, growing and building their own army against them.

Briseis turned toward her fireplace then and noticed the fire going down, a small chill creeping up her bare arms.

"Endora!" she yelled continuing to pace at the foot of her bed.

Moments later the door knocked and opened allowing her handmaiden Endora to enter.

"Endora get that fire going properly. It's freezing in here!"

"Yes, your highness," the young girl rushed to the fireplace and immediately got to work.

Briseis could have easily used her powers to do this but she needed someone else around her, some activity to take her mind off her frustrations.

She finally took a seat at the foot of her four-poster canopied bed staring at Endora who for all she knew could be the warrior.

Briseis laughed at her paranoia as she knew, from her reading, that any Samai born while their power source was not in the hands of their ruler would not be blessed with their gifts. Endora was only fourteen years old, too young to have been around before the power shift from Samai to Man.

During her father's short reign, gifted human children were suddenly emerging all over the country. Some were not able to handle their new-found gifts and either went crazy or in some extreme cases, died.

Others found ways to get rid of the power by not using or acknowledging it; not wanting to be associated with anything of the old ways but there were a few, strong enough to maintain the power who were sent to the castle; to Briseis.

Here, Briseis trained, nurtured and sculpted them into what she hoped would one day an unstoppable magical fighting force.

Their main weakness however was their age - the eldest only sixteen years old – and that there were not many of them; only a handful in seventeen years.

In time they would be a significant defence against the Redeemer and any other threat to the realm but right now, they were nothing more than children.

Briseis saw the irony in that she regarded people only a few years her junior as children. There was of course a maturity that came with more than age. It came from knowing you were alone in the world and that no one was looking out for you except you.

Curian had been less than a father to her growing up, instead spending many years away from the castle on some crusade or other against the various races that had or might oppose him. She had realised, even at six years old that she needed to get her father's attention and so, while he was away fighting in some war; Briseis asked the castle Swords Master to train her.

At first, he agreed only to humour the little princess but when Briseis began to display true skill, he began to take her seriously.

By the time she was fourteen she had bettered him in every way and by then, she no longer cared about impressing her father. By then she had decided that her time would be better spent dealing with the Samai threat and since then she had devoted her energy to that cause.

Endora had finished with the fire and rose up from her knees to stand in front of Briseis, eyes cast down.

"Is there anything else you need Princess?" Briseis looked her over from head to toe. Her simple maids uniform suddenly an irritant because even in the plain grey of the shapeless dress, Endora was still one of the most beautiful girls she had ever seen.

The Samai were notorious for their outstanding beauty in both the men and women but Endora was something else entirely.

"Wash your hands and then come and brush my hair." Endora curtsied then scurried out of the room. When she returned moments later, Briseis was sat at her vanity table, her large skirts draped across the cushioned stool and Endora immediately began to brush. Briseis looked at the young girl in the mirror, concentrating on her task.

"Are you loyal to your king Endora?" there was a small pause in her brushing movements, but Endora continued without looking up.

"Yes, your highness."

"Are you loyal to me?"

"Yes, your highness." The girl didn't skip a beat.

"Do you flatter me? Do you say yes to my face then plot my demise behind my back?"

"No, your highness."

"How can I believe you?"

Briseis continued to watch Endora in the mirror and until now Endora's eyes had remained firmly fixed on the back of her head. Now, her eyelids lifted revealing her large green eyes that connected with Briseis' grey ones. Her thick long black hair framed her face as she stared back at her,

"I am of a loyal people. I am bound by my honour as well as my fear to serve you…your highness." Briseis laughed, "As opposed to my treacherous heritage you mean?" Endora said nothing and finally looked away. Briseis was angry, "I wish to be alone…leave."

"Yes, your highness."

Endora placed the hair brush back on the vanity table, curtseyed with her eyes low and quietly left the room.

Briseis decided to get herself ready for bed later that night, not wanting to be around anyone.

She lay in her large bed and decided that the next day, she would consult the Samaian history books again and hopefully find something that could help locate the Samaian heir.

She would find them and she would kill, even if she had to destroy Mortania along with it.

***

Baron Lyon Dreston lay awake in bed troubled.

It was the early hours of the morning and still he had not managed to fall into his usual peaceful sleep.

He'd had more than enough entertainment at his banquet, but it had run its course and he had consequently dismissed his guests and Lady Clara to retire to his private bed chambers.

Even now, a satisfied grin appeared on his face as he recalled he humiliation he had caused Lord Priya. After his time with Clara, they had exited his private quarters in full view of the other guests, and he handed her back to her red-faced husband.

No one would ever dare bring it up to him, but they would all know what had taken place.

He understood that making an enemy of someone as influential as Tyus might not be a great idea, but he would rather have Tyus hate and fear him then for Tyus to simply hate him and believe he could harm him.

In their fear he would have their obedience and once he had Baron Erik on his side and consequently, Thelm then he could begin his plan to overthrow the crown.

He had to make sure that the Barons and Lords he recruited into his immediate circle had more to gain then they had to lose by supporting him. For that, he needed to make a lot of promises in the way of social advancement and of course, wealth. Gold he had but influence was another matter.

There were still many houses, big and small that he would need to connect with to advance closer to the crown. No one would believe he could elevate them if he himself was not elevated; no matter how wealthy he was. Men wanted titles, any fisherman could make some coin but influence and a name to last the ages was what drove them more than anything.

Lyon immediately sat upright in his bed, his brain ignoring sleep as it continued to work overtime.

Baron Thelm had a daughter, a quiet little thing who had made a formal visit to Dreston some years ago; she had been twelve or so at the time.

What lasted longer than the names of kings…or queens? Lyon mused over in his head.

If he proposed to Thelm that he would make his daughter Queen, then the man would undoubtedly be on his side to cement his daughter's position. The excitement that bubbled inside of him was uncontrollable. He swung his legs out from under the thick fur covers of his bed and marched out of the room into the candlelit hallway. His waiting guards jumped to attention,

"Lord Dreston?"

"Have Master Lineas make a trip to Thelm and do a portrait of Baron Erik's daughter."

"Yes Lord" Lyon laughed heartily as he stepped back into his bedroom and shut the door. Before getting into his bed, Lyon pulled on a short rope hanging from the bed canopy.

Nothing happened for a few moments before a small door adjacent to his bed opened and a young woman stepped out.

She was naked but for a sheer strip of gossamer material running from around her neck, over her shoulders and falling down the front of her to cover her modesty.

The piece of material was held at the waist by a thin gold chain that was connected to two golden chains around her ankles.

She had long brown hair, graceful in elegant waves over her heart shaped face as she hung her head low.

"Look at me." Lyon commanded, and she did so. Her eyes were a shocking blue that startled him every time he laid his own eyes on her. Lyon held out his arms, "Come to me Alaina."

Alaina walked towards him obediently, coming to a stop directly in front of him. Slowly, Lyon reached into the neck of his night shirt and produced a small golden key at the end of a chain. He used it to free her of the chains around her ankles then pushed the material aside, so she stood bare in front of him.

She didn't utter a word as he ogled her, silent as ever.

"You are most beautiful," he complimented her softly, but the endearment did nothing to bring life to her eyes.

If not for her blank expression on her face, anyone would think this an exchange between two lovers, both willing but this was not the case.

Yes, Alaina was his favourite; she had been since she had arrived at the castle a year ago when she was fifteen with three other young girls from the city. Her beauty was her gift and her curse as Lyon had not been able to leave her alone since she arrived. Despite robbing her of her innocence and having her chained like the slave she was, Lyon gave her everything. The best clothes, the best meals; even her chains were made of pure gold.

"I will be married soon," he told her as he circled her, taking in her supple flesh. He took pride in the knowledge that he was the only man to have experienced her. Alaina said nothing as he knew she wouldn't unless told to.

"Speak,"

"I wish to serve you for however long you wish it Lord." Lyon smiled.

Perfect.

Without another thought, Lyon took her hand and led her into his bed.

THE PROPHECY

Hours later, after Thorn had left her with the memory of his kiss, Trista lay in her bed wide-awake going over the last few days.

Her time at The Grange had been well spent and now that her engagement was public knowledge, there was a clear acceptance of her amongst the townsfolk. She was someone to be revered and respected now and it felt wonderful; to finally be on the inside instead of an outsider.

Her impending marriage to Thorn along with prestige, brought a level of responsibility that she was excited to take on. Having something to do with her time was stirring to say the least.

She lay awake listening inattentively to the heavy raindrops hitting against the thin glass of the window and as her eyes became accustomed to the dark, she began to make out the ghostly shapes of the furniture and across the room, opposite the dresser she saw...a *woman*.

Trista bolted upright in her bed, widening her eyes but whatever she had seen was gone.

She scanned the room frantically then back at the spot that she thought she'd seen the figure before gingerly pulling her covers back to get out of bed. Her feet were cold on the stone floor and she quickly pushed her feet into a pair of slippers conveniently placed by the side of her bed.

She wrapped the housecoat that lay at the bottom of the bed around her, tied the waistband and walked towards the dresser. The figure was long gone, but she looked anyway, convinced there had been something there.

Trista took a steadying breath before she felt something brush her shoulder and as she spun around, now facing the closed bedroom door she came face to face with a bead of white light.

It was the light from her dreams!

She stood dumb struck staring at it, waiting when suddenly it begun to move.

It made its way to the door and right before her eyes, it opened, and the light floated through it into the hallway.

Trista rushed to the door, staring out at the light that hovered waiting for her and without a second thought she stepped out after it.

She followed it down the hallway, down two flights of stairs and completely out of the house.

When she stepped out the front door however, everything was…different.

There was no courtyard, stables or trail down the mountain into the town square but instead she was surrounded by a large array of trees that didn't look like any forest near Remora she had ever seen.

Trista made her way towards, then through the trees and bushes that had begun to get dense, scratching her arms and tearing little holes in her housecoat. The wind from the chilly night air beat at her clothes and low hanging branches caught in her hair, but she didn't stop walking.

She only cared about catching the light.

She had no idea how long she had been walking when suddenly the light stopped and she found herself at the opening of some sort of cave.

It appeared out of nowhere but there it was, both the entrance and the light beckoning her to enter.

Trista edged forward as she watched the light enter the cave but this time it didn't wait for her. Trista bolted after it, gaining speed in thick darkness with no thought to what was around or in front of her.

Her heart pounded so furiously in her chest, she thought it would break out but still she ran. Her legs began to ache and when her knees and ankles threatened to crumble beneath her, the light came to a sudden stop.

Trista tripped and fell to the floor after the sudden stop, laying on her stomach and writhing in pain. When the pain finally began to subside, Trista slowly got to her feet. Her hands had shallow cuts and along her arms were scratched but as far as she could tell there was no lasting damage.

Once she'd finished checking herself over, Trista looked around for the light. She found it now, above her and it slowly started to get larger.

She watched in fascination as it grew and floated toward the ceiling that she could see was a few immeasurable metres above her.

The light gradually cast over the enclosure and brought everything into clear view.

The cave seemed to stretch out and above forever and Trista could immediately see that all along the rough walls were markings.

She took a step toward the wall closest to her and pressed her fingers against the cold rock. Looking closer, she realised that there were symbols and pictures that kept recurring. The beginning of the symbols - she assumed it was the beginning - showed a faded white circle with lines coming out of it.

She knew instantly that it was her light, the light she had been following and this had to be its story.

The light symbol was eventually joined by pictures of water, trees, vegetation, animals and finally...people. People were eventually joined by something she struggled to identify but looked like winged dogs.

Trista stared in wonder at the symbols until she staggered, suddenly feeling lightheaded. She held the wall to steady herself, but the floor seemed to turn to water beneath her.

Trista fell to the floor, unable to hold herself up and where she sat, holding her head trying to stop the nauseating feeling; the light began to change; to mould into a figure...of a woman.

The Great House will deliver a child,
To remake the world once more.
Lines of magic chosen,
For the truest power to be born.
To Make the strength needed,
To balance the world of Men.
Beasts of fire will soar the skies,
Purely once again.

What the words meant, she couldn't say but she knew they were meant for her as the cloudy figure came closer and looked down at her.

Open your eyes Trista. Do not be afraid.

Slowly Trista opened her eyes and felt that the nauseous feeling had gone. Feeling better, she slowly got to her feet and looked at the cloudy figure that even in this state, looked so familiar...

You have been chosen, the cloudy figure said. *To return magic to the world.*

Trista was confused,

"What? What magic?"

Believe in yourself Trista, the figure said again. *Believe in who you are.*

"Who am I?" she called out desperately. "Who am I?"

As the question left her lips, sharp images seemed to slam into her mind of people fighting, people fighting with fire that seemed to come from their very hands.

The pictures raced through her mind, confusing her; making her head hurt especially when the most monstrous creature reared its head into her vision.

Believe in who you are

Trista fell to the floor again, her head screaming in agony as the images subsided and all she could see was the cold cave floor in front of her eyes.

When she finally looked up, her heart racing the figure was gone and she was laying in her bed at The Grange.

ASCENSION

Trista knew she was lying down because her mother, her father and Avriel were looking down at her.

Gradually, she sat up in the bed and as she did so, she watched her parents step away from her. Trista outstretched her arms,

"Mother...do not be afraid. Our family have been chosen."

Gwendolyn looked at her daughter and fell to the floor in a faint. Matthias rushed to her side instantly,

"It is time then." Trista said nothing, apparently unphased as Avriel approached her, hands outstretched for her to take,

"What do you mean...what happened?" Trista asked, clearly confused.

Her father was now standing with a firm look on his face with her mother in his arms who was crying.

Before they had a chance to answer, information unexpectedly began rushing back to her and she knew where she had been and what she had witnessed but she still didn't know what any of it meant.

"How long have I been away?"

No one answered her,

"Answer me!" she yelled at them.

Matthias took one look at her before letting go of Gwendolyn and marching completely out of the room.

Believe in who you are, the figure had told her.

Trista looked toward her mother and asked,

"Who am I?"

Avriel looked over to Gwendolyn,

"This is not yet my place."

Then she too left the room.

Trista repeated her question.

She had learned too much in that cave for her mother to continue to lie to her, it was now or never.

Gwendolyn walked toward her daughter and took hold of her hands that were resting neatly on the bed covers. Gwendolyn stared into her daughter's face and even though it would hurt her to tell Trista the truth; she knew the time had come.

"I've fought to keep this from you Trista, not to harm you but to protect you."

Trista remained quiet, needing all the answers that she felt Gwendolyn would now provide. Her mother left her for a moment and walked over to the dresser in the corner of the room.

There was a wooden box on top of it that Gwendolyn lifted into her arms and returned to the chair beside Trista's bed with it on her lap.

"You've been asleep for four days Trista. When I realised what was happening to you, I returned home…for this."

Gwendolyn ran her fingers along the top of the box, looking at it then back at Trista.

"Sixteen years ago, a woman came to our home and spoke to me. In her arms she had this box and a small child…you."

Despite expecting it, Gwendolyn's answer still came as a shock. Gwendolyn looked so tortured that Trista didn't know what she could have said at that moment even if words hadn't failed her.

"I am barren Trista and for your father, his family and mine I was a disgrace. I had no choice but to find any way in which I could please my husband and my family and when that opportunity arrived, I took it. You were asleep at the time and one look at your beautiful face and black hair after a long childless marriage, seemed to be the answer to all my prayers."

Gwendolyn looked back down at the box then back up at Trista.

"She said that she was a warrior who had been given a special task she was not able to carry out. She gave you to me Trista in the hope that I would care for you as my own…and I did." She leaned forward. "She said that one day you would be called for something bigger than anything I could imagine and that when that day arrived, I must give you this." Gwendolyn handed her the box that had her name engraved on the side,

"She was not your mother, that she made clear, but she did look a lot like you; you all look alike so they say."

"What do you mean?" Gwendolyn sighed,

"We know what you are Trista, your father and I. We know that you are a Samaian. In Remora, we don't know much about them and we've never had any Samai live among us. The elders told us stories about the ruling race with magical powers but to us, they were just that…stories. The King and Queen were Samaian, but we had and would never lie eyes on them to know what that meant."

Gwendolyn took a deep breath before continuing,

"What we did know, was that King Curian had made being Samaian a bad thing and that woman made it clear that if you were found, people would try to hurt you. You know the King despises them."

"Us,"

"Excuse me?"

"You said *them*, but I am one of them." Gwendolyn sighed heavily and closed her eyes as though trying to block out something then reopened them.

"We didn't tell you what you are because we didn't want you to have to worry or be afraid. We wanted you to be normal."

"I've never been normal!" Trista suddenly erupted at her mother. Annoyed at the naivety of the woman who had raised her. "I've never had any real friends here!"

Suddenly a thought occurred to Trista,

"Is that why the town doesn't like me, why they've always treated me differently?"

"Remora is a small town, but the elders must know the Samaian stories. I can't help the prejudices people might have Trista, or what they teach their own children."

Trista ran her fingers over the box and was amazed and slightly afraid to find the same symbol representing the light that she had been following engraved on the front.

"She said nothing else?"

"All she said was that the Lady would understand. I've only learnt since you've been sleeping that she was referring to Lady Avriel. Until now I'd never even looked at that box again."

After a painful silence, Trista uttered her emotionless question,

"Would you ever have told me?" Gwendolyn sighed heavily,

"I didn't think there would be anything to tell! Trista please understand that your father and I love you very much and didn't want anyone or anything to take you from us."

Trista nodded because as much as she had wanted to, she didn't hate her mother and she could understand the situation she had found herself in.

Had she not been the outcast of Remora, fighting to find something to make her one of them?

If she had been her mother's ticket to acceptance that was otherwise almost impossible to come by, then how could she blame her for that?

A lone tear escaped Gwendolyn's eye and she seemed to realise that it was time to leave and that Trista needed space.

Gwendolyn got up from the chair by the side of the bed and walked over to the door. She opened it and stepped outside but before she closed it, she took one last look at her daughter and smiled,

"Happy Birthday Trista."

Trista sat in the bed with the box on her lap just staring at it minutes after her mother had left.

It was her eighteenth birthday and instead of celebrating she was being hurtled through a web of confusion and fear.

What she had seen in the cave had helped to confirm what her mother had said but she still had no idea what had happened to her or what any of it meant for her now.

And, despite all that; all Trista could think about, was Thorn.

Where was he?

Did he know what had happened to her?

Seeds of doubt and uncertainty now plagued what should have been a time of celebration and she had no idea how she was going to explain to him what she didn't understand herself.

Trista looked down at the box in her hands.

It was made of a dark wood she couldn't immediately name and engraved into the side was her name.

She pried at the lid and struggled to open it at first until the top finally gave way and a blinding blue light shot out of it, then instantly disappeared.

When her eyes had regained focus, Trista gazed into the box with apprehension, excitement and fear.

Bordering on disappointment, all the box contained was a ring, a folded piece of parchment and one half of a pendant on a chain that as far as she could tell; would create a sphere when reunited with its partner. She put the pendant around her neck before taking out the piece of paper.

Written in clearly a rushed hand were names and places in Mortania:

Rayne (Dreston)
Gorn (Priya?)
Council (Thelm)

She placed the paper on the bed beside her before reaching into the box again and retrieving the ring. She turned it over slowly in her hand and saw it was made of silver and had a dark sapphire set in the top. Moulded over the top of the smoothed stone was the letter 'A' also in silver.

Suddenly with an uncontrollable urge, Trista placed the ring on her right ring finger.

A sudden wave of heat rushed over her, rising from the tips of her toes to the top of her head. The heat resided there for a while, pulsating violently until the pain of it threw her backward onto her bed.

Trista's body jerked against her bed until she stopped with her chest heaving in and out heavily. Trista clamped her eyes shut, waiting for the feeling to pass and when it did; she lay there in bemusement.

Slowly, she got from her bed and walked over to the bowl of water that was placed on the dressing table. She splashed some water onto her face, then drank some from her cupped in her hands. Feeling somewhat better, Trista went to sit back on her bed but when she passed a mirror on the far wall, she stopped abruptly. Trista rushed over to the mirror, staring at the person looking back at her.

"What in the Gods…"

Her hair that was usually wavy, straight on a good day was now a cascade of tight black curls that stopped just below her elbows. The cuts and bruises she had acquired from the forest were all gone, and she looked…beautiful.

Everything about her face had changed somehow and for want of a better word; all she could think was *perfect*. Her eyebrows were perfectly arched, her skin clear and her eyes bright.

Trista peered harder into the mirror and saw with astonishment that there was a ring of blue flames circling her green pupils.

"What the…" she raised her fingers to her eyes, peering her eyelids this way and that, trying to understand how there could be fire in her eyes when her hand erupted into flame.

Trista stumbled back, falling to the floor, shaking her hand trying to out the flame but it wouldn't budge.

Do not be afraid

She didn't know where the words came from, but she knew she must listen to them. Trista looked down at her hand, her heart beating rapidly in her chest and ever so slowly, the fire spread. The blue flame spread like a mist up her arm until it covered her entire body and she sat, on the floor surrounding by fire. Trista got to her feet once again to look in the mirror and she was entirely up in flame.

Do not be afraid.

Trista closed her eyes and took a deep breath and when she opened her eyes, the fire was gone.

***

Briseis bolted upright in her bed and stared into the darkness.

With a wave of her hand, the candles dotted around her room were immediately alight and flickering.

"Guards!" she called out and within seconds, three large men stood at her bedchamber door,

"Yes Princess?"

"Assemble a team of men and have them ready and waiting to set out for Remora."

"Remora your Highness?" one of the guards asked quizzically.

"Yes you imbecile, it's a little spit of a town west of here within the mountains. There you will find the warrior we've been looking for and when you do; kill her!"

"Will we go in the usual way Princess?" Briseis nodded as excitement coursed through her veins. She felt the hair on her arms rising from the anticipation of it all.

"I will have the necessary spell to have you there soon but until then be ready to leave when I give the call."

"Yes Princess!" the three men chorused and filed out of the room, closing the door behind them.

Briseis smiled to herself as she lay back on her pillows.

Now she knew where the warrior was hiding, there was nothing that could stop her.

ABUSE OF POWER

She could *feel* her.

Briseis did not know what had changed or how she knew who it was, but she could now feel the Samaian Redeemer.

She felt connected to her somehow and as enlightening as this knowledge was, it unnerved her that the Redeemer could possibly feel the connection too. If she did, did she know how strong Briseis was and was planning to become?

What was abundantly clear from the connection, was that the power she felt was significantly weak. Whether from distance or that the warrior was just not powerful enough, if Briseis could find her and kill her before she grew into those powers, her ascension to the throne would be smoother than expected.

Nevertheless, Briseis knew she had to devise a way to get rid of this woman if for any reason her men failed. She had to do it before the Redeemer became too powerful to kill or even control.

For now, she had to focus on getting her men to Remora. It wouldn't do to wait around too long; the warrior might discover she was being pursued and then flee and Briseis might have no way of knowing where she was headed next.

Quickly getting out of bed, Briseis outstretched her arm and a black hooded robe flew out of her closet and into her waiting hand. She put it on along with thick black fur slippers that sat beside her bed. Once she'd fastened the big silver button just below her breasts, she marched out of her room, into her meeting chamber and into the dimly lit hallway.

The guards posted outside her door twenty-four hours a day jumped to attention,

"Come!" she commanded and led them down the long corridor that led from her room to the steps leading into the west wing of the castle.

Swiftly she made her way down the wide steps then back up the adjacent stairway towards the main library. She had purposely made her own chambers this close to the library once she discovered what there was to learn there.

Swinging the doors open with her power, Briseis continued to march into the enormous library without a change in her step, her guards still close behind.

She finally stopped at a wooden desk, where a large leather-bound book lay open on top of it. The book was open to the relevant page as she'd rarely used any other spell from within it.

She had used this spell many times before but usually had time to make it brew before using it. She was in no mood to wait this time and set to work making the strongest and fastest concoction she could. She wouldn't let the Redeemer slip through her fingers, not now that she could feel her and her power.

As if she had heard something, Briseis suddenly stopped and looked around her in confusion and growing rage

"Where did it go?!" she screamed.

Her guards looked at each other warily as they were accustomed to her random outbursts and knew that nothing good would follow. Briseis began to pace with her eyes closed and her fists clenched by her sides.

As she paced and grew steadily angrier, grey flames began to gather at her hands until eventually they engulfed her whole body.

"WHERE DID SHE GO!" as she let out an ear-piercing scream, the grey flame streamed out of her knocking her two guards to the ground and setting them on fire.

The men screamed in their armour, Briseis ignoring them as she continued to blaze with fury.

Decidedly, Briseis clicked her fingers and her flames subsided. She waved her hands towards the two guards writhing in pain on the floor and the fire extinguished.

They lay whimpering in pain,

"Get yourselves to the Infirmary!" the guards groaned in agony as they tried to get to their feet. Once they staggered out of the door, Briseis slammed it behind them with her powers before slumping into a nearby chair.

Her black robe gathered around her on the floor like a sea of darkness leaving nothing exposed except a few escaped golden tresses and her beautiful face beneath the large hood.

It was gone.

The connection was gone, and she had no way of getting it back. She knew now more than ever that she needed to get the spell done and catch the Redeemer in Remora before they moved on. She had to be smart about it she knew. She couldn't let her rage and anxiety consume her so much that she used the magic the way she had just now for no reason.

A few parlour tricks here and there to scare her father into submission were one thing, but to lose control of the power inside her just out of anger was something else entirely.

She had to control the power, or it would consume her, and she couldn't allow that to happen.

***

The Antonides Legacy I

Being an Empath was to have great responsibility for the emotions of those around you as well as your own.

An Empath had a duty to respect the wishes of others and not reveal their most inner desires even if it seemed that they were screaming to let it out. Without someone's express permission to exhibit those desires or feelings, being exposed could become a torment all on its own.

Lamya had learned to deal with the responsibility of keeping someone's secrets in the early stages of her training but even she had trouble keeping some things to herself, especially when she knew it to be important.

On this occasion she was lucky not to be around anyone she had to keep this news from though she knew it to be incredibly significant.

Momentous may have been a better word, Lamya thought to herself, as she lay in the back of a horse drawn cart being driven to the nearest dock of the Agmantian province where she had been living for the last year.

Once there, she would take her place on *Storm's Breath*; the ship that was to take her to Mortania, a trip that would take days.

She had travelled by sea many times but no private cabin on a rocky vessel for seemingly endless nights was ever going to be as comfortable as her room at the inn.

Lamya had sent her things on ahead the day before, most of which she would have to sell when they reached Thea's Point, the biggest trading point in Mortania, so she could buy passage towards Thelm. While packing, she had already arranged what she could part with and replace and what she could not; a task that had not been easy. She had accumulated a lot of valuable information and trinkets along her travels and hated having to part with them for any reason.

On the journey from the inn in the late hours of the night, Lamya had a lot of time to think about what would happen once she found the Redeemer.

She hadn't realised until this very moment, that the Redeemer hadn't even Ascended and that was the secret she must keep. She had felt the change in the air, that the balance of power that was all around had once again shifted towards the Samai. She had also felt that the holder of this power, the Keeper to all who understood that meaning, did not know what they had inside of them.

It was a raw energy, waiting to be moulded into the phenomenal power that it needed to be.

Lamya knew the Council had wanted her to advise the Redeemer but she had no idea that she would be doing it from scratch. She knew the child would have been in hiding but she also thought that they would have had some incline as to who they were and what they were destined to become.

It was painfully obvious from the weak power that Lamya felt now, that this revelation had only just occurred. There was still no guarantee they knew who they were or what had happened to them.

Lamya instantly felt sorry for the young woman she was to meet, realising then that this must be an incredibly lonely time for her unless she had someone to confide in. She was no stranger to being different, her own intellect surpassing those of her peers in the training academy; the reason that she had been accepted onto the Council at such a young age.

Overnight she had gone from being the reserved young woman with amazing empathic powers and a broad intellect amongst her peers, to someone who told them what to do. Their initial rejection of this change in authority did not go down well and Lamya had been forced to take on a new personality to deal with their torment and jealousy. Admittedly this didn't last very long because the Liya by nature were not an aggressive people and simply because she became so good at being a Councilwoman, they had no choice but to respect her.

With that thought, Lamya became even more determined to see this thing through. She owed it to the quiet little girl inside her to help the Redeemer realise their full potential and earn the respect that position deserved.

Lamya closed her eyes to drown out the noise of the passing countryside. Nocturnal creatures scurrying about in the trees and on the ground looking for their latest kill and the warm summer breeze moving through the leaves. It was weird being able to feel animals as well as humans, but she had come to realise over the years that they were just as important as everything else in their world, that everything had its place.

The cart tottered along, dipping in and out of holes in the road making her journey an uncomfortable one but soon enough, she arrived at the astutely named The Dock.

Agmantian's were not known for their imagination, the way they were known for their steel. Many of their establishments were named after what was sold there. With only one of each tradesman in most villages, it just wasn't necessary and made life much easier for passing travellers.

"Woah!" the young man driving the cart brought it to a stop and Lamya sat up to look around.

"Here already?" she yawned, rubbing the sleep out of her eyes and sending herself some healing essence to wake herself up.

It had been a long ride of almost three hours from the village she was staying in, to The Dock and she needed to be alert before she got aboard the ship and had a chance to retire to her cabin.

"We are here," her driver said getting down from his seat at the helm to help her out. She had been lying on a sack of flour that although better then laying on nothing, had not been kind to her back. Lamya straightened out as her feet touched the ground and her black hooded robes gathered around her feet.

"Thank you very much," she reached into her purse to pay him and he accepted kindly.

"Will you be needing anything else miss, it is kind of late. You never know who could be in these bushes." Lamya smiled at his warning, knowing that there was nothing and no one in the trees, that could do her any harm.

"Thank you for your concern but I'll be fine. I'll wait a few hours in the inn before my ship leaves at dawn. I've already bought passage," he nodded his approval with a kind smile and walked with her to the front of his cart before climbing back into the seat.

"Well you be safe now you hear? Wouldn't want anything happening to a nice young lady like yourself, would we?" she shook her head with the kind flirting smile that had won her the trip in his cart for less than the going rate.

"I'll be fine, thank you. Have a good night."

The dark-skinned man tipped his wide brimmed hat to her and went off in the direction of the neighbouring town that bordered the harbour. Lamya instead walked towards the water, making her way to the closest inn.

The inn was quiet, as was to be expected at this time of night but she still had a while to go before her ship set sail.

Lamya made her way to the bar and pulled her hood back, revealing her long mane of bright red hair. When the barman finally looked at her, she saw the shock in his face as well as the attraction within him so she smiled.

"What can I get you sweet darling?" the brown skinned man smiled gleaming white teeth at her, making his eyes crinkle at the corners. This was a man who smiled often,

"Just some water please,"

"You come to an inn for water?" he replied in disbelief even as he turned to get it,

"I have a lot of reading to get through before my ship leaves in a few hours. I shouldn't cloud my mind with ale." He shrugged with his back to her before returning with a large mug of water.

With her hood now down, Lamya felt the desire from the few men in the room and Lamya smiled to herself as she handed the man a copper coin.

"Thank you,"

"So," he said setting up camp behind the bar in front of her, busying himself with wiping down the bar top. "Where are you headed?"

"Mortania." He visibly took a step back, his deep brown eyes flashing with concern and...fear? Nervously he ran his hand over his tight dark curls,

"Why would you want to go there?"

"It's not a matter of want I'm afraid. I'm needed there, by a friend."

The barman whistled his relief as he made to wipe down some glasses,

"Must be a darn good friend for you to go back to that place."

"Really?" he continued to wipe down glasses then begun on the bar top again.

"Of course, 'aint nothing up those parts but faming and fighting. My eldest got back not three months ago and said he would never go back."

"That bad?"

"That bad," he confirmed putting his cleaning cloth into the front pocket of his apron. He wiped his hands down the front of it. "Of course, the rich folk 'aint doing a darn thing about it. Making all their excuses and such the like, blaming it on the Samai." Lamya was instantly intrigued.

"How so? I thought Mortanians were above petty superstition, at least now?"

"Most, but you know people. They just want somebody to blame."

"It's that wretched king who's to blame!"

A gruff voice from the corner of the tavern yelled across at them. Lamya and the bartender turned in its direction.

The voice came from what appeared to be an old man wearing a weathered and brown hooded cloak and worn leather gloves where two of the fingertips had holes in. He rose unsteadily from his seat in the corner and limped uncomfortably towards Lamya and the barmen.

As he drew near her, Lamya felt an intense pain radiate from him and watched as his face grimaced while he made his way haphazardly to the bar stool beside her. He let out a laboured breath as he took the vacant seat. Lamya and the barman said nothing as the old man pulled the hood away from his head, revealing an untidy mass of dark blond hair. He raised his head and looked Lamya straight in the eyes, electric blue suddenly clashing with her large hypnotic hazel.

She could see now he was a young man, no older than thirty but his body was aged. He was hunched over, clearly in pain but Lamya still said nothing,

"That king will destroy us, every last one of us!" he said, more loudly than needed. He banged his fist on the bar top in clear frustration.

"Take it easy Morn, we don't need any of that around here."

"I'm not doing nothing Jediah," he placated him but not taking his eyes off Lamya.

He seemed to be studying her, weighing up his options but still, he remained wary. He leaned toward her, raising his eyebrows when she didn't lean away from him as she imagined most were accustomed to do.

"He's evil and we'll be the ones paying the price for it," he said. "The day he took the throne was the day our country died!"

"Why do you say that?"

"The land!" he yelled at her, waving his hands wildly. "All around us the land is dying and so are the people. I'd be dead too if they never sent me back."

"Sent you back from where?"

"The city," he snapped as though she should have known exactly where he meant. "We all went there, looking for work and hope of a new life…" he seemed to go into deep thought as he looked away from her. Lamya looked over at Jediah who shrugged.

"Morn, maybe you need to get some rest,"

"I don't need rest Jediah I need revenge! Look what they did to me, look!" he screamed causing the remaining patrons to look over uneasily as he pulled up his sleeves, displaying blackened and blistered arms.

"Look what they did to me with their magic and their power, power that they stole!"

Lamya looked over his burnt arms and wondered what in the world could have done this to him.

"Got told to fight…got told to fight and we'd be rewarded but we got nothing. Putting us in harms way like that and not evening bothering to explain, to tell us…to warn us…" Morn struggled with anymore words and Lamya took pity on him. He had clearly been through something terrible at the hands of King Curian, proven not only by his extensive wounds but his questionable state of mind.

Lamya had witnessed only the beginning of Mortania's torment when Curian took the throne. She could have never imagined that he would allow the power he possessed to hurt people other than through the destruction of the country. This man had clearly come too close to a level of power that was beyond his comprehension.

Curian was being reckless, as reckless as he had been when he began his descent on the Samai all those years ago. She reached out and placed her fingers lightly onto his exposed arms and watched as his eyes widened in alarm then closed as the gently, soothing feeling of healing came over him.

Lamya felt the pain slowly ease from his body, giving him some peace. When she took her hands from him, he opened his eyes and looked at her with serenity in his eyes.

"Get some rest Morn. A change is coming my friend…and you will live to see it." Morn nodded slowly, then limped considerably less painfully back to his chair and his ale in the corner. Lamya looked out the window of the inn and saw the tell-tale signs of the coming morning.

It would soon be time to leave and witness what had broken this man beyond repair.

HEIR TO THE THRONE

Trista placed her feet into the slippers by her bed and tightened the housecoat around her body before leaving her room.

She made her way along the quiet hallway and towards the stairs that led to Thorn's room. She had to see him, talk to him and tell him what was going on.

With a candle in her hand, Trista arrived on the upper floor and nearly fell back down the stairs as she came face to face with Avriel.

She noticed immediately that Avriel's hair was not wrapped in its usual headscarf and she could now see that the woman had long black curly hair just as she now did.

"Your hair, its…"

"I am Samaian," came her simple reply.

Trista didn't have time to be shocked, but was somehow offended,

"Why didn't you tell me?" she accused her, not bothering to question why Avriel was even there at that time of night.

"It was not the time."

After what felt like an eternity of silence, both staring into each other's eyes that were so alike, Trista spoke the three words that wouldn't leave her.

"Who am I?"

"Then you are ready," Avriel said quietly. "Your mother would be proud of you."

"You knew my mother?" Trista asked and Avriel nodded,

"The greatest woman I ever knew. Come."

Avriel led Trista to the first-floor study where they had been conducting her lessons and shut the door.

Avriel took a seat at one of the large oak tables and Trista sat beside her, eager to get the information that she knew Avriel would have. She watched as the older woman, took a deep breath and begun.

"I don't know what you saw while you were sleeping but I do know that you learnt things about our people and our magic that I could never begin to understand."

She paused for a moment, seemingly thoughtful about something before continuing.

"Over a thousand years ago, the First Keeper, Thea was taken away from her village and when she returned, she had with her a great power that she gave to her people and her country. The Samai, through Thea had been chosen to rule Mortania as kings and queens if they agreed to use and distribute the power fairly."

"They were entrusted to protect that power and they did so diligently until the reign of King Alexander XII and his Queen Rowan. It was during this time that an uprising began and a group of Men calling themselves the Prophecy, led by Curian Greybold, revolted against our king in a bid to steal the throne for himself."

"As a direct descendant of the First Keeper, Alexander was also the Keeper of the Everlasting."

Trista's mind was reeling but she continued to listen intently.

"The Everlasting is the maker of worlds, an entity of pure unlimited power. We were sworn to protect it...but we failed."

Avriel took a moment then, when something like anger appeared on her face. Trista didn't know what to make of it but said nothing, eager to hear the rest of the story.

"The Greybold and Samaian armies fought viciously during the Battle at The Wide, and during that battle; King Alexander was killed. He lost his hold on the Everlasting and it was transferred to Curian, as the new Keeper."

"What does that mean?"

"It means that all the power and responsibility of maintaining the balance of magic in this world was taken by Curian when it should have gone...to you."

"What?"

Avriel looked directly into Trista's eyes and firmly said,

"The power and responsibility of Keeper is passed down generation to generation through the first-born child when the parent dies...Alexander was your father Trista."

Trista felt her heart stop and her throat go unbelievably dry. This wasn't right, it couldn't be true.

Believe in who you are

"My...father?"

"Yes," Avriel looked over at her but it felt to Trista like she was looking down at her.

"As the first born, the Samaian heir, the ultimate power of the Everlasting and the responsibility of Keeper must return to you or our world will continue to deteriorate, and we'll lose our power altogether."

Trista shook her head and stood up definitely,

"No, no wait a minute. I don't understand any of this, how is a king my father?" Trista panicked but Avriel just looked at her patiently,

"You were born a few months before the Battle at The Wide, but fighting had erupted all over the country even before that. Curian had become such a threat that the celebrations of your birth were put on hold and you were not openly named or crowned. You were brought here to Remora, just before your mother disappeared."

"Disappeared?"

Avriel stood then and began pacing so her face was away from Trista.

"Once Curian murdered your father, he sent men looking for your mother...Rowan. He had to get rid of you so that no one could contest his right to crown or revolt against him in your name."

"Your mother fled Tirnum but after arriving in Priya, Curian found out somehow and she had to act quickly. By then you were about eighteen months old and she fled so that you could both survive."

"Where is she now?" Trista asked.

She realised that she had been given a lot of information but all she could focus on was that her mother was still alive somewhere...possibly.

"No one knows," Avriel said finally turning to face her again. "She disappeared so you could survive long enough to grow into your powers and take your rightful place...as Queen."

Even though she had somehow accepted that Alexander and Rowan were her birth parents, Trista had not made the connection that this made her the next in line to the throne.

"I'm no queen!"

"It's your destiny Trista. You must save Mortania from this destruction Curian has placed it in." Trista shook her head defiantly,

"No, why should I? Why must I accept a destiny I only discovered two *seconds* ago? Why must I fight for a mother I never knew...and who didn't even want me?"

Trista's heart was pounding with the overflow of emotion and information that was coming her way.

"Rowan did what she had to do Trista," Avriel's eyes were one of such dismay that Trista almost felt bad for having said it. Still, her mother had given her up, she had to know why.

"Rowan did what she had to do so you could survive, and your destiny be fulfilled. We have to believe it was the best thing for you."

There was no emotion in what she said, nothing to help Trista determine if this were true or not. Avriel had never been one for extravagant displays of emotion but this was disconcerting.

It was a few moments before Trista responded, her heart and mind heavy with what she knew her next question would bring.

"What do you expect me to do Avriel?"

Avriel approached her and lifted her right hand, displaying the silver and sapphire ring that sat there.

"This ring is the connection to your family." Avriel turned Trista's hand this way and that, looking intently at it. "It enhances your powers when needed…amongst other things I would imagine."

Avriel dropped Trista's hand,

"You'll need it when you travel to Tirnum City and fight Curian and Briseis for the throne."

Trista looked up at Avriel as a crushing realisation came to her.

"I can't go to Tirnum, what about Thorn? We're getting married!"

Avriel's expression didn't change,

"That no longer seems to be the case does it?"

"What do you mean?" Trista watched as Avriel formulated the words that would ultimately change her life.

"You and Thorn can never marry. It is not your destiny."

Trista was angry. How dare Avriel dismiss her engagement like this?

"What does destiny have to do with anything? I love him!"

Avriel did not seem to be phased by Trista's obvious disgust at the thought of leaving Thorn behind.

"You can't make me leave him; I won't do it!" Trista banged her small fists on the table beside them and began to pace.

"I have not asked you to do anything Trista…you came to this conclusion on your own."

Trista felt disgusted as she stopped pacing to stare into Avriel's irritatingly calm face. Seconds ticked by and still they stood staring at one another,

"You knew this would happen. You knew I would have to make this decision, so why did you let us get engaged?"

"If I had protested against your engagement Thorn never would have forgiven me."

"So, you've left it for me to break his heart!" Avriel didn't reply. "I love him Avriel."

"This is much bigger than that." Trista scoffed

"Where is he?"

"Asleep. You may speak with him in the morning if you wish."

"Why hasn't he come to see me, I know he wants to see me!" she demanded,

"He understands that you're going through something that he cannot be a part of and is respecting my wishes."

"What about *my* wishes? I want to see him!"

"No!"

Trista stared at her defiantly but when she realised she was getting nowhere, she collapsed back into her chair and buried her face in her hands.

When she raised her head again, her face was wet with tears.

"All I've ever wanted is to be accepted for who I am, to know who I am and now that I do...I wish it would all just go away."

Avriel walked up to Trista,

"It won't go away Trista, none of this will disappear. You must embrace your destiny."

Trista's heart ached from the impending reality that she had to leave Thorn, but she was slowly beginning to accept that she was doing this for a higher purpose.

She was doing this for herself, her parents but most of all; she was doing this for her country.

She finally belonged to something that right now, needed her and she wasn't going to turn her back on that; she couldn't.

"What must I do?"

Avriel smiled as she sat back down, and Trista followed.

"You must save Mortania and the Everlasting from Curian, more specifically his daughter."

"The princess?"

"She is *not* the princess Trista, you are. You must accept this. When Curian murdered your father, Alexander's abilities as the Keeper of the Everlasting were absorbed into him but because it was taken illicitly, the power has been corrupted. You can see it in everything around us, the way crops are struggling and the dramatic changes in the weather. If the power stays with Curian and then moves consequently to Briseis when he dies, then Mortania will eventually destroy itself and everyone in it."

Trista tried her best to hide her shock at the devastation Mortania was falling in. She had heard her father discuss matters like this briefly with her mother but never thought it had anything to do with the king; no one had reason to.

Living in Remora made her privy to Mortanian gossip but that's all it ever was, gossip. No one had been to the capital or seen Curian's power. Curian himself remained to be seen for most people, as since the rebellion, he had all but locked himself behind the walls of the capital city.

"You and Briseis are the first-born children of Keepers. You're both co-existing; sharing the power until it can settle in either one of you. You must kill Briseis and Curian to return the power to yourself, before they kill you and return it to them. If you are killed Trista, the power will belong to Man permanently and Mortania will perish."

"But you still have powers and I've only just found out I even have any" she questioned.

"We have our powers because we were born while the Everlasting was under the protection of the Keeper. Any Samaian born now or since the power passed to Curian will not have our abilities."

Trista said nothing, trying to come to terms with the fact that she could die for something she didn't fully understand. She realised how important her task was and now where she belonged, but there was still uncertainty, a need for the finer details.

It was one thing to accept that she was meant to become the saviour of a race but the prospect of dying for that cause was another.

The survival of the Samai and their entire world depended on her defeating Curian and Briseis and she didn't know if she was capable of that.

She wanted to be, she wanted to be able to look Avriel in the eye and say that she was ready, but she couldn't seem to find the words.

Luckily Avriel spoke instead,

"You have a long journey ahead of you Trista but once it is over, everything will be perfect. For now, I want you to get some sleep and we will begin plans for your departure in the morning. Now that you have Ascended, Briseis may know where you are."

Trista understood her to mean the change in her appearance as ascension into her powers but didn't ask any more questions.

With nothing else to add Trista nodded in reply and made her way out of the study. As she opened the door she took one last look at Avriel,

"Thank you…for everything."

"You're welcome …and Happy birthday."

Charlotte Murphy

BIRTHRIGHT

The king stood bathing in its radiation, closed his eyes and took a deep and laboured breath. He exhaled slowly as he opened his eyes again and took in the magnificence of what lay before him, around him and even through him.

The Everlasting, the physical manifestation of the magic, was a beautiful sight to tired, troubled eyes such as his despite his means of acquiring in it. Despite the wars he had fought and the lives he had taken, Curian had firmly believed that he had done what he did with the best intentions. For too long the Samai had ruled Mortania and he had done what no Man before him had achieved by taking their power from them.

Here, in the depths of Tirnum Castle guarded both physically and magically the glorious sphere of shining light rested.

He could feel the power emulating from it, feeling the way it did when it first entered him and gave him his powers. The energy that had raced through his veins was indescribable and he knew then, as he knew now that this was what he was born for. He was born to yield this power, to use it to better his people but with constant obstacles his task was becoming increasingly hard to do. The unknown Redeemer and the absent presence of Queen Rowan continued to plague his dreams, taunting him with the very notion that they were yet untouchable.

Curian walked around the dark circular underground chamber, never taking his eye away from the spherical light atop a triangular pillar of pure gold.

The pillar was in the centre of the chamber, embedded into a marble floor that was in fact a highly detailed map of the Known World.

Around the edges of this were marble cylindrical pillars carved with the names of every Samaian ruler since Thea the First. The letters had faded over the years but what was left had been protected by a magical shield to prevent any further deterioration.

The Samaian rulers for the past thousand years were able to look up their ancestors, know their names and read their stories. Curian wanted that for his own people; the chance to etch his family name in stone until the end of time.

From this far side of the chamber, it looked as though the Everlasting were sitting on top of the pillar, but he knew that it was hovering just above it. Pure energy kept it there, an energy that even he couldn't touch, an ability that was beyond Man but not the Samaian royal family.

Hate surged through his heart as he accepted just how foolish he had been by not finding Rowan the same day he had murdered her husband. She had managed to slip through his fingers and for months evade him before disappearing off the face of the earth! She and the child, a daughter from what he had been told, had been in hiding since the start of the rebellion and he'd not laid eyes on them the entire war.

He had last seen Rowan when his officers had advised him on a diplomatic route as opposed to a physical one and he, Rarno and his own father had come to the castle for an audience with the king. She had been serene then but there was energy about her that he couldn't explain…

***

TIRNUM CASTLE, THRONE ROOM
999 AE

"What you ask is as preposterous as it is impossible. I will never give up my throne, to you or to any other man."

Although he hadn't raised his voice, in the few minutes they had been speaking, King Alexander's voice carried with it, a potent authority that none could deny. This came from a lifetime of knowing that you were better than everyone else, that you were special and did not have to work or struggle for anything Curian decided as he watched the dark robed man rise from his throne, and step down from the marble dais towards him.

Alexander was in a long black robe embroidered with silver thread along the cuffs of his sleeves, hem and the high collar. Silver buttons adorned the front and the cuffs and even the tips of his black boots were tipped with the same metal.

He was a tall man, over six feet with a lean but muscular frame, accentuated by the sharp fitted cut of the robe. His black hair was pinned back from his face in a long and thick braided ponytail that reached to the middle of his back. A sapphire ring was on the ring finger of his right hand and a matching necklace sat low on his stomach; another sapphire set in silver.

Behind him on the adjacent throne was the most beautiful woman Curian had ever set eyes on; Alexander's queen, Rowan.

She was also wearing black, a dress that fit firmly against her generous bust and flowed out like an elegant tent that gathered on the floor at her feet. She had a large diamond and sapphire necklace that rest comfortably on her chest, the centre and largest stone forming into a tear drop that rested subtly near the crevice of her breasts. On her head, on top of a mass of thick ebony curls was a simple diamond tiara and another large sapphire in the centre.

Sapphires were their gem, Curian knew and realised that they had dressed this way to display their power, but he refused to be phased by their grandeur. If anything, it proved how they were running the country: on the backs of the common people and living an affluent life of riches and jewels.

Alexander was now directly in front of him, obstructing Curian's view of the taller man's beautiful wife. Curian fought to tear his eyes away from her to look Alexander straight in the eyes.

"I suggest you return to your homes and forget this idiocy. I agreed to this meeting simply to look into the eyes of my would-be opponent. I have to say; I find him to be less than formidable."

Curian could feel his blood boiling.

Who did this usurper think he was talking to?

He was nothing but a thief who had stolen the rightful place of Man and he had to be stopped. Alexander was a pompous, condescending tyrant and Curian wanted nothing more than to destroy him.

Curian clenched his fists together by his side as Rarno stepped forward,

"My king is a worthy match for any Samaian warrior and will display as much on the battlefield."

"So worthy in fact that he must let his guard dog speak for him." Alexander had not looked away from Curian even as he addressed Rarno.

It was then that Rowan spoke, before Curian could reply, raising from her throne as she did so. Curian was in awe of her as she walked gracefully down the marble steps of the dais towards the four men.

As she drew closer, the thirty or so palace guards that lined the central walk way of the great hall shifted ever so slightly, their stances more alert, ready to protect their queen.

"My husband has forgotten his manners Curian Greybold. At this moment in time, you are our guest and should be respected as such."

"It is you who are our guest, a foreigner in our homeland." Rowan smiled, though the act did not reach her eyes,

"A guest, for over a thousand years?" the answer was in her question.

She believed they had every right to be there as much as Curian believed that they did not. Rowan was finally by her husband's side and as if to taunt him further, Alexander placed a possessive hand around her waist to rest on her now obviously pregnant stomach.

Curian had had no idea that the queen was expecting and for some reason this angered him more. That this extraordinary beautiful woman was ripe with Alexander's seed made him want to rip the man's throat out.

He didn't deserve the crown or this power.

He didn't deserve *her*.

"You see, other than being bound by the chains of duty, honour and of course my birth right, I have a much more personal reason to hold on to my throne." Alexander said condescendingly. Curian looked from Rowan's stomach, to the queen then back to Alexander's judging eyes.

"Then we have nothing left to discuss." Curian made to leave when the queen said,

"Goodbye Cur."

Curian looked at her intensely and was angered, how dare she do this him?

The Antonides Legacy I

With a last look at Rowan, Curian turned on his heel and marched out of the great hall with his father and Rarno in tow.

When they were out of the castle and mounting their horses, his father Magnus turned to him.

"What will you do now?" Curian thought instantly of the delicacies of Rowan's face and her swollen belly that carried another man's child.

"We will destroy him...and take everything he holds dear."

That night Curian had made passionate love to his wife and nine months later, Briseis was born.

The months following that encounter had been uninterrupted preparation for the war. Before that meeting, there had been petty battles amongst common men and Samai in the streets of Tirnum and the then surrounding towns and villages. Curian had been rallying men to his cause, building an army that would eventually help lead him to victory over Alexander at the Battle at The Wide.

He had indeed taken everything Alexander held dear, his kingdom, his life and his wife.

His advisors and guards had told him that she and the child must have been killed but he knew better. There was no way that Rowan would have allowed herself or her child to die and there was no way he was going to let them destroy him or his own daughter.

Briseis.

Briseis was another issue altogether.

It troubled Curian that despite her shortcomings as a loving daughter and filthy attitude toward the power she possessed, he still loved her with all his heart.

In all but attitude she was the very image of her mother and looking at her made him feel closer to his late wife.

Myrenda Greybold had died giving birth to Briseis and he had raised his daughter as best he could. Despite his best efforts, Briseis had grown into a vicious, manipulative and cruel young woman with an insatiable thirst for power. In a son, he might have admired this, even praised and goaded it but in a woman of seventeen it was ugly. It was unfair he knew, to judge her actions by her sex and not by the destruction that ensued but there was a time and place for everything and this wasn't it. He needed things to change with his daughter and soon.

He looked to the Everlasting now for answers, knowing they wouldn't come. It didn't think him worthy and now, after so many years, he had started to believe it.

Although it had given him the power, he knew it did not want to be there.

He knew in the way he struggled to control it sometimes that it felt foreign in his body. As if to defy it, he focused his will and channelled the power through him. Black flame immediately emerged around him then gathered to just appear on his hands and immediately shot out of them towards the ball in the centre of the room.

The fireball bounced off an invisible field surrounding it that rippled then became still almost instantly. Curian shot out another ball of flame then another and another that all disintegrated as they touched the force field, getting nowhere near the Everlasting.

It was no use, he knew. Only a member of the royal family could touch that orb or give express permission for it to be touched.

Once again, something he couldn't do, he couldn't *have* that Alexander could.

Well, he refused to let him continue to win even in death. Once he found Rowan and her child, he would kill them so that he could finally be the king he was born to be.

FOLLOW YOUR HEART

It took Trista a long while to get to sleep after her talk with Avriel but once she finally did, it felt as though she were instantly woken up.

She didn't know why or how, but she instinctively knew that she was in danger.

The feeling was palpable, almost a physical thing in the pit of her stomach that she couldn't ignore.

She rushed out of her bed, dressed quickly and rushed out into the dimly lit hall way outside of her room. She was barely down the stairs, heading desperately towards Avriel's bedroom, when the older woman suddenly appeared on the stairs.

"Something's happening to me!" she cried, rushing into the woman's arms.

"What's wrong Trista?" Avriel placed her arms on Trista's shoulders to stand back from her and look into the young girl's face.

"What happened Trista?"

"I-I don't know. I just feel like I have to get out of here, that I have to leave!"

"Leave and go where?" Avriel was so calm it was almost infuriating even though she knew she had to remain calm to figure out what was going on. Trista took a deep breath as she tried to explain,

"I was woken up by a...a feeling, a feeling that I was in danger and that I had to leave Remora. That's it, that's all I have."

Avriel looked thoughtful,

"It may be that your powers are manifesting in new ways since your Ascension, but why would you be in danger?"

"I don't know Avriel, aren't you the one who's meant to know about these powers?" Trista was shocked that she snapped at her and seemingly Avriel was too.

She removed her hands from Trista's shoulders,

"Now that you've Ascended, Briseis may very well know where to find you. Maybe that is what you're feeling."

As Avriel said the name of the princess, a sharp pain stabbed into her head making her double over.

"The princess?" she barely got out the words as her head pounded,

"Yes, you're connected somehow."

The sharp pain hit her again and suddenly Trista heard a very clear female voice ring through her mind,

Get to Remora immediately. I want her dead. Do you hear me? Dead!

Avriel was right, but how was this happening?

"I have to leave here," Trista doubled back onto the stairs to her room,

"Where will you go Trista?" Avriel was following close behind her as Trista staggered to her room but didn't offer to help her.

"Dreston," Trista said decidedly. She suddenly remembered the box her mother had given her and inside was a name and a location.

"The box said something about Dreston, I'll start there."

Trista finally got to her room and rushed on the first set of clothes she could find. She packed her box and the few items that had been left in the room with her since she'd lay comatose for four days at The Grange.

"What about your parents Trista, what about Thorn? Don't you want to say goodbye to them!"

Trista stopped for a moment as she rushed her small things into a bag she had found,

"There's no time."

Trista replied regrettably before turning around to look at Avriel,

"My parents will never understand; they'll never accept this." Trista explained even though she suspected that Avriel already knew.

"Please tell Thorn that I'm sorry. Tell him, that as much as I care about him…that I can't marry him right now."

Avriel seemed to expect her response and simply nodded,

"I need a horse." Trista said and exited the room expecting Avriel to follow.

They got to the bottom of the stairs and out into the courtyard where a young boy sat carving something,

"Boy, we need a saddled horse with small provisions, any will do."

The young boy jumped to attention, confused clearly as though this was usually the quiet shift and he'd never expect to be needed.

"T-there's o-only Master Thorn's horse ready my lady," the boy stammered.

"It will do," Avriel demanded and the boy scurried off.

Trista took a deep breath as they waited for the boy to return.

It was finally happening; a little sooner than expected but she was finally leaving Remora.

It was all too real and she suddenly didn't know if she could handle it. Her heart began to race as she looked at the boy finally coming toward her with the saddled horse. She went to turn back into the house but Avriel was standing in the doorway.

"I can't, I can't do this!" she screamed hysterically and burst into tears.

Avriel quickly pulled her into a tight hug and rubbed her head gently.

"You must do this…there is no other way."

She pulled away from Avriel, who uncharacteristically wiped the tears away from her face,

"I want to say goodbye to Thorn, I can't just leave him like this!"

"He'll only try to make you stay"

She was right of course but still Trista didn't know what to do. She was too afraid and too nervous to think of retaliation so instead she was silent.

Avriel clearly took this as acquiescence

"You should get anything you may need from your home, Dreston is a long way away."

Trista nodded her understanding before turning to mount the Palomino mare. Trista looked down at Avriel and smiled to which the older woman smiled back, a true genuine smile,

"Take care," Avriel said softly as Trista gave her one last look, waved goodbye and headed down the hill.

Avriel watched as Trista disappeared down the hill and the smile fell from her lips as she looked down at her hands where distinct grey smoke clouded around them. She turned and looked up to the second-floor window where Thorn was banging his fists against the glass and no sound was coming from it.

Avriel snapped her fingers and instantly, Thorn's screams and pounding could be heard,

"You'll see her again soon enough my son," she murmured before stepping back into the house and with a swipe of her hand, closing the door behind her.

The ride into the town square was a quick one and when Trista raced through, there were only a few people around.

The butcher and the fishmonger were up arranging their new commodities for the day and some of the wives were up too. No one paid much attention to her and the people who did just acknowledged her with a polite hello as her horse trotted by.

When she finally made it up the path to her house and dismounted, she was surprised to see Dana Black sitting on the small bench beside their front door.

Trista ran up to her,

"Dana, what are you doing here?" Dana stepped aside so Trista could open the door,

"I'm here to start the wedding plans with you and your mother. As your Maid of Honour, it's my duty. Where is your mother, I was surprised she wasn't here?"

"We've been at The Grange. Dana, I can't deal with any of that right now,"

Trista ran into the house and up the stairs with Dana following close behind. She entered her bedroom and immediately went rummaging for extra clothes, shoes and anything else that might need on her trip,

"Why not, what's going on?"

Trista continued to claw through her things and pack them into small bags she had at the bottom of her wardrobe. She had placed the weird shaped pendant around her neck from the night before and the ring on her finger along with the sheet of old paper. The box she had packed with her other things,

"Thorn and I aren't getting married."

"What, why not?" Dana was mortified but Trista didn't answer straight away.

She continued to pack and was about to leave the room when Dana held her back.

"Trista stop and talk to me! Why aren't you getting married and *where* are you going?"

Trista didn't want to cry. She didn't want to have to explain to Dana that she was leaving the one person in the world she cared about behind and that she was doing this for a purpose she still didn't fully understand.

She knew where she needed to be and that somewhere inside she wanted to do it, but was it worth giving up Thorn for? Dana looked at her waiting for an explanation. Trista turned to her only real friend in this whole world and said,

"I can't marry Thorn because I found out that I am not my parent's real child. I'm going to Dreston to find my birth parents."

It wasn't entirely the truth, but it wasn't a lie either. In some ways, she was trying to find Rowan.

"Birth parents?"

"Yes, and now I have to leave. I'm sorry Dana...I really am."

Trista ran out of the door leaving Dana stunned for a moment before she regained her composure rushed out of the room after her,

"Trista, Trista wait!" she found her once again in the kitchen packing any food she could carry easily into one of her bags. Fruit, bread, a block of cheese. It would have to do until she found things less perishable. Trista brushed past Dana and back outside leaving the front door wide open before strapping her bags securely and mounting the house once more.

"Trista...you can't just leave!" Dana was at a loss for words as she stared up at her,

"I have to Dana."

"Then I'm coming with you."

"What?" Trista looked down at the only real friend she'd ever had, and her heart broke all over again.

"I'm coming with you. Dreston is days away, you can't go alone."

"I have to go alone it's my desti…" Trista stopped herself before she said too much. "Dana you can't come, it's too dangerous."

"Why would it be dangerous?" she didn't have an answer for her.

Dana stared up at her waiting for an answer and all Trista could think about was the time they were wasting. Whoever Briseis was sending after her could be here at any moment.

"I can't explain Dana, just know that I have to go, and I have to do this alone…I'm sorry."

Without giving her a chance to speak, Trista turned the horse around and rode out of the clearing, down the hill; through the town and straight out of Remora.

DO WHAT MUST BE DONE

She hadn't been riding for twenty minutes before Trista knew she couldn't do what was required of her. She contemplated for the millionth time that she was finally leaving her home and the life she was accustomed to, to indulge in a fantasy that could more than likely get her killed.

She was entering a game with far more experienced players who wouldn't hesitate to take her life. As much as she had dreamed of leaving Remora and doing something new and exciting, this was more than she had ever bargained for.

Trista rode hurriedly down the mountain path even while her heart told her she would never survive whatever she found at the other end.

Suddenly, the distant sound of galloping hooves reached her ears, and an immobilising fear paralysed her atop her horse, bringing it to a stop.

Could they have made it here already?

Trista looked ahead of her at the road that led into the open lands of Mortania then back to the mountain trail that would take her back to Remora.

The galloping was getting closer but she couldn't tell yet from which direction as it seemed to echo all around her.

She forced herself to focus on the sound and not her fear and realised that it was in fact coming from the direction of Remora.

Eventually the horse and its rider came into view, coming at a great speed until Trista could see that it was Dana.

"Trista!"

Trista watched as Dana came racing towards her, before bringing her horse to a sharp stop. Trista dismounted, and

Dana followed suit before Trista pulled her into a hug then almost instantly pushed her to arm's length to look her in the eye.

"Dana what are you doing here?" Dana smiled, unsure of herself,

"I saw the way you left the town and I couldn't let you go alone. I got some supplies from home and here I am. I'm here to help you find your parents."

Trista immediately felt guilty that Dana had come all this way on a lie. She couldn't tell Dana that she had lied to her but she couldn't tell her the truth either.

"Dana, as much as I appreciate you looking out for me, you *can't* come."

"Why not?"

"It's dangerous…I could die!"

"All the more reason not to go alone. How you could die searching for your family though, I have no idea!" she said with a giggle, making Trista roll her eyes.

"I'm not looking for my family I'm…"

Trista was cut short as a deafening clap of thunder erupted from above them.

Both girls ducked instinctively looking up into the clear, blue early morning sky then back at each other. They turned slowly in the direction of the kingdom as the thunderous echo of armoured steeds and riders escalated towards them.

This was it, they were coming for her and she was powerless to stop it.

As if in answer to her deflating thoughts, her right hand began to twitch, and Trista looked down at where her ring was now glowing faintly. If there was ever a time to prove herself to Avriel, to her parents and more importantly to herself then it was now.

The Antonides Legacy I

She knew she had to be brave; she knew she had to take on whatever was coming towards her and face it with all the power she had been told she could possess.

She could feel it now, coursing through her hand and breathing through her skin but how to let it out she still wasn't quite sure. Taking a longing look at the ring on her hand, Trista knew she had to act quickly.

The riders drew nearer,

"Get on your horse."

"W-what?"

"Get on the horse Dana, *now!*" Trista commanded as Dana nodded in fear and climbed back onto her horse. Trista handed her the reins of her own horse then stood in front of both them and Dana. The riders were visible now, charging towards them like an ominous wave of destruction and terror; a patch of darkness surrounded by light and life.

She knew they had seen her now but they didn't show any signs of stopping.

First, Trista stood with her arms by her sides, closed her eyes and concentrated. She focused on what she wanted to do, on the tens of men coming towards her, their horses; their weapons. The familiar and now welcome feeling of being weak came over her and she knew whatever she was doing was working. Harder she focused, trying to keep her thoughts entirely on the soldiers approaching her. She could feel their power, their determination, their thirst for blood; *her* blood and knew that this had to end.

"Trista?" came Dana's worried tone but Trista had to ignore her.

"Trista...Trista!" as Dana let out an earth-shattering scream, Trista opened her eyes.

In that instant, her entire body was cloaked in light blue flame with a ring of flame around her pupils. Their horses reared and stepped back from her, unsteadying Dana but she held on as she stared in amazement and terror. Trista raised her right hand towards the approaching army just as she had done in Remora and as she did so, the army collided into a solid wall of…nothing.

Trista stood in full blaze, palm outstretched as the army crashed into the invisible barrier she'd created between them.

One by one, the men and horses crashed into the transparent wall with a thunderous din and collapsed in a heap at the base.

The noise was deafening as screams from men; animals and the collision of steel and cracking bones added to the ruckus.

As the last of the soldiers met the wall or the crushed army before them; the flames subsided, and Trista fell to the floor unconscious.

***

"What do you mean you can't find them?"

"There has been no word from them your highness. No one has been able to reach them and we've received no raven."

"They cannot have just disappeared off the face of the earth Gardan!"

Gardan Beardmore, the Captain-of-the-Sentry shifted in his stance unsure of what to say or do.

It unnerved him that a grown man such as himself could be afraid of a young woman, but still he knew better. Gardan stood in front of a few of his men and waited for Briseis to speak. He felt shuffling behind him and instantly the princess turned her attention to the movement behind him.

"What did you say?"

No one spoke, unsure of whom she was referring to but Briseis continued to stare into the group of men.

"You," she stretched out her arm and gradually a parting was created between the men as a young guard named Enam was dragged between them from the back of the group, all the way towards Briseis.

The rest of the men watched as he was pulled towards her by some unseen force, the tips of his boots not even touching the ground. Enam hovered there, inches above the floor directly in front of Briseis as she lowered her arm to fold it across her chest.

She glared at him through grey irises with a look that he understood meant trouble.

"What, did you say?"

"N-nothing Princess!" he stammered as he hovered above the ground held up completely by her magic.

"Do not insult me by lying, I don't have the patience. You want to know why you have to take orders from a little girl do you?" he knew better than to reply but it wouldn't save him from her wrath.

Briseis smiled devilishly and tilted her head slowly to the side as Enam's neck began to twist. The skin on his neck became misshapen as his head turned slowly to the point where it could not go any further, then with a quick blink; it twisted that little bit more and snapped.

Enam dropped to the floor and the rest of the guards backed away from the body but said nothing.

"That's why." Briseis turned away from her guards and placed a hand on the chair in front of her, taking deep, slow breaths.

"I want to know what happened to them Gardan. I want to know where they are and whether they have killed the warrior. Do I make myself clear Captain?"

"Yes your highness!" Gardan left the room before she could bark any more orders that he wouldn't be able to carry out.

Leaving his men to return to their posts while he went to his own quarters to devise some kind of plan, Gardan marched forcefully toward the entrance of Sentry's Keep making sure that things at least in the castle were running smoothly.

As Captain-of-the-Sentry, he was tasked with the day to day running of the city and Briseis' personal guard. It was a newly acquired position and he hadn't understood why no one wanted to put themselves forward for it in the beginning. It was because, he found out later, that Briseis was such a tyrant. Gardan had previously provided his services in the king's army where not much took place, but where he saw the opportunity to head his own men, he gladly took it.

Working for a sadistic woman like Briseis, was the price he had to pay for moving up in the world. He was from humble beginnings and so moving from lowly soldier to captain, was a welcome move.

Almost an hour after his audience with Briseis, while he was sat behind his desk trying to determine how he was going to find men who had disappeared off the map one of his lieutenants rushed in.

"What is it Minen?" Minen saluted as was appropriate,

"A soldier from the Remora expedition, they've returned." Gardan clapped his hands together triumphantly,

"Finally, some good news. Let's see what he has to say shall we?"

The Antonides Legacy I

It had only been a few hours since soldiers had been sent to Remora using Briseis' magic and she had been demanding answers that so far he had been unable to deliver, maybe now was his chance to please her.

Gardan laughed to himself, making his way to the main entrance of Sentry's Keep, knowing full well that there was nothing in the world that could make that young woman happy. Her anger and distain could be suppressed for a while but complete happiness? Not in this lifetime.

He was unsure what had made Briseis the way she was and didn't particularly care as long as it didn't get him killed.

He approached the entrance where his First Lieutenant Minen was waiting for him, having run on ahead of giving his message.

"Where is he?" Minen saluted him again

"Jero has just arrived Captain, he has news from Remora but it's not good."

"Bring him in."

Minen exited the small entrance chamber to Gardan's work area and returned minutes later with Jero. Gardan was taken back momentarily but did not let it show on his muscular and rigid face.

Jero, a healthy strong and loyal man of about nineteen was now less than a shell of himself. He looked as though he hadn't eaten in days and had been through the war of the worlds. Blood was stained across his face and over the armour that wasn't covered by a large blanket they had given him. His helmet was missing and his hair tussled and thick with dirt and grime.

"What happened? Where are the others?"

"Dead Captain...all dead." Gardan's eyes widened in disbelief,

"All *eighty* of you?" Jero nodded,

"A woman...a woman was there on the trail. It was the Redeemer."

Gardan's eyes narrowed,

"Are you sure? Speak man before I kill you myself!"

"Yes, it had to be her; she had power just like the Princess." Jero's eyes were all over the place, shaking in terror, his face contorted and confused. "What she did...the power was unbelievable!" Jero was clearly in shock as he recalled what had happened to his fellow soldiers. Gardan and Minen listened intently as unwelcome fear crept up inside them.

"Where did she go, where is she headed?"

"I don't know Sir, the collision knocked me unconscious and when I woke up she was gone. Everyone was dead but me and Gibson but his heart soon gave out. I knew you would need this information so I used the magic the princess gave us to get back here. It did this to me," Gardan hadn't noticed before but Jero was missing an arm.

On their many expeditions to find the Redeemer, if there was any information that was deemed imperative the princess have, then the leader of that expedition was given a source of power, a spell to use. It would immediately transport the user back to Tirnum Castle where they could then deliver that information. Because the garrison were but normal men, using the power had severe side effects, some mental and some like Jero, physical. It was too dangerous to use often and required a skill that Jero clearly hadn't been trained for.

"Get this man to the Infirmary immediately. I have to speak to the Princess."

Minen rushed Jero out of the guardhouse and away to the infirmary as Gardan sank deep into a nearby chair.

The Antonides Legacy I

Although he had spent his entire time in the princess' service searching for the Redeemer, he had never thought they would find them. He'd thought the princess' vendetta a pipe dream and even found himself hoping that they would never find the Redeemer and that the princess would give up on her futile mission.

Of course, he knew the stories and legends, growing up in Thea's Point he'd seen Samaian rule first hand and knew the stories…and Mans destruction of it.

He had heard tales of distant lands where man had taken over from ruling kings and destroyed the very land they had claimed to want to protect from the Samai and any other enemy that they came across. Despite being Man and growing up amongst their teachings, Gardan was often unsure of whether he was fighting for the right side.

Was this Redeemer really such a bad omen?

From the stories, he had heard of their ability to bring forth peace and a better Mortania, he didn't think that they were. He wasn't stupid, he saw the cold weather that crept up from the coast at Thea's Point. His own mother told him how her crops were failing this season. It wasn't a coincidence that once Briseis' father was in power; things had gone terribly wrong.

Making his way back into the castle, Gardan knew the princess would go insane once she found out the news and he was not in any rush to tell her considering the state he'd left her in only hours before but it was his duty.

With a heavy heart and a mind plagued with doubt and growing fear, Gardan went in search of the princess.

He heard her battle cries before he saw her.

The in-palace guards had informed him that Briseis was now in the eastern courtyard training; she had been since her audience with him but two hours before. He walked steadily along the arched stone walkway until he appeared in the enclosed, open aired courtyard. Briseis and her trainer were at the far end sparring. Both were in full armour, Briseis' moulded to her elegant frame. Gardan watched her for a moment as she ducked, weaved and attacked her trainer with both force and grace.

She was agile even with the armour, the finest Phyn leather that was so hard to come by. The Phyn were an unsociable race at the best of times but to catch one and get beneath the seemingly impenetrable surface of their skin to the thick flesh beneath to make the leather was widely unheard of.

Briseis moved swiftly to avoid her teacher's next heavy blow and continued to match his expertise as she danced around him wielding two short swords.

She took her stance as her trainer took his and raised her swords, crisscrossed above her head. Then without any obvious warning to Gardan, she stepped forward while simultaneously slicing outward causing her trainer to lose his balance.

In the second he lost his form, she used her right hand to slice across his chest, then her left to slice back across then spun around so her back was to him before jutting them out behind her so that he trainer couldn't advance on her.

As he stumbled back, her left arm stayed where it was as she stepped away from him and brought her right sword up over head. She stood there for a moment as her trainer composed himself then came at her again. She parried with ease before performing an intricate manoeuvre that brought her teacher crashing to the ground.

She raised both swords above her head and brought them down into his chest, when Gardan stepped forward,

"Princess!"

Briseis stopped with the tips of her blades, piercing slowly into her trainer's breastplate. Without easing up she glared at Gardan through tendrils of blonde hair that had escaped her ponytail. Gardan bowed low as he approached her,

"Princess, I have news of the Redeemer."

He saw her body shift and slowly, even dangerously she straightened up.

Her teacher, a man of about forty looked obviously relieved and wasted no time getting to his feet. Two servants appeared from seemingly nowhere and rushed to her side. One relieved her of her swords while the other stripped the leather armour away from her. In seconds, she stood before him in just her undergarments, unashamed although Gardan and the rest of the guards had the sense to look away.

Her indecency was short lived as the servant undressing her, placed a cotton robe around her shoulders and Briseis tightened it at the waist. She turned and walked away,

"Speak," she commanded as Gardan followed in her footsteps.

"One of the men, Jero, he returned with the use of the reserved magic; everyone else was dead." He was now beside her and Gardan saw her cold eyes shift to glance at him but she said nothing, so he continued,

"He says that the Redeemer was there and killed them all with power such as yours."

They were walking towards the bathhouse where more servants would be waiting to attend their princess.

"Jero was knocked unconscious and only came to when the Redeemer was gone. He has no clue as to her next destination."

Garden concluded his report as he waited for the princess to respond. They had reached the bathhouse and a huge door opened inward, revealing a lavish room housing a large marble tub. Steam rose from it and Gardan saw various women inside preparing to do their duty. Finally, Briseis turned to him,

"You and your men have done well but there is much to be done."

"Princess?" Gardan was confused; he had expected her to be angry.

"I will know soon enough where the Redeemer will be next and when I do we will find her there and attack. I have been drained by this first expedition Gardan I will admit, but I will soon be at full power and have the necessary resources to kill this woman."

"I have every faith, Princess," came Gardan's dutiful reply.

"For now, I want your best men trained to be better. When my power is restored, I will need them ready."

"Yes, your Highness," Gardan bowed low and turned to leave her.

"Oh, and Gardan?" he turned, "My weapons tutor should buy you a round of ale; after all, he does owe you his life."

Briseis winked at him and sauntered into the bathhouse.

ALLEGIANCES

When Trista woke up it was dark.

She waited a few moments for her eyes to adjust the darkness then realised she was laying by a small fire. She tried to sit up, but someone was immediately by her side and she looked up to see Dana smiling down at her.

"Don't get up, drink this."

Dana offered Trista a cup of what turned out to be water and she gladly took a sip of. When she was done, Dana took the cup away from her lips, placed it on the ground beside them then took a seat next to her. At that moment, Trista could not have appreciated Dana more and so she took a deep breath and said,

"How long have I been out?"

"A few hours…basically the whole day."

Trista nodded although she was confused.

She'd been unconscious the whole day from the use of her power. It was clear she needed to be more careful with it or something worse could happen to her next time.

"Where are we?"

"The end of the Remora trail. I didn't know where you'd want to go so I set us up at the end of the trail until morning." Trista nodded her thanks as Dana waited patiently for her to explain

"I'm a Samaian." Dana turned to look at her, her expression never changing and waited for Trista to continue. "Years ago, Mortania was ruled by a Samaian king, my father. Our people ruled Mortania for a thousand years with the help of a power called the Everlasting. As the first born and heir to the throne…it is now my job to protect the Everlasting, use it to destroy Curian, bring Mortania back to its previous glory and…take my place as Queen."

Dana said nothing for the moment,

"And what happened earlier…that was the power you've been given?"

"Yes."

"How does it happen?"

"I don't know exactly, but its channelled through this." Trista showed Dana her ring. "It was left to my mother. I don't know where she is but if I find her, maybe I can make sense of all of this."

Trista turned the ring around her finger,

"Until then, the only lead I have is Dreston. I'm going to go there and figure all of this out."

"We better get some sleep then. It seems we have a long journey ahead of us," Trista looked at her in shock.

"Us, you're still coming?" Dana smiled as she leant down to Trista to hug her.

"What kind of a friend would I be if I left you now?"

The following morning, Trista was feeling significantly better than she had done the night before.

Her body still felt incredibly weak and her breathing had become laboured, but she was grateful that she could now move. The two girls packed their belongings and continued into the kingdom. Dana had set up camp for them at the end of the Remora trail and so there was nothing but land ahead of them for miles. A vast plain of trees and rocks could be seen in the distance, with hills and mountains, littered with rivers and streams lay before them reeking of danger and the unknown.

Trista looked up into the sky, at the sun shining overhead and took a deep breath. It was now or never and she chose now.

After consulting a basic map that Trista had taken from home, the Trista and Dana determined they could reach Dreston in a little under three days if they kept a good pace

There were geographical obstacles that they would have to deal with, but they would cross that bridge, or in this case, plateau when they came to it. Not wanting to waste any more time and the weather on their side, they rode steadily across the wide wasteland known as The Plains towards The Triplets, three rivers that joined into one and flowed into the Alzo Sea.

"We follow the main road until we see the Alsan," Trista said, referring to the first of the three rivers that flowed south into Dreston. "If we keep it behind us, we can avoid getting lost in the desert."

Dana had agreed and even though it added time to their journey, they would rather be safe then lost by going directly across The Plains with no mapped route.

They set off in the direction of the rivers, the mountains of the Northern regions, far off in the distance. The sun beat overhead, hotter here than in most of the kingdom she had been told, warming them to their bones.

They'd dressed lightly once they set off but even with loose dresses, the girls baked in the sun.

They rode steadily into the vast open space and despite all that had happened, it was admittedly a welcome change to the confinements of Remora.

All her life Trista had longed to leave and find adventure and now that adventure had finally found her, despite her reservations she was elated.

With Thorn and her parents momentarily forgotten, Trista was able to appreciate the opportunity that had been laid at her feet.

She was going to learn about her life, her heritage and of course, her powers.

She was still feeling weak from her ordeal on the Remora trail but slowly she was coming back to some form of normality. With her new outlook on live, everything looked brighter, newer somehow. Even the sand that slowly emerged beneath the horse's hooves was rich and sparkled like gold.

Almost as though to prove she didn't have the right to feel happy, Thorn came to mind again. She felt guilty for feeling good about herself and her situation when she had left him behind.

Will I ever see him again?

If she did, what would she say, and would he still care for her?

Thorn not wanting to be with her was more than she was willing to think about right then, so she simply decided not to.

"What happens when we get to Dreston?" Dana asked as they made their way toward the river.

"Find someone named Rayne, it's not much to go on I know." Dana didn't say anything and Trista didn't push her to although there was something clearly on Dana's mind,

"What is it?"

Dana sighed and turned to look at her friend,

"Do you think you can do all this?"

"You don't think I will?"

"No, I'm not saying that it's just well, this is so much bigger than anything we've ever done. How is a girl like you supposed to deal with all this, powers or no powers?" Trista didn't answer straight away,

"I guess what I'm trying to say is, do you think this is even worth it?" Trista was confused for a moment, her response to her own capabilities aside.

"Saving Mortania isn't worth it?"

"Is saving Mortania by giving up your life worth it?" Trista was taken back,

"What life am I really giving up Dana? I had nothing in Remora, nothing and no one!"

"Is that what Thorn thinks?" Trista didn't reply immediately as her guilt returned. She knew she had left Thorn behind, but Dana had to understand that she had a bigger purpose.

"Thorn doesn't matter anymore Dana. Thorn was a silver line on a very dark cloud and I wish with all my heart that I didn't have to leave him but this, saving Mortania is bigger than him and anything that I ever felt for him."

"Trista that doesn't sound like you."

"And what if it doesn't? What am I going to do, turn back? Whatever I had or didn't have in Remora is gone now. I'm here, doing this and this is what I have to focus on. There is nothing more important than reclaiming the Everlasting and saving Mortania. If you don't understand or believe that then why are you even here?"

Dana sighed heavily, looking guilty but replied with sincerity,

"I just don't want this to all be for nothing. I saw what you did back there and I saw what it did to you, what it took out of you. I hope that kind of sacrifice is worth Thorn because I don't want you to have given up your one silver line for a dream that might never come true."

"What dream?" Trista snapped

"The dream of finding out who you are," Trista narrowed her eyes at Dana. "I've known you your whole life Trista, I know how the others treated you. Don't act like this isn't a mission to finally belong to something."

Trista had nothing to say.

Was she really on this mission to save the Samai or just to get out of Remora and finally belong somewhere having spent her entire life as an outcast?

"You're right," she finally said. "You're right and I'm sorry for…I'm sorry." Dana smiled,

"No I'm sorry, I didn't mean to upset you. I just want you to be clear about what you want going into…this."

Trista smiled her gratitude and looked out onto the land, thinking about what her future would hold.

They rode the entire day before setting up camp at the side of the road. There were no inns or outposts marked on their map and they'd past no other travellers the whole day. Though the terrain was pretty much bare, they had found a small cluster of withering trees that would have to serve as shelter. They tied the horses to one of the available branches and proceeded to taking out their bedrolls. Dana rubbed her hands together as she arranged the blankets she had brought,

"It would be great to have a fire right now, but I don't think these pathetic excuses for trees have enough wood." Trista nodded in agreement as she looked at the feeble branches that the horses had been tied to. Dana continued organising her bedding as Trista looked at the trees then down at her hand. Her ring had a faint glow to it and a smile appeared on her face.

Trista reached up, broke off a branch and set it down in the space between herself and Dana,

"What are you doing?" Trista didn't answer as she tried to clear her mind and concentrate on what she wanted to do.

She sat there for a few minutes and simply willed for fire.

She didn't know what else she was supposed to do but on both occasions, she had used her power, she had needed it and it had happened. She hoped that this would be the case now.

She pictured the branch in front of her and willed it to catch fire. As she sat there, eyes closed, her mind suddenly went blank a wave of nausea overwhelmed her and instantly her eyes opened.

As they opened, the branch set alight, sending a pillar of flame straight up into the evening sky knocking both the girls backward.

The girls stared in horror as the pillar continued to blaze letting off an intense heat,

"Trista stop it!"

"I don't know how!" she screamed, backing further away.

As Trista scrambled to her feet to get away from the fire, she took her eyes away from it and the pillar snuffed out.

"Thank the Gods!"

Dana crawled over to Trista and the horses and both girls stood soothing the large beasts as well as themselves.

Where the pillar of flame had been was now just a scorched circle of earth with thin tendrils of smoke rising from it and small embers.

"I need to learn how to control this and soon…or I'm no help to anybody."

"Trista don't say that,"

"Why not, it's true. I can't even make a simple fire and they want me to go up against this princess. I can't do it!"

"If you think you can't do it then of course you won't be able to. You have to believe in you before anyone else can," Dana reasoned.

"You don't even believe I can do this, don't try and give me your encouraging talk now." Dana stood there gawping like a fish.

Trista turned and slumped herself on her bedrolls and stared into the black space where the fire had been.

"I didn't mean to make you feel like that Trista and I apologise. I have my doubts I admit that but I stand by what I said just now and you need to believe in yourself if any of this is going to work." Dana came and sat beside her.

"I was wrong to doubt you, but I made a choice to come on this journey with you because regardless of powers or prophecies, I believe in you as a person. I believe in you as a person who deserves to be happy and if finding your parents or fighting this princess or whatever you need to do is going to do that, then I'm with you all the way."

Dana reached out to pull Trista into a hug,

"I don't know how I'm going to explain any of this to my parents," Trista looked at Dana in shock and realised that she hadn't questioned her about what happened when she left Remora. She asked her,

"I took my father's horse; he always has it packed and ready for when he goes into the kingdom for supplies. I took some food from the kitchen, added it to the saddlebag and left before anyone saw me. My mother was in the wash room," she added the last bit sadly.

"I'm sorry that you had to give up your family Dana, you will see them again." Dana nodded but Trista had a feeling that she didn't quite believe it.

"We should get to sleep; we have a long day ahead of us." Dana nodded again and went over to her own bedroll.

Disappointed, guilty and tired, Trista took one last look at the blackened outline and sighed. As she did so, the circle erupted into a small fire. Trista looked at Dana and Dana looked back in amazement then they both burst into a fit of laughter. Trista looked at her ring just as it stopped glowing and kissed it,

"Thank you," she whispered into the night.

***

"Thelm, do you have news of the capital?"

Baron Erik Thelm looked toward Baron Lyon Dreston, abandoning his conversation with the most recent Coznian ambassador. He was trying – once again – to persuade Erik into trading slaves from Rolania to Thelm; Rolania being the largest shipping port in Coz.

Baron Erik thanked the Gods for the intervention and made his excuses to approach Baron Lyon. The Baron, who was sitting in a small corner of the room surrounded by guards, had staged a party of sorts to accommodate the most influential men in the kingdom.

Since his now public humiliation of Lord Priya, many of the men present were reluctant to be in Lyon's company, but as with most powerful men they were drawn to more power. They couldn't resist being close to a person who had the most money or the most influence and of the former he had plenty.

It was the latter that was to be desired.

"Not news, Lord as much as gossip."

"What gossip then?"

Thelm was the closest city to Tirnum, the thin pass named Thea's Reach connecting the north of the country to the South. Nestled between Thelm, the Great Forest and The Wide and overlooking Crescent Bay, Thea's Reach was large enough for travel but had begun to deteriorate in the years since the rebellion. Due to its volatile state, Thea's Reach was rarely used except for official messengers, people instead travelling the longer way around by ship into Thea's Point in the South.

The land set neatly between Thea's Peak, The Wide and Tirnum City was known as the Imperial Lands. Since the rebellion when the Samaian aristocrats had been forced out of their homes and lands, no one had lived in that part of the kingdom, forcing people inside the gates and out of the city completely.

City gates were set to crumble as cities expanded, threatening to burst at the seams. There were not enough resources to feed the growing populace and the entire south of the kingdom now had only Thea's Point to rely on for trade.

A large, though not large enough trading point to the south governed by Lord Weilyn was straining under the pressure of being the only major trading point in and out of the capital.

The Wide was steadily dying anyway, and the decay was spreading, creating a barren land that was dangerous to travel and impossible to cultivate.

Thelm was the closest to this expanding deterioration, and through his need for resources, Lyon knew he could get him on side.

That, and the promise that his only daughter would one day be queen.

"The city feels as though the king is doing nothing for the kingdom Lord," Thelm said.

"This is both true and common knowledge," Lyon replied in annoyance.

"Yes, Lord but there are those who feel their allegiances would be better placed."

"With whom?" Lyon now gave the Baron his full attention.

"Her highness Princess Briseis."

The Antonides Legacy I

There was a mixture of shock, agreement and confusion around the room. Lyon raised an eyebrow and took note of the men who had been aware of this and those who had not. He rose from his seat at the head of the large table.

"Baron Thelm, I will hear more of this. My lords Rinly, Balkin and Weilyn, would you please join us?"

DRESTON CITY

The murmurs rose considerably as the remaining numbers wondered why they had been overlooked and sent curses to the ones who had not.

"Please, gentleman. Eat your fill and drink to your heart's content. Many of you have long journeys to make to your homes so make sure you get some rest."

They knew they were being dismissed but they were no longer of any consequence. Lyon knew who had their ear to the ground; he knew who he needed on his side.

Stepping out of the alcove he had sat himself in, Lyon led the Barons through an adjacent door that led to his private rooms. As they entered, a young girl draped in very sheer silk stood up from a bed in the centre of the room. The silk was an attempt to hide her naked form beneath it but did nothing to hide the shackles around her neck, feet and hands.

Lyon went to a large round table at the far end of the room and took a seat in one of the five chairs around it. He motioned for the other men to sit, but they stood in shock, staring at the naked girl.

"Some entertainment for the evenings," Lyon said dismissing their attention towards her. "Bring refreshments!" he barked, and the young woman immediately moved to do as she was told.

"Come," Lyon said to them and they all hurried to take a vacant seat.

The men were not old but were still far from young. The evidence of their glory days in battle were now present in the jewels at their sword hilts that they had stolen from wealthy Samaian families and some even from Tirnum Castle.

Their fine clothes were made of the best materials in the kingdom at the expense of the kingdom itself. The people were all but starving, the land slowly diminishing and not producing anything worthy to live on.

As the weeks went by, Mortania was beginning to swallow itself whole; decaying from the pollution its ruler had thrust upon it by stealing the Everlasting.

None of this mattered to them of course as they helped themselves to the glasses of wine that the slave girl had returned with.

"You are dismissed." Lyon said sharply without glancing at her.

The girl returned to the bed and sat at the end of it, her hands in her lap, staring straight ahead.

"Now," Lyon took a sip of his wine. "Tell me of the Princess."

Baron Thelm cleared his throat.

"Her highness is an exceptionally gifted warrior as we all know and the realm has come to respect her for it."

"The people have always loved a good soldier," Lyon agreed.

"Her highness does possess a certain ruthlessness unique to her person,"

"A cruelty if you will," Lord Balkin of Illiya interceded. Lyon's eyebrow raised and he continued,

"Briseis knows no mercy. I have witnessed her sentence a man to death for merely looking at her in a way she did not think appropriate."

Lyon loved her more every second. He made it a point not to meddle in kingdom gossip which was why he had not thought to discuss the princess before but wondered how this girl's actions had managed to escape him.

"And the people love her?" Lord Weilyn of Thea's Point offered his response this time. The man was of Agmantian descent and so had smooth dark skin and had a voice so deep, it shook the people around him.

"We use the word loosely. Those who see her potential to…develop the kingdom love her." He chose his words carefully,

"Those of us who hold considerable power and can understand her importance in any major changes to the kingdom, respect her." Lyon laughed at Weilyn as he downed his drink then promptly poured himself another.

"So, in other words, the country hates her, but the rich politicians know she is worth having in the event of another rebellion."

The baron and lords shuffled uncomfortably in their seats, eyes darting everywhere but at him.

"It is treason to speak ill of the King Lord," Lord Rinly of Crol and the Northern pastures replied, eyes downcast.

"Come, we are among friends are we not? We commit no crimes by discussing the issues of our beloved realm."

The other barons nodded their head in agreement,

"Our dying realm." Lyon added coldly.

He drained his glass once again and looked at them each in turn, his intense fiery gaze burning into their souls like the fires of damnation.

"Our lands have suffered at the hands of that low born usurper and now we must pay?" Thelm, Balkin, Rinly and Weilyn were silent.

"I paid," Lyon continued. "I paid thousands in gold to fund his campaign. *My* armies took that throne. My armies killed that poisonous Samaian king but, yet it is my lands that suffer!"

He hadn't realised he was standing until then. His hands clenched into fists on the large round table, leaning towards the four men who looked on in fear. It was treacherous to hear much less repeat what Lyon had just said, the rage and bitterness clear. Still they sat, unable to move, wishing they could undo hearing his bitter revelation. Lyon took his seat,

"I would speak to the Princess. Bring her to me."

All four men gave weary looks to one another,

"What is it?" Lyon demanded from their silence.

"You think you can summon royalty?" Thelm questioned, clearly bemused at the notion.

"In any case, one does not summon a Princess, Lord," Rinly added before Lyon could answer.

"No one summons, *this* Princess." Balkin said with finality.

Lyon looked to each of the others who shook their head with an obvious fear that almost made him laugh.

Who was this young woman who struck fear in the hearts of men twice her age?

"Very well, Adrianna!"

The momentarily forgotten slave girl jumped up from where she had been sitting on the bed and was by Lyon's side in seconds, head bowed, arms at her sides.

"Find my scribe, I wish to send a letter to Tirnum."

"Yes Lord," and she ran off to do as he asked.

Lyon turned back to his guests as they continued to sit in silence, still unsure of what position they were in and therefore what card they should play. Lyon poured himself another glass and with an absence of anything else to do, the other men followed suit.

"How is your daughter Erik, Geneiva I believe her name is?" Erik was immediately all ears to the conversation. When

Lyon Dreston spoke of one's daughter, it was not usually in the best context. Erik cleared his throat,

"She is a good girl…as is my wife. She just turned sixteen this spring."

"Interesting age sixteen. Have you any suitors in mind for her at such a delicate age?" Erik straightened that bit more in his chair and placed his full glass of wine back on the table.

"Not now Lord. She has expressed her desire to serve the Gods." Lyon laughed,

"Why on earth would she do that?"

"Daughters as devoted and innocent as Geneiva tend to go towards that path Lord."

"Why would she do that when there are so many marriage opportunities in place for her…namely my own."

"Lord?"

Lyon stood up from the table they occupied and bowed graciously to Lord Rinly, Balkin and Weilyn.

"I will be in touch gentlemen, there is much to discuss before you return to your homelands, but I would like a private word with Baron Erik."

The three men nodded and quickly vacated their seats, happy to have a reason to leave such a dangerous gathering. As they got to the door to leave, Lyon stopped them,

"My lords…I trust there were no misunderstandings about what was said here today. I would hate for any differing accounts to reach the king's ear."

All the men nodded and chorused,

"Yes, Lord."

Lyon sat back at the table with Baron Erik and smiled his most accommodating smile, but it didn't do much to relax the baron.

"Forgive me Lord but I must confess, I'm not sure why you have kept me behind."

"Of course, you are Erik, I made it clear enough."

Erik was hesitant before he spoke,

"You wish to marry my daughter?"

"Yes,"

"I am flattered Lord but...why?"

"I need a queen and why not one as beautiful as your daughter?"

Lyon had received Geneiva's portrait just under a week ago and had been pleased with what he saw.

Geneiva Thelm was by no means the most heart stopping beauty seen but she was from a wealthy enough family and would make an appropriate queen. Erik cleared his throat, clearly uncomfortable with the way this conversation was turning out but Lyon could see his mind working. There was too much of an opportunity here for him to not at least listen to a proposal.

"My daughter is indeed as beautiful as any queen should be, but that position is already intended for another."

"I am set to marry another?" Lyon said slyly with a grin on his lips as he took another sip of his wine and then poured his guest another.

"Lord I..."

"Leave us!" Lyon called out suddenly, cutting him off and guards that Erik had not even noticed were there, filed out of the room. They had been positioned in doorways and discreetly beside curtains so silent and still that they had practically been invisible.

"You are a rich man, that I know," Lyon said looking at Erik once his men had left. "I know there is not much I can offer you in the way of riches but what of glory?"

"Glory Lord?"

"Yes Erik, for your name to live through the ages not as Barons or Lords or locked away in some Gods forsaken nunnery but as Queens and Kings!"

"We have a king!" Erik snapped with more force than he clearly intended.

"A king you would gladly replace with his own daughter so why not do so with yours?" Baron Thelm had no answer. Lyon approached Erik and looked down at him.

"Marrying Geneiva will bring our families and our names together in a way that will strike fear into the hearts of any men who tries to oppose us. Join me Erik, join me in ridding Mortania of this parasite and replacing him with someone of your blood. My son, your grandson ruling Mortania as Man was born to do!"

Erik said nothing for a moment before rising from his chair and stretching out his arm for Lyon to take. Lyon grasped the other man's forearm in a strong hold and looked him in the eye.

"Geneiva can be here as soon as you will it."

***

The girls were up, dressed and packing the horses when three riders were seen heading towards them.

They were not blocking the riders' way and so they ignored them until the riders approached and suddenly stopped opposite them in the light of the early morning sun.

The three men looked down at them and so Trista and Dana smiled politely even as they continued to pack their belongings.

The Antonides Legacy I

"Morning," they said politely, continuing with their tasks as quickly as possible.

The man closest to them was tall, even on the horse as his stirrups were so low down. He had a toothpick in his mouth and a large hat to protect him from the sun. His clothes were worn in but clean and he had an untidy brown beard that took up the bottom half of his face so that before he spoke, you couldn't see his lips.

"What are you two doing out here?"

"Leaving," Trista replied curtly.

What business was it of theirs why they were there?

The horses were packed and so with a quick look to Dana, Trista led her horse back towards the travelled road.

The two men behind the bearded man dismounted and stopped in her path,

"Excuse me," she said firmly, looking straight in the eyes of the man closest to her. The other had stopped, of course in front of Dana,

"No," the man said. "I don't think I will."

Trista said nothing and turned to walk away from him but he stood in her way again while the other man, without saying a word reached out and grabbed Dana,

"Get away from her!" Trista snapped as the man cornering her stepped towards her.

Instantly angry and without any coherent thought, Trista turned and pushed with her right hand at the man and sent him flying clear across the ground. He landed almost a foot away, clutching at his chest as he writhed on the ground.

She turned to where the other man had grabbed Dana and with her same hand grabbed at the air in his direction and pulled her fist towards her.

The man was tugged viciously forward, landing on the ground and smacking his face on the hard, dry dirt.

"What in the Gods!" the first man, still on the horse, backed away as he looked down at her with fear.

Trista narrowed her eyes at him as she made a sweeping motion with her hand and the man was knocked off his horse to the ground, hitting his head as he landed.

She didn't bother to check if any of them were seriously hurt and quickly mounted her horse. Running to catch up, Dana did the same and two girls headed off at speed into the open plains.

They didn't stop riding until they felt no one could be following them and by then, both the horses and the girls were exhausted.

They brought the horses to a stop along the side of the road and silently took out their small amount of water to give to the animals.

"Trista…"

"Don't," Trista cut Dana off. "Just don't. We're okay and that's all that matters."

"It is, but are you okay?"

Trista looked down at her hand and flexed her fingers.

She was fine, much better then when she had used her powers to stop Briseis' would be assassins. Maybe she only had trouble using her powers for big things.

"I'm fine," she finally replied as she rubbed her horse's smooth neck.

For once, using her power had felt…good.

She had felt powerful and strong and in control and she loved it. The fact that she had hurt those men, maybe even killed them didn't bare thinking about.

The Antonides Legacy I

She had done the right thing she knew, but like Dana had said, at what cost?

Dana pulled some dried meat from her saddle bag and handed it to Trista who took it gladly before putting her water skin away and getting back onto the horse.

When the Alsan finally came into view, the girls rushed ahead to fill their water skins and bathe.

The Alsan was a large river, they could barely see to the other side but they could see smoke rising from the mountains further north.

They washed quickly before setting out again and heading downstream towards Dreston.

Mortania was beautiful, Trista thought to herself; never having seen so much variation of land before. The way the sky and the earth beneath it looked so different at dawn then when it did at sunset. At the colours on the horizon and the very feel of the air in the hot and dusty lands of The Plains.

After their third day on the road and exhausted nights as they had taken shifts with sleeping; it was a welcome sight when the walls of Dreston City finally came into view on the horizon.

Dreston seemed to have sprouted from nothing, as there was nothing and no one around it for miles. This part of Mortania had always been this way however, a dry spot surrounded by mountains and green once other cities were in the vicinity.

The large, sand coloured walls rose high into the sky where from far away the red and brown roofs of the many buildings within could be seen.

The closer they got, the more caravans and wagons and stalls on the outskirts of the city came into view, leading up to the large double doors that led into the city.

The girls approached wearily when the two armed guards patrolling the front came up to them,

"What do you want?"

Trista had to stop herself from asking him where his manners were but decided to let it go. She smiled at him as best she could and spoke sweetly,

"My name is Fallon and this is my sister...Fern, we've been sent by our father to buy cloths and linen." Trista wasn't sure why she lied about their names, but it just seemed the right thing to do. The taller of the two guards examined them for a moment, Trista for a bit longer then was necessary before raising his hand and yelling,

"Two, open the gate!"

Both the girls looked up where just above the city gate were two guard posts. They watched as a man in each post, either side of the door began to move, and the large doors opened inward with ease.

It opened just enough for their horses to enter and closed as soon as they were safely inside. Trista sat astride her horse and stared in wonder at the activity going on in front of her.

There were people *everywhere*.

Men, women and children of all ages ran in every direction, buying, selling and yelling. They were at the start of a long central road with taverns and market stalls lining either side. There were other roads leading off into unknown territory and at the far end amid a very rocky hill, she could see castle.

She had never seen anything like this. The diversity of people and smells and intense colours that surrounded her was overwhelming.

"This will take a little getting used to" Dana chuckled beside her as they continued to stare into the cosmopolitan city.

"Definitely, but we should keep moving." Trista pointed out.

She had already noticed people beginning to stare at them. She was also aware that if they stayed gaping around any longer, it would be even more obvious that they didn't belong.

She immediately felt that Dreston was a place where it was best to stay inconspicuous. Quickly, the girls dismounted and led their horses on foot through the crowded central marketplace.

All around them, street venders yelled and bragged about the quality of their wares and the discounted prices. She rode past fish, meat and bread stalls; jewellery stalls and stalls that sold coloured materials. Everywhere someone was busy doing something or talking to someone and as she rode silently through the din it was then she noticed her.

Standing outside what looked like a bookstore was a little girl with long jet-black hair and the biggest green eyes she had ever seen apart from her own. She had a book in her hand and before stepping into the road; she looked up from it to check the traffic in front of her.

As she did so, she caught Trista's eye. Trista had expected some surprise or shock to register on the little girl's face but instead she smiled and continued to cross the street in front of them. Trista followed the little girl with her eyes and watched her meet up with an older girl with the same long black hair and green eyes.

"Trista...they're everywhere," Dana whispered to her and sure enough, everywhere she looked she saw more and more Samai.

They were selling fruit and vegetables; they were haggling with customers and scolding their children. The majority of the people surrounding her were Men of course but never in her life had she seen so many people that looked like her.

Tears welled in her eyes as she watched her people live their lives in this diverse city, free from shame and ridicule.

"I know," she was silent for a moment, too stunned to speak or look away.

Trista shook her head as if to put her senses back together,

"We need to find this Rayne person but let's get something to eat first, I'm starving." Dana nodded her agreement and they continued down the muddy market street.

A few minutes later, the girls came across an inn called The Swan and headed over because it had a small but clean looking stable next to it for the horses to be looked after. They dismounted outside, and Trista approached a young man that was sitting outside the door on a stool. He was no more than fourteen but was muscular and had a lean face that showed a good life but filled with hard work.

He was tall with bright red hair and light blue eyes that seemed to shine brighter in the sunlight.

When she approached, he smiled broadly and stood up from the stool to greet her,

"Can I help you Miss?"

"My friend and I, we need shelter and food for ourselves and the horses, can you help?"

"Sure, I'll just get my Pa," the young man walked into the inn after some other men and disappeared. Minutes later he reappeared with a tall burly man behind him. The man was bald but had a thick large red beard and small blue eyes that wrinkled at the corners when he smiled at them,

"Malachi here said you were pretty, but I didn't believe him!" the big man bellowed with a joyous laugh and slapped Malachi on the back. Malachi's cheeks flushed red,

"Pa!"

"Hush boy," he laughed ruffling his hair. "So, you two young ladies want food and lodging?"

"Yes sir, if it's not too much trouble. We've travelled a long way,"

"I pay no never mind to what you did before you got here, just so long as you can pay your way and don't give me any trouble while you're here."

"No Sir, no trouble at all." Trista replied eagerly as the big man stepped forward,

"Well then, since you are just as pretty as Malachi says I'll put you and the horses up for a gold coin a night, meals included. That's pretty reasonable for the two of you unless you want to go someplace else?"

"No Sir, one gold coin is fine,"

"Good. I'm Joe or Joseph if you're highborn and this here is my boy Malachi," he ruffled Malachi's hair again who looked as though he wanted the ground to swallow him whole. "He'll look after your horses and I'll get you settled inside when you're ready."

"Thank you," the girls chorused together as Joe turned and went back inside.

THE CITY WATCH

The girls followed Malachi into the adjacent stables where they unloaded the horses and got them settled into the nearest space. The saddles and saddlebags were hung neatly beside their horses while the girls took everything else, they would need to clean themselves up. There were two other horses housed with their own, chewing away at the abundance of hay around them.

"We saw a lot of people in the market. Is it always this busy this early in the morning?" Dana asked Malachi as he soothed the horses,

"Always, Dreston is a main city, hundreds of people pass through here every day. Some important; some not so important but they come through anyway."

"Well I'm actually looking for someone, their name is Rayne. Do you know anyone by that name?" Trista watched as the kindness and joy in Malachi's eyes instantly faded and anger replaced it,

"You told Pa you didn't want any trouble," he snapped at her.

"I don't, we don't!" Trista protested, completely confused as to why he was so upset.

"Then don't be asking about that witch. You're lucky you didn't ask anyone else or you might be a head shorter if you catch my meaning."

Trista nodded and looked over at Dana who merely shrugged her. Malachi began to brush the horses down and as the girls turned to leave with their personal supplies, Trista rested a hand on Malachi's shoulder,

"I'm sorry I upset you Malachi, I meant no harm." He turned to look at her and smiled shyly,

"No harm done Miss," he said sweetly and turned back to the horse as his cheeks began to flush red.

Trista and Dana entered The Swan a few moments later and saw Joseph at the bar at the back of the room serving drinks.

It was a large and airy place, packed with people all laughing and talking in their various groups. There were large round wooden tables for people to have a meal as well as more intimate tables to have a few mugs of ale or just talk.

A couple were in the corner holding hands and kissing while in another corner a group of men were playing a game of cards. The girls approached the bar cautiously, but none of the other patrons paid them any mind.

"This here is my daughter Bess," Joseph said as they took seats on the bar stools immediately opposite him. A tall red headed girl with a thousand freckles over her face who had been serving tables, stood next to her father.

"She'll show you to your room." Bess smiled at them and lead them away from the bar and up two flights of stairs. On the landing, the sounds from the bar immediately ceased,

"You can't hear anything," Dana said in amazement,

"It's why we get so many customers wanting to stay here," Bess said. "You can get a decent night's sleep and not have to worry about the drunk's that roll in here all hours of the night."

The girls laughed as Bess opened the door to a small but comfortable room with two single beds, a dresser and a washtub in the corner. There was a window that looked out onto the city and from it; they could see a large castle on the highest hill. Trista walked over and looked,

"What is that place?" Bess's eyes grew dark as she spoke,

"Dreston Castle...where the Baron lives."

"The Baron?"

"Baron Dreston, he owns everything. Of course, there are businesses like ours but not everyone is so lucky. The Baron takes anything from anybody and charges them huge sums to do it."

"Why would he do that?" Dana asked in horror,

"It's just his way. His family's wealth is older than Mortania they say. He made a whole lot more of that money during the Civil War."

"Civil War?" Bess laughed,

"Where have you girls come from, don't you know anything?" Dana and Trista laughed their ignorance away but Bess continued anyway,

"The war between Man and the Samai. It had been going on for months but Baron Dreston helped dethrone the last Samaian king. He's favourites with His Majesty now,"

"Curian?"

"Yes," Bess giggled. "You sure are a funny pair. I have to get the breakfast out soon anyway, come down when you're ready for something to eat." With a cheery smile, she exited the room and shut the door.

Dana collapsed on the bed behind her and blew out a long breath,

"As hungry as I am I think I could sleep for a week," Trista laughed as she took a seat on the opposite bed.

"I know how you feel but I think we should eat something. We haven't had a proper meal in days. My magical fire didn't really hold up when I wanted it to." Dana sat up and looked at her,

"If you master any power before we leave here, please let it be that," she laughed. Trista smiled with her until both looked at each other questioningly.

"Why do you think Malachi reacted that way when I asked about Rayne?"

"Who knows but I think he was right about one thing, don't go asking too many people about her."

"Then who do I ask?"

"Anyone who isn't Man," Dana said simply.

She was right obviously; if anyone was going to know where Rayne was then it had to be one of the Samaians.

"I just want to eat and sleep. We can think about all of this later,"

"Now that's a plan I can deal with. We need to think about some new clothes too."

The girls instinctively looked down at their dresses.

Both had left Remora in such a hurry that they hadn't dressed appropriately for a cross country adventure.

"You're right but as I said, we'll sort it all out later." Trista fell back onto her bed and closed her eyes to drift off to sleep.

When she opened her eyes again, it was dark and she was underneath the bed covers.

Trista sat up frantically when she looked over and spotted Dana's empty bed.

It was unmade so she knew Dana must have been in it but where was she now?

Trista got out of bed and went over to the washbasin. She had a quick wash of the important areas and her face and changed into a light blue dress that her mother had made her. She attempted to tame the mass of curls on her head but eventually gave it as it clearly had a mind of its own. Once she had her shoes on, she left the room in search of Dana.

When Trista stopped at the bottom of the stairs, she felt as if the entire inn had gone quiet and was staring at her.

For a few seconds, every eye in the place was on her and as quickly as they were, they weren't. Everyone went about their business, trying desperately to not look her way. Uncomfortable, Trista scanned the room for Dana but before she spotted her, a small voice called out to her,

"Trista," she saw Malachi walking towards her through the crowd.

He smiled that big smile that was beginning to grow on her. "Trista, Dana is in the kitchen with Bess."

"Thank you," she smiled appreciatively.

"I'll take you," he offered eagerly, and Trista just smiled, letting him lead the way.

They passed the inquiring eyes and stepped through a back door that opened into the kitchen where Dana was sat with Bess and another woman who was cooking.

"There you are, did you sleep well?" Dana said cheerily,

"Really well actually, where did you disappear to?" she asked with only a hint of attitude.

They were in a brand-new place with people they didn't yet know if they could trust and Dana had just run off.

"I came down here, had something to eat then started to help Bess until her mother kindly asked if I wanted to stay in the kitchen with her, away from all the men."

Trista didn't miss the ridicule she was getting by not acknowledging the other woman in the room and cleared her throat, instantly ashamed.

"Good evening miss, I'm Lorna. I hope the beds were comfy," the older woman said politely. Trista smiled though a little embarrassed.

"Good evening, the bed was lovely thank you, I'm Trista."

"Trista, Ma's been teaching Dana how to cook a few things for when you're on the road." Malachi piped in.

Trista sat opposite Dana,

"Has she now?" Malachi nodded and went to the stove where his mother was standing and came back to Trista with a bowl of some kind of stew and a few slices of thick bread.

"Oh you shouldn't have gone through any trouble," Trista protested.

"Heavens child we run an inn. Cooking is what we do, besides, we've all ate and Dana says you haven't had a proper meal in days." Trista shook her head and began to eat.

Trista ate while Malachi, Bess and Lorna talked their ears off with an occasional contribution from Dana. The inn was still open so although she spoke until the cows came home, Lorna was constantly making pot after pot of stew and rice and other things.

They were introduced briefly to the other young girls who came in to collect orders, but Bess came in and out regularly; more in then out and got involved with the gossip. Every now and then, Joseph would pop in with some quip about women being in the kitchen where they belonged then mockingly scolding Malachi for being in there with them and dragging him out. Minutes later, Malachi could be found back in the kitchen sitting beside Trista.

The five of them were still in the kitchen talking when suddenly the door burst opened and Joseph rushed in,

"Come to put us in our place again eh Joe?" Lorna giggled but Joseph wasn't laughing.

"No Mrs Joe, guards are on the hill headed this way." The colour drained from Lorna's face.

"Why now?"

"I don't know, is everything in place?"

"Yes Joe, as always."

"Good, well stay in here until they leave."

Lorna, Bess and Malachi all nodded but Dana and Trista sat bewildered. Trista felt Malachi sit a little closer to her,

"What's going on?"

"The Baron," Bess said through gritted teeth. Bess didn't say anything else so it was left to Lorna to offer the explanation,

"Every so often the Baron's men go through the city and take from the people."

"What do they take?" Dana asked,

"Anything they want, money, food, cattle…people."

"*People?*" Dana and Trista were horrified.

"They take the boys as slaves and the girls as…" Lorna didn't need to finish the sentence. Trista looked at Malachi and then turned to look at Bess who was standing close to her mother although her face was defiant.

"They can't do that!" Dana said outraged,

"They can and they do Dana." Bess stepped closer to her mother then and Lorna pulled her into a hug.

As the five of them sat in the kitchen, they heard commotion outside the kitchen door. It didn't sound like trouble but they could distinctly hear the unsheathing of swords and deep rumble of male voices clearly in the act of intimidation.

Suddenly, raised voices echoed through the door and Trista reached out to take Malachi's hand when she saw it shaking.

As she did so, the kitchen door swung open and a guard stood there; head to toe in black leather.

Trista had seen city guards when they'd arrived in the city of course, and although they looked intimidating, this man was clearly of a different kind.

The sword attached to his hip he held readily, hand on the hilt. He was a tall man with long brown hair tied back in a ponytail and dark brown eyes that were almost black. He scanned the room and when he laid eyes on Trista, he stepped forward, so she stood up. He looked her up and down with clear contempt,

"Pity," came his deep grumble then turned to look at Bess. "You will do."

"No!" Lorna screamed, pulling Bess closer to her as the girl began to sob.

The man went to step around Trista, but she blocked his path,

"Touch that girl and it will be the last thing you ever do."

The guard looked at her with curiosity as well as anger. He had made countless raids and it was nothing new to have someone try and stand up to him to protect their friends, but it had never been a woman.

This green eyed, raven-haired woman stared at him, unmoving. He knew what she was, it was why he hadn't taken her; the Baron didn't take kindly to their kind in the castle. He wasn't about to anger the Baron no matter how beautiful this woman was. She was breathtakingly beautiful and if it wasn't for his allegiance to Man and the Baron, he would have been happy to claim her as his own personal slave and not just in a domestic capacity.

She continued to stare him down and as he looked back, he could have sworn he saw her eyes flash with blue flame. He had heard the stories about the Samai and their powers, but he had never seen it in real life, it was forbidden in Dreston.

"What did you say girl?" he said stepping closer to her as Trista continued to stare,

"Turn around, walk out that door and never come back here again."

Trista looked directly into the man's eyes with clear intent and focus. She was not going to let him take Bess away. She repeated to herself as her eyes ignited with a thin ring of fire,

"Turn around, walk out that door and never come back here again. Do you understand me?"

"Yes. I understand."

The guard was looking in her direction without really seeing her. His eyes had glazed over as he looked directly into nothing.

"You won't remember anything that happened here tonight, and you won't remember me or my friends, do you understand?" the man nodded,

"Yes. I understand."

"Now leave." Trista commanded him to exit and he did without another word. As he walked out, Trista collapsed into her chair and Dana rushed to her side.

No one said anything for a long time but minutes later, Joseph burst into the kitchen looking around frantically for his family.

"Bess?" Bess ran into her father's arms, as did Malachi and Lorna. "What happened, did they hurt you?"

"No Pa," Bess said quietly.

Even though Malachi, Bess and Lorna looked at Trista no one said anything about what had happened. With Dana's help, Trista stood from her chair,

"Thank you for the food," she murmured quietly, feeling like she would collapse at any moment. "I think I should rest now."

Dana helped Trista out of the kitchen and Joe and his family followed out after them.

Most of the customers had left but a few lingered in the corners, drinking the last of their ale and keeping their eyes to the floor. Trista noticed, even in her weakened state that two of the waitresses were missing. She may have saved Bess, but she had clearly missed her calling for the other girls.

Malachi went behind the bar and poured his parents a drink while they sat at a vacant table with Bess. Just as Trista and Dana got to the bottom of the stairs, the door to the inn flew open and a hooded figure stood there.

Joseph rose from his chair,

"What do you want?" he demanded as the cloaked figure just stood there unmoving. The few people still inside stared at the person, clearly afraid of an encore of the previous events. As they stared, the person's right arm rose slowly and pointed in Trista and Dana's direction.

"I want her." The voice was female and as she spoke, she raised her head, pulled back her hood and stared at Trista.

"Good evening Trista…my name is Rayne."

VIGILANTES

Joe was immediately defensive,

"We don't want no trouble in here Rayne, we don't need your kind in here." Joseph replied sternly but Rayne just laughed.

"My kind? Then what is she?" she was clearly amused as she stood in the doorway.

The older woman stood tall with long white curly hair that still had strands of black at the temples. Her eyes still burned a fierce green like the fresh new leaves of spring.

"You know what I mean witch!"

"Witch? If you're going to insult me, please do it right. I'm a sorceress, not a witch."

Rayne stepped further into the inn and approached Trista who was still at the bottom of the stairs.

"What you did just now, was a wonderful but stupid thing. That took a lot of power and not many of us can do it."

"How do you know what I did?" Rayne only laughed,

"What don't I know child. Now, are you coming with me or not?"

"She can't come with you now, she's very weak and she…" Rayne's eyes turned to focus on Dana,

"Forgive me but I don't remember asking for your opinion."

"Don't speak to her like that!" Trista stepped in. "Dana is my best friend and she's looking out for me!"

Trista snapped with a lot more energy then she felt,

"I don't know who you *think* you are sorceress, but who you are to me remains to be seen. I may have travelled for days to find you, but I can wait one more night to be acquainted with your less than welcoming attitude."

Trista turned and began to walk up the stairs with Dana faithfully by her side. Rayne stared up the stairs at her quizzically before she turned on her heels and left.

***

No matter how many times she sailed the open water, Lamya would never get used to it. She enjoyed travelling by ship, the salty breeze, the never-ending stretch of beautiful ocean water and on occasion, breath-taking scenery was more than enough to make her love sailing but it was so uncomfortable.

The past four days had lacked in the way of scenery, the Dyam islands too far west and The Rock, a mountainous island between Agmantia and Mortania too far east and so she had been confined to her room or in the Captain's quarters when he had kindly extended her an invitation. This seemed to happen more often than usual as she was the only woman on the ship, but she did not mind as the captain was a kind old man who had confided in her that this was to be his last voyage before retirement; not counting the return trip to Agmantia.

Lamya had just left one of these meetings with the captain, enjoying a late supper with him and his First Mate and was on her way to her own cabin when some talk amongst the crew caught her attention. Not wanting to seem as though she were spying on them, she changed direction and went to stand against the port side of the ship, looking out into the dark night time waters.

"...came back with no arms and legs they say."

"Then how'd he get back at all?"

"With that magic the princess is using obviously!" the first man said angrily, clearly annoyed that the second was questioning the validity of his story. He continued swabbing the deck as he spoke again,

"Got back to the castle and said she was coming to kill us all."

"Who?"

"That lost Samaian, the one they took the crown back from!" the first man was getting annoyed again. "Don't you know anything?"

"I know plenty Juba; I just don't be listening to every little thing that comes out of Mortania. I've got better things to worry about than them rich folk over there!"

"Well you better be worryin' about it cause we won't survive if that Samaian gets her hands on that power!"

"You think they will?"

"Why not? Them Samai are evil enough to rob our fathers of their rights, why not try to steal it back?" Juba said conclusively.

"Well, I don't know Juba. Mortania hasn't been the same since that Alexander died."

Juba stopped swabbing and Lamya instinctively paid closer attention, even shifting her footing to mask her attempt to shift closer.

"What do you mean by that?"

Juba moved closer to the other man, clearly trying to intimidate him and instantly Lamya felt his worry at what Juba would do next. She had learned over the years to silence the feelings that were constantly around her but sometimes, there were some things she couldn't ignore and this other man's instant reaction to Juba was one of them. She felt his regret at having said anything at all,

"Well we all know we wouldn't be doing this extra work if the land hadn't been dryin' up,"

"You sayin' that's the kings doin'? That Man did this?" Juba's voice rose considerably and as he took a menacing step toward the other man, Lamya took a step toward them and pretended to slip on the hem of her robe.

Her movements alerted them to her presence as the other man rushed to her aid,

"Are you okay Miss Lamya?" she fiend weakness as the man held her steady and Juba looked on with menacing eyes. She didn't question how the unknown man knew her name. As the only woman aboard the ship, she had been the topic of interest for the first few nights of the voyage.

"I'm okay thank you..." she paused for a name.

"Rick,"

"Thank you Rick, I think I'm a bit more shocked then anything. My apologies for interrupting your work." Rick smiled at her but still had not let her go. She didn't mind as she felt that there was not anything perverse about his intention but instead, relief. She smiled back at him,

"You were a welcome interruption, wasn't she Juba?" Juba made an incoherent noise but said nothing. She could feel his growing animosity towards Rick and knew it would escalate if she didn't do something to intervene.

"I think I can make it back to my cabin from here Rick," she went to walk away from them but as she stepped, she pretended to falter again and once again, Rick caught her. Lamya giggled,

"Perhaps I had a bit too much ale with the captain. Rick, would you be so kind to help me back to my own cabin?"

"Of course. I think the decks can wait." Rick said light heartily. "I'll be back Juba."

Once again there was the incoherent mumble from Juba who had continued to swab as Rick helped her back to her room.

The short walk was spent in comfortable silence. Lamya felt Rick's apprehension at being alone with her and smiled to herself at his innocence. He was a young man, not yet thirty perhaps but life as a seaman had clearly made him appear and act much older. She had found on her travels; that men with influence, power and titles were less worthy of those titles and the broad shoulders to bare them, than the men who worked the land and sea.

They arrived at her cabin and Lamya opened the door before stepping inside.

"Would you mind terribly waiting with me a while?"

Rick's eyes widened but he simply shook his head as Lamya made her way over to the small desk and chair bolted to the right wall opposite her bed and took a seat. Rick stood in the doorway awkwardly not saying a word but Lamya could sense intrigue in him.

He was nothing like Juba, in no way aggressive or overly opinionated and she had been right to intervene. The rising anger she felt from Juba would have got Rick into trouble she doubted he could get himself out of with the much bigger man.

"You seem fine now," Rick commented and Lamya smiled and nodded.

"Yes, thanks to you."

"Come on Miss Lamya, I know there wasn't much wrong with you but thank you just the same." Lamya smiled with mirth,

"Was it that obvious?"

"To me but I don't think Juba knew much...he was much too angry."

The Antonides Legacy I

"I realise that...care to explain why?" Rick was silent for a moment before stepping completely into her room and closing the door behind him. The room felt immediately cramped with another person in it.

"Juba is a nice man, he means well but sometimes he doesn't know his foot from his elbow!" It all came out in a rush making Lamya laugh.

"What do you mean?"

"I'm Man and even I know that what's going on is our fault!" he hissed his response as he looked around as though what he was saying was treacherous.

He came further into the room and sat on the bed directly across from her.

"Excuse me for being on your beddin' like this but I feel like I can say this to you...I can say this to you, can't I?"

"Of course, you don't have to hide your feelings from me."

"I don't want to go back to Mortania. I don't want to be anywhere that that mad king has any power. Since he took the crown from the Samai the country has gone to the wolves."

He was still whispering but she heard the anxiety and anger in his voice.

"I want to make it clear Miss Lamya that I know my place, I know what I am and I'm not trying to support no Samai but after this trip, I'm going back to Agmantia and staying there."

"Is that the right thing for you, being away from your home?"

" I got a little one on the way"

"Congratulations," Rick smiled and nodded his appreciation.

"Two weeks to go. Wife thinks it's a girl but I think it's a boy. I want my first to be a son."

"First time father? Well double congratulations. I'm sure you'll do a wonderful job."

"I have to," Rick was suddenly pensive as he looked past her and at the wall. "I don't want my son growing up in war. Constant fighting and blaming the Samai for what the king caused. I don't know how he did it but things definitely changed back home after he became king so it must be his fault!"

Lamya didn't say anything, realising that he had wanted to get this off his chest for a while.

"The land is dying Miss Lamya, you can't grow anything good and if you do, nobody's got the coin to buy it for what it's worth. You can't even work enough to feed your family properly and I don't want that for my boy or my wife."

Lamya stood up to stand in front of Rick and placed her hands either side of his head, channelling some healing and good luck into his being. He closed his eyes as she did so and when her hands left his head, he opened his eyes with a welcome smile.

"Thank you,"

"You are most welcome Rick."

He stood up, causing her to step back so they were not too close together.

"I best be getting back to Juba. Thank you again Miss Lamya."

"You're welcome Rick." He backed away from her and turned to open the door but when he did, Juba was standing there.

How long had he been standing there?

"Juba?"

"I came to see what was taking so long. Them decks aint going to clean themselves!" he snapped and marched back up the stairs to the main deck. Rick looked back at Lamya who smiled reassuringly. Rick nodded last thanks and left the room, closing the door behind him.

Lamya stared at the closed door for a long while before she pushed the chair back under the small desk and got ready for bed. Once she was in her night dress, she blew out the bedside candle and climbed into bed.

Staring into the dimly moonlit room, Lamya closed her eyes and began to meditate. It was easy enough to do on a ship at night as the swaying instantly made her calm. She focused on her inner self and giving herself the needed energy to continue with her trip. She had learnt a lot in the last four days about the morale of the crew members and therefore the representation of the Mortanian population.

There were men like Rick, including the Captain who understood that there was clearly correlation between Curian's current reign and the destruction of the country.

Some were ready to blame him and take the side of any opposition against him to save the country but there were others; like Juba who were not so inclined to see the truth. Some were so passionate about their loyalty to Curian that they were ready to fight for him and not just in Mortania. Being in Agmantia for the months that she had, she had seen that men were fighting in the name of the king on matters that had nothing to do with them. They were simply using his name and his rebellion as a means to fight and plunder against their enemies. Now, it had not taken too much flight in Agmantia other than in a few small towns and villages but once wind of it reached Mortania and Curian knew that other countries were on his side, who knew what he might do.

Agmantia of course had its own ruler, their own human ruler for hundreds of years.

The current monarch, Queen Nucea Voltaire was a quiet woman who rarely concerned herself with matters of war and strife but that would have to change if her own country was beginning to fight amongst themselves.

The irony was that it was not even Agmantians that were starting these fights, but immigrant Mortanians making a name for themselves overseas.

Moving slowly out of her meditative state, Lamya was suddenly anxious to get to Mortania. She could feel the energy building in everything around her and knew that big change was coming.

Whether Mortania, Agmantia and people like Juba would be able to handle it without rebellious behaviour was another matter altogether. She took a deep breath and turned over in her bunk to sleep.

The next morning, she knew immediately that something was wrong. Washing and dressing quickly, she left her cabin and ran up to the main deck.

As the top of her head immerged on the main deck, the wave of hurt, confusion and fear almost hit her like she'd run into a stone wall. She stepped back and took hold of the railing to steady herself with one hand and placed her left hand on her chest that had begun to feel tight.

Breathe Lamya, Lamya

Something was terribly wrong for her emotions, her genuine personal emotions to feel this way. Stepping fully onto the main deck she saw the other crewmen going about their daily business but not in their usual merry way. She made her way towards one of them, Esta and tapped his shoulder,

"Esta?" he turned to look at her and although he smiled, the gesture did not reach his eyes.

"Morning,"

"Esta what's wrong?" he looked at her with pained eyes.

"Death on board,"

"Death!" she exclaimed clutching her chest again and closing her eyes, the despair was overwhelming. "Who?" she whispered but as the word left her, she knew who it was.

"Rick. Found him hanging from the boom early this morning and a goodbye note."

"What goodbye note, no! He wouldn't *kill* himself!" she shook her head in disbelief eyes still closed as she refused to accept what she was hearing.

"He did miss, said he couldn't bear to work so hard for nothing and wanted to end it."

"He has a wife...a baby..." she whispered.

She could feel her heart breaking. She hadn't known Rick for half an hour, but this was not what was meant for him. Rick had not killed himself; she knew he hadn't.

Esta continued, having not heard her.

"Three of us had to pull him in before you and the captain and other guests got up."

"You pulled him in?" Esta nodded and she patted his shoulder comfortingly, however futile that was.

"Thank you Esta," she said softly and let him get back to his work.

Lamya walked slowly up to the poop deck but the captain wasn't there.

Looking down onto the rest of the ship she sought out and locked eyes with Juba but as he saw her looking, he immediately looked away.

RAYNE

The royal family were at breakfast.

The king sat at the head of the large table that almost dwarfed the dining hall it was placed in and the princess sat in the seat to his right.

His late wife would have occupied the vacant seat to his left but since her death, a single white rose was placed on the plate to remember her. The elaborate spread of scones, jams and cold and hot meats were eaten in silence as father and daughter avoided any conversation with each other. The attendants stood by uncomfortably waiting to do their duties, breakfast being their least favourite mealtime of the day.

At least at dinner the various advisors and noblemen would be in attendance and provided noise other than clashing cutlery.

As father and daughter ate, a young man wearing a green tunic displaying his post as a messenger entered the dining hall in a hurry toward the king.

He bowed as was appropriate,

"A message for His Majesty!" he announced as both Curian and Briseis looked up from their plates. The messenger handed the letter to the king who scanned the page quickly then handed it back to the boy,

"Put this in my study, I'll deal with it later."

The messenger bowed again and exited the dining hall as quickly as he had entered. Curian turned back to his breakfast,

"What was that?"

"Another request for money. Crops aren't growing and so the food supply is short."

"From who?" Briseis demanded.

"Priya,"

"Don't give them anything," Curian looked at her and raised an eyebrow.

"And why not?"

"Why would you give them any more money, what does Priya do for us?"

Curian looked at his daughter in pure disbelief. That she could be so dismissive of the people who made the kingdom function was unfathomable.

"Where do you think our manpower comes from? Where do you think the *taxes* comes from, if not from the citizens of the realm and the Barons and Lords who govern them?"

"They're expendable. The people would still have to pay taxes to the crown without some jumped up man in a shiny suit telling threatening them to do so." Briseis stated defiantly.

"I guess you're the only one who can threaten anyone?" Briseis smirked but said nothing. Curian clenched his hand into a fist and took a deep breath.

"How do you ever expect to be a good queen if you don't respect your subjects, your country and the people who help you run it?"

"Are you giving me a lecture on the respect and sanctity of human life, really?" Briseis laughed and took a sip from her glass of orange juice. Curian sighed heavily as he fixed contemptuous eyes onto his daughter's face.

"What I did before this has nothing to do with what we do now," Briseis burst out laughing and looked at him as though he were the crazy one.

"It has *everything* to do with it! If you never made promises to those stupid advisors of yours to be barons and lords, then they wouldn't be asking you for money now. You gave them titles that meant nothing without the Samaian wealth behind it and now you can't deliver. All you had to do was take the throne and get rid of them, they played their part."

"Then where would the other cities be now without leaders?"

"In ruin. Oh...wait,"

Curian said nothing as he stared his daughter in the eye and she stared back defiantly. A smile spread across her face as she pushed her chair back and stood up.

"As wonderful as this exchange is father, I have more important matters to attend to."

Her long blonde hair that was tied back with intricate braids, swayed gracefully across her back as she strode toward the door,

"Briseis!" she stopped but didn't turn. "I can disinherit you...at any moment. I can disinherit you."

"I'd love to see you try,"

Briseis left the dining hall.

Briseis made her way swiftly to her rooms and found her own letters waiting on her desk.

She had requested that her own mail be delivered here as she did not want her father taking note of anything that she may receive. He may then come under the impression that it was any of his business.

Opening the first few she was mildly interested in the various requests to join her Sentry as well as sightings of men that had shown signs of Samaian power.

It wasn't until a small letter written in an unknown hand at the bottom of the pile that she became intrigued.

Tearing it open, she realised it was a letter from Dreston; marked as such with its official seal. More importantly it was from the Baron himself:

The Antonides Legacy I

To Her Royal Highness, Princess Briseis Myrenda Greybold of Mortania, Duchess of Dyam and Lady of the Imperial Lands.

Briseis rolled her eyes at the use of her extended title but continued reading:

To her most gracious majesty Princess Briseis,

Despite my various dealings with your father the king, I have not had the pleasure of personally meeting your acquaintance. Although I have visited the castle, our paths have not yet crossed so I write to you to discuss the matters that have recently come to my attention.

I have concluded that we may be able to assist each other in ridding ourselves of that which threatens our great land and its future prosperity. Plainly put, I have been informed that there is unrest amongst the Mortanian leaders. Our people look to a new face to govern them since the one chosen does not seem to be able to bear this burden.

The people look to you Princess, as do I.

With your position and power, coupled with my gold and influence amongst the leaders, we can be a true force to be reckoned with. I speak frankly as I believe you are a woman who will respect my honesty as well as the position we and our country are in; due to the failing efforts of a small few.

I anticipate word from you.

BLD

It was signed with his official seal and signature. A bold move Briseis thought with a smile as she leant back in her chair with the letter still in her hand.

She could have him beheaded for this letter and he knew it but believed that she wouldn't...why?

What had Baron Lyon Dreston been told that he thought he could proposition her to overthrow her father and she wouldn't charge him with treachery and put him to death?

Briseis stood then and began to pace. Did the people really wish to put her in her father's place? She had never cared about the country leaders or councilman and the low born even less so. She knew she would inherit her birth right and so their opinions did not matter because once she became queen, she would do everything her way anyway.

If the Mortanian people however were getting tired of her father and wanted her in his place, then maybe her ascension to the throne would be sooner than she thought.

Before she could even begin to put her mind to appropriating her father's crown, she had to find the Redeemer who had managed to evade her Sentry and her powers.

The failed mission to Remora made her feel sick to know that the Redeemer had just narrowly escaped her grasp. All she needed to know now, was where they were headed next.

She hadn't felt the Redeemer use their powers in a long time but that did not mean it wasn't happening. She could only hope that the feeling came soon and then she would have something more solid to work from but until then she couldn't afford to work on hopes and maybes.

She needed a clue as to where the Redeemer was and once she knew, she would kill her once and for all and put an end to the inconvenience that was the other woman's existence.

Baron Dreston could have her attention after that.

***

The following morning, Trista awoke feeling rested and for the first time relaxed.

She turned in bed and saw that Dana was already awake sewing the hem of a dress. She didn't say anything for a while, not wanting to disturb her, until Dana turned and saw Trista watching her. Dana smiled without saying anything and Trista returned the gesture as she sat up.

"Do you think we'll have any trouble with Joe this morning?"

Dana shook her head as she placed the dress beside her on the bed.

"No, he didn't object to us staying last night."

"True, but that doesn't mean that he wants us to stay any longer." Dana nodded her understanding. "Maybe we can make peace with him somehow?"

"What other way do you need then saving his daughter from sexual slavery?" the reality of what she had done came back to her and Trista looked down guiltily.

What *had* she done?

Like all the other times she had used her powers, it was all instinctive.

She had wanted the man to leave and so she'd told him to do exactly that. She didn't know how or why he had listened or even that it would last.

"Do you think they told him what happened?"

"What if they did? If anything, he should be grateful," Trista looked up at Dana and they both knew that that would not necessarily be the case.

If their one night in Dreston had taught them anything, it was that although the Samai were accepted; their powers were not.

Trista threw the covers back off the bed and got out. The wooden floor was cold on her bare feet, so she quickly found her boots then turned to Dana.

"We have to get moving any way. We need to know if we can stay here and then I have to talk to Rayne."

Dana rolled her eyes,

"That wretched woman. I can tell you for free, I have no desire to see her again," Trista laughed,

"Neither do I but she's the first piece of this puzzle and as much as I hate to admit it... I need her."

Joseph had no problem with them staying at the inn if they didn't start or bring any trouble into his establishment. Lorna had told him what Trista had done for Bess and he was more than grateful.

After a hearty breakfast, Trista and Dana went back up to their room to get changed.

As they laced up their boots and gathered their shawls, the door knocked, and Bess entered the room.

"Is everything alright?" Dana asked as the young girl stood timidly in the doorway. Bess nodded unconvincingly but closed the door behind her.

"I...I wanted to thank you for what you did last night."

"I didn't do..." Trista tried to interject but Bess held up her hand to silence her.

"I know there are certain...feelings towards the Samai and their power but when it's used to help me and my family...I can only be grateful."

Trista smiled humbly.

"I didn't get to say thank you last night so, there it is."

"There was no need but you are very welcome."

As Bess turned to leave the room, Trista called out to her,

"Bess, may I have your help with something?"

"Anything Trista," Trista cleared her throat.

"Do you know where we could find Rayne?" Bess was clearly upset by her question but her contempt was silenced by her gratitude.

"She lives but four stalls from here, in a large house next to a tailor."

"Thank you, I'm sure we'll have no trouble finding it." Bess nodded and left the room without another word.

The Antonides Legacy I

Trista and Dana found Rayne's residence with ease.

She indeed lived in a large house, sandwiched between another small inn and a tailor's shop.

The house looked more like a shop then a house but the primly kept rose bushes at the front of the window gave a homely look to the front.

Above the door was the symbol for the Everlasting that Trista had seen in the cave. Dana gave Trista a reassuring look as they approached the door and it instantly opened, swinging inward.

No one behind them seemed to have noticed but cautiously the two girls entered.

As they stepped over the threshold, the door closed sharply behind them and they were engulfed in darkness.

As their eyes adjusted, the girls began to make out a collection of items, some familiar but most foreign to them. There were vials of multi coloured liquids and jars of preserved plants and dissected animals.

There was a musky smell to the large reception room they stood in, as though no fresh air had been in the room for the past hundred years. They continued to look around and saw doors and archways at the sides of the room, leading off into the unknown.

As Dana stepped forward to inspect a jar filled with eyeballs, a voice spoke through the silent darkness.

"I wouldn't touch that if I were you," Dana stopped immediately with her arm outstretched. "To drop dragon's eyeballs would be to lose your hair and any sons you bare to be deaf, dumb, blind and mute and wander their retched life in eternal damnation." Dana calmly stepped away from the jar.

"There are no such things as dragons" Trista replied plainly although she could not see Rayne.

"Not anymore."

Trista and Dana looked at each other in disbelief as one by one, candles dotted around the room came alight and the room was overcome in an ominous glow. Dana instinctively stepped closer to Trista, who smiled reassuringly although she wasn't entirely sure there was nothing to be afraid of. As much as she had been instructed to seek this woman out, since meeting her she had been anything but welcoming or kind.

The girls watched as from a narrow spiral staircase to the right of them, came Rayne.

The older woman looked almost regal as she descended the stairs, something that made Trista instantly think of Avriel. There was something about the two Samaian women that she had met and even the ones she had encountered in the street that exuded poise and grace.

Although they had clearly fallen into hard times since the time of the Samaian rule, they still maintained the airs and graces of their ancestors that made them stand out.

As she watched her, Trista hoped to be like this one day; to radiate beauty and power and know unconditionally that you were special despite countless attempts for that to be proven otherwise.

Rayne's long white hair adorned her like a cape and as she stood in front of them, Trista and Dana gasped as her hair collected itself into a ponytail, plait itself then rest neatly over her shoulder.

"Showing off?"

"Child's play." Rayne shot back. The girls rolled their eyes at each other.

"Listen, I feel we've got off on the wrong foot here. I've travelled a long way to find you and ever since we've met you've been completely rude. What have I ever done to you?"

"You have done nothing,"

"Then what may I ask is your problem?" Rayne smiled at her dubiously then turned and walked away, heading for a room at the back of the house.

"Would you like some tea? It's always best to discuss bringing down an empire over some tea."

Without another word, the girls followed her into the other room.

Charlotte Murphy

A MOTHER'S LOVE

Thorn sat in one of the studies that he, Dana and Trista had completed and continued to ponder on the last few days.

The image of Trista fleeing on her horse was etched into his mind like a scar. He had banged on the window until his hands were bruised but she hadn't even looked up, like she couldn't hear him.

He'd asked himself over again why he hadn't run out to her but whenever his mind took him in that direction, everything went blank. He remembered banging on the window for her to see him and that was it…nothing else after.

He couldn't escape it even now, when he was awake. It had started as seeing her face in his dreams and watching her disappear. Now, her rejection of him taunted him during the day.

He searched his mind trying to understand what he had done wrong, why she had left so suddenly after agreeing to marry him. Even if they had not been betrothed, he just didn't understand how she could have left when she was supposed to love him; marriage or not.

He knew she loved him; he'd known the first time he had spoken to her at the Summer Fete when they were just ten years old. He'd known then that he loved her too. There was something about her that drew him to her and he had waited his entire teenage life to propose to her.

It was all he had ever wanted.

Not Adina, the young woman who if not for her overbearing mother and moderately important father would have been the town whore if the young men had enough coin. No, he had the most coin and that was why she wanted him. That was why she was here now; trying to coerce him into some activity that she thought would make him want her. How could he want her when the one true love of his life had disappeared into the night like a phantom?

No explanation, no note; nothing to explain why she thought to break his heart this way.

"I'd like you to leave."

Adina's nonsensical conversation was cut short as she stared up at him in confusion.

"Excuse me?"

"I'd like you to leave, Adina, now."

"I don't understand," she said with a smile on her face. "I thought we were…"

"You thought wrong!" he snapped at her. Adina stepped back and looked on at him in disgust.

"This is about her isn't it? This is about *Trista*," he didn't need to answer her. She scoffed, "She left you Thorn, she's not coming back!"

"So you thought everything would fall into place and I would take you as my bride?" Adina stood gaping like a fish.

"I thought nothing of the kind" she protested but the lie did not reach to her eyes.

Although he had known his whole life that Adina was not a nice person, it was not until this moment that he utterly despised her and every manipulative bone in her body. Thorn rose from his chair and walked towards the door. He reached out to the handle, pulled the door open and held it there for her. No words needed to be spoken as Adina picked up her shawl and her pride and walked out.

Thorn exhaled as he closed the door and went back to his seat. He hadn't been sitting long when the door opened behind him. Expecting Adina to be back, Thorn spun around in a rage,

"I said get out, Adina!"

"Sorry to disappoint," his mother said calmly. "It is only your mother."

Thorn didn't relax even as his mother stood there,

"What do you want?" he snapped at her. If she was affected by his outburst she didn't show it.

"It seems my presence is an equal disappointment," she said calmly as she stepped further into the room. Thorn ignored her as she took the seat that Adina had vacated. Avriel looked at her son and sighed,

"Thorn, I…"

"Just leave me alone, Mother!" Thorn banged the table top in anger and pushed away from it. He went to storm out of the room but was stopped in his tracks as he collided with an invisible barrier. Gingerly, he reached out and watched as his fingers made ripples in the air like water on the surface of a poll. Thorn turned to look at his mother,

"What is…are you doing this?" he turned to look at his mother sat calmly in the chair behind him.

"Yes."

He couldn't even begin to care to ask her how. His mother had surprised him recently with her actions and this was just something else.

"Another thing you neglected to tell me?"

"I never specifically omitted telling you about my powers, Thorn, it's just never been a topic of conversation."

"Spare me the big words and smoke and mirrors Mother," he replied in clear disgust. "What the hell is going on?" he was facing her fully now and she motioned for him to take a seat. "I think I'll stand."

"Stop being stubborn Thorn, do you want the truth or not?" Thorn eyed her suspiciously then quietly took his seat again, his eyes still filled with obvious contempt.

"Despite your grievances Thorn, I am still your mother have some respect."

"Respect for a woman that lies to me?" Avriel said nothing. "Is the truth going to come out of your mouth anytime soon? If not, I'd rather not be here!" he made to stand up again, but an invisible force slammed him back into his chair. Thorn stared at her wide eyes but said nothing.

"Are you ready for this?" she said quietly.

"I have to be. If it will help me understand why Trista left, then of course I'm ready!" in an instant his whole demeanour changed as he looked at her with pleading eyes.

"Mother…please." Avriel sighed and looked him straight in the eye.

"Trista chose to leave."

"What?"

"Trista was given a choice; her love for you or her duty. Her decision is evident by her absence."

"What are you talking about, what duty?"

"Her duty to her people, *my* people." Thorn narrowed his eyes at her.

"You made her do this!" he accused.

"No," she replied evenly. "Trista chose to leave to pursue her destiny."

"You're lying! I saw you from the window. I saw her turn back, I watched you convince her to leave!"

There was the faintest look of shock in her eyes before her steely gaze returned.

"If you saw so much, why didn't you stop her?" Thorn sighed, clearly distraught.

"I tried, I…I went to the door and I…I tried but…" His last words faded into nothing as he tried to remember something that seemingly wouldn't come to him.

Avriel shifted in her chair,

"You would have only been a distraction...she said so herself." Thorn' eyes widened in obvious disbelief,

"That's not true."

"Isn't it?"

"No! She wouldn't do that to me. She loves me!" Thorn yelled with a lot more conviction then he felt.

"Whether she loves you or not, it didn't stop her from leaving you did it?"

"Why are you saying this?"

"You wanted the truth," she raised her eyebrows at him.

"This isn't it! Trista would not have agreed to marry me if she thought she would have to leave me."

"Her actions say otherwise."

Thorn ran his hands over his head in exasperation,

"What Trista is...*who* Trista is, is bigger than you or me. She knew this and chose accordingly. I'm sorry if you cannot accept that you were used."

Thorn would never have believed that his mother could be so cruel. Where was the woman who had nursed and cradled him when he scrapped his knee as a child? Who told him that everything would be okay and that no one would ever hurt him? Avriel rose from her chair and crossed the small space to stand before her son. She placed her hand on top of his bowed head.

As Avriel stood there, an unfamiliar though painfully unmistakable feeling of guilt threatened to consume her as she heard her son begin to sob beneath her touch.

She knew she had been harsh, but she needed him to forget about Trista.

She never thought he would be affected this much. She had known her lies would come at the expense of her son's trust, but she never thought she would feel this bad. Avriel thought the certainty that she was doing the right thing would subdue her guilty conscience, but she had been incredibly wrong. He would hate her a lot more before this ordeal was over, so she had to trust in her belief that she was right.

"Hush," she couldn't bear to see him this way. Avriel stood there and was momentarily taken back as his arms suddenly curled around her waist and he pressed his face into her stomach and cried.

She realised then, that his anger was his coping mechanism, his dam holding back his flood of pain. Now that she had broken it, it was her duty to put it back together as best she could. Even if she would have to hurt him again before she did so.

A distinct smoky mist creeped around Avriel's hand as she placed it gently onto her son's head and watched the smoke seep into his head.

WILL AND CONTROL

Dana and Trista sat with Rayne in the large kitchen at the back of her house drinking tea she had brewed with magic.

It seemed every little thing she did around them, she did with magic just because she could.

"Who are you?" Trista asked her once the tea was between them and everyone had a cup.

"My name is Rayne, I'm a Samaian sorceress," she smiled to herself. "A very powerful Samaian sorceress once upon time. I lived and worked in the castle with you mother and father for the entirety of their reign."

"Okay, why was I sent to find you?"

Trista explained about the box she'd been given and what she had seen before her Ascension.

"You were sent to find me so I can teach you how to use your powers. I can't begin to, explain what you saw or where you went but I can give you all the knowledge I have available to me. What happened to you only happens to the heir, and no one else. When we Ascend, it just happens, one day you wake up and your powers are open and ready for you to shape as you will. For you, it's a very different story."

"What is my story?" Trista pleaded. "I made my friend do something just because I heard him think it. I stopped a wild horse before it ran over a child, I stopped a guard from stealing a girl to take back to some castle. How am I doing these things, how does all of this work?"

Rayne seemed to find her panic amusing,

"It's called Compulsion, it's a very easy thing to do once you know how."

Rayne turned to look at Dana,

"Put a thousand teaspoons of sugar into your tea."

Trista watched as without question, Dana reached out and began to spoon the sugar in,

"What are you doing, stop that!"

"I'm demonstrating,"

"Not on my friend! Stop it!"

"You stop it," Rayne said simply.

"I don't know how!"

"Just will it," Rayne replied unhelpfully.

Panicked, Trista turned Dana's head to look at her; she still spooned the sugar into the tea.

"Stop spooning the sugar and forget Rayne ever made you do this."

Immediately Dana stopped and shook her head in confusion,

"What's wrong," she looked at Trista weirdly. "Why are you looking at me like that?"

Trista sighed heavily but Rayne merely laughed to herself,

"Let's get started, there is lots to learn!"

***

Though large, beautiful and insanely intriguing Rayne's house had become a prison.

Meals came at set times and if Trista didn't achieve some seemingly impossible goal during her training sessions, sometimes she didn't eat at all.

The Driving Imperative Rayne called it, when Trista asked on her fourth night how she was supposed to concentrate without having any food.

She and Dana had moved into Rayne's house the night before, so Trista could have around the clock tutelage.

"Worry less about eating and more about how to get the food."

"What are you talking about?"

Trista groaned as for what felt like the millionth time that day, she had failed to stop Rayne from sensing her powers.

She had a headache from lack of food, was feeling weak and was not in the mood for any riddles.

It had been like this for the past few days and it was wearing thin.

She needed Rayne to teach her about her powers, her history and her family, but they didn't seem to be getting any closer to that.

Rayne continued her tirade,

"If you want to eat, you know what you have to do."

"I can't do that if I don't eat!"

"If you don't do it, you never will."

Rayne's reply was blunt. Trista's eyes widened as her heart began to beat faster,

"You can't starve me!" Rayne said nothing as she continued to stare at Trista from across the room.

They had been conducting most of their lessons in Rayne's study; a large room with walls lined with books and scrolls as high up as Trista could see.

"Now," Rayne said firmly. "Try again,"

"I can't," came Trista's exhausted reply.

Rayne stormed towards, her face rigid with rage. She grabbed Trista by the shoulders and shook her violently,

"Your power stems from your emotions; anyone who must deal with power knows that. The power wants what you want; it does what you will it to do. Will it to hide from me, block it Trista!"

"I don't know *how*! You're telling me to do something I have no idea how to do. You're supposed to be teaching me and instead your starving me and treating me like a prisoner!" Trista fired back at her.

"How did you stop that horse in your town?"

Trista went to speak but Rayne cut her off.

"How did you hear your friend's thought when you wanted him to pick Dana for Selection? How did you stop those soldiers on their way to kill you or create fire when you needed warmth?"

"I…I…" Trista stuttered,

"You did it because you wanted it, because you needed it. The Everlasting came to your aid and you have no more training now then you did then. Want this Trista; want to learn to hide your powers!"

"I do!"

"You do not!" Rayne spat at her as Trista backed further away from her. "You want to run home to your parents and curl in your bed and cry because it's too hard. You want to go home to Thorn and weep in his arms, because it's all just too much. You want to be weak; you want to be insignificant and lonely like you have been your whole life living in that immaterial mountain town where no one respects you and no one cares about your existence."

Trista hadn't realised how much Rayne's words had hurt until she felt a lone hot tear, sear down her cheek.

She hated that this terrible, cruel woman had made her cry when she had spent her entire life not letting bullies affect her. She had grown up a lonely child in a town full of judgmental children and adults who rejected her just because she looked different. She had buried her insecurities inside her, telling herself that it didn't matter that she didn't have any friends, willing herself to be strong when their cruelty threatened to break her down.

Now, she knew, she could no longer hide from those feelings not only because Rayne had so cruelly thrown them back in her face but because she wasn't that lonely little girl in Remora anymore and she had no intention of allowing Rayne to make her feel as though she was.

Trista straightened up, wiped her tears and looked Rayne straight in the eye,

"Now, hide your power. Will it to be hidden from me and it will be."

Trista closed her eyes and looked into herself as Rayne had taught her on their first day.

When she did this, she could feel her energy, her powers floating around and inside of her. She felt dizzy with it but continued to look deep inside herself, searching for her powers.

Her powers were a light, the light that had guided her to the cave on the eve of her eighteenth birthday. When she found it, she did as Rayne had said and willed it to be hidden.

Nothing happened.

Trista cursed under her breath at her failure but tried again.

No one respects you and no one cares about your existence

Insignificant and lonely like you have been your whole life

The words flashed in her mind's eye and she winced as she remembered how the other children had made her feel.

Although her physical eyes were still closed, her mind looking inside herself had closed her eyes in fear. If she could do this, she could prove they were wrong, that she was special, that she was meant to be here.

When her minds eyes opened, it couldn't see the light; she couldn't find her power. Terrified that something had gone wrong and she destroyed it, Trista, physical Trista opened her eyes.

"I can't find it!" Rayne smiled at her warmly, "Neither can I."

***

A fifth day went by and a sixth that were all increasingly more forgiving than the one before it. Now that she was able to shield it, Trista was now able to use her power.

Not being able to shield her powers made her vulnerable anytime she used it without the proper restraints. Rayne had said it partly explained how she was nearly captured in Remora.

"Briseis can detect your powers," she said one evening as Trista practiced in the living room. "The reach of that is more difficult to tell and whether she can personally sense you or has taken to abusing the Everlasting to do so."

The anger that escaped Rayne at that last possibility didn't go unmissed. She harboured resentment for the royal family that went beyond explanation. What she saw as the rape and pillage of her home, country and position was not going to be forgiven lightly, if at all.

Trista was attempting to light a fire in the hearth using her magic when she asked Rayne if teaching her was just to get revenge on Curian and Briseis.

"Yes," was her curt reply. "You should want that too and you would if you knew what was at stake." Rayne clicked her fingers and a blanket appeared that she quickly wrapped around herself.

"Why don't you tell me?"

"I shouldn't have to. You should want to fight this battle and win this war because you *feel* it, not just for my vengeance, however justified. Now hurry and light that fire before we all freeze to death." Trista smiled, dismissing Rayne's attempt at chastisement. She turned her attention back to the hearth, concentrated and within seconds the fire roared into life, knocking her back then sucking back into itself.

"Control Trista. We are but mere animals without control." Trista rolled her eyes at Rayne who was now reclined on the chair under the blanket with her eyes closed.

Turning back to the fire once again, Trista stared in frustration. Rayne had practically beaten into her that their power came through their will. The Everlasting fuelled their power, but their will controlled it, moulded it, and made it perform how they wished. The Everlasting was a natural source that could therefore be shaped by whatever persons will consumed it. If you were a good person then the Everlasting heightened those qualities. If you were someone like Briseis, the evils were unimaginable.

Rayne had explained that while the use of their power was mainly through thought and will, the actual power was molecular.

It was channelled from The Everlasting and because the Everlasting powered the known world, power could be found all around if you knew how to find and harness it even though it was by no means unlimited. Using too much of the natural energies around could drain someone to the point of depletion which had fatal consequences.

One of the most important things about their power, Trista learned was the use of the Flame.

"When we use our powers for the day to day, with the right training this should take very little energy," Rayne had said. "Little children can freeze objects or create wind for example, but the skill is in the quality, size and control of your magic."

"When we need to lock into the Everlasting to use more power than we personally hold, this is called Enflaming."

"Is it bad if I use it too often?" Rayne smiled reassuringly and shook her head,

"No, but it is costly. Enflaming means you're using too much power and therefore draining yourself of it."

"That's why I pass out," Trista said. "I'm using too much power while running on empty."

"Or using too much too quickly," Rayne agreed. "Enflaming is for big use of power or spells and if you can achieve these without enflaming then you are very powerful indeed."

Rayne's explanation had stayed with her and she tried every day to complete tasks and use her powers without enflaming. The best way she had found to do this was to use her pain as the fuel for her magic.

"Can you do large spells without Enflaming?" Trista asked and although she laughed, Rayne simply nodded.

"Yes Trista, I can." Rayne suddenly looked very sad and looked away from Trista to look down into her hands. "I haven't had to in a very long time. It might be…difficult now."

Rayne looked back at her again with a sad smile on her face, "I have the will…and that's what matters."

Trista now knew she had the will to fight.

She had been taken from her family and that was before she had been forced to flee Remora. Curian and his less than gracious offspring had brought nothing but disruption to her life before she was even born. They had taken her father from her before she had a chance to know him. They had made it necessary for her mother to disappear to who knew where and for all she knew, had died in the last sixteen years.

Rowan was her last link to a family she might never be a part of and Curian and Briseis had made it that she didn't belong.

Yes, she was Samaian; there was an entire race of people that she belonged to and was eventually expected to rule but she would never meet them all.

They couldn't replace a mother's lover or a father's protection.

Even if they welcomed her with open arms as their leader and exalted ruler, they would never be her immediate family. Her birth parents, her parents in Remora, her rights to a normal life had all been taken from her because of Curian, by events that had been unfairly out of her control.

This fight, however, was not out of her control. She now fought for the family she never knew, the family she had been forced to leave behind, for Rayne and her vengeance and for the thousands of exiled and broken Samai that were no longer able to Ascend into their birth right. Also, she thought sadly, she wanted this for Thorn so that one day, if he still loved her, she could return to him.

"You care for him."

The statement brought her out of her thoughts.

"Who?" Trista tried to deny. Rayne only smiled and tapped the side of her head.

"There isn't a lot you can hide from me Trista, but if he can make you do that," she pointed to the now flickering fire in the hearth. The flames licked gently against the now crackling wood, "Then he cannot be a bad thing."

Although she had created the fire, there was an immense sadness that came with her achievement. She had found her will, but it stemmed from her pain and she didn't want to be a slave to that torment. She didn't want to feel sad or hard done by every time she wanted to be powerful.

Trista watched as Rayne fell asleep in the armchair then went to find Dana. She was in the kitchen making a hot drink.

"Can I have some?" Dana turned to her with a grin,

"I don't think you want this,"

"Why not?"

"It's Griffin Tonic."

Confusion was evident on Trista's face, but Dana only laughed teasingly,

"Griffin Tonic helps the bowels, along with indigestion and inflammatory infections or any cysts you may have in there."

"How do you know that?" Dana handed her a large leather-bound book and Trista read the title,

"Potions, Tonics and Ointments?" Dana took the book back.

"Rayne gave it to me and told me to study it." The happiness that spread across Dana's face was contagious. "There are amazing things in here Trista, things to make your hair grow or to cure diseases, even make blind people see again. Obviously, I wouldn't be able to do that because I'm not a Gifted, but you'd have to have trained for years to even attempt that and I'm not even Samaian, but Rayne says that…"

"What?" Dana stopped babbling and looked at Trista in confusion. "What's a Gifted, what are you talking about?"

"Well Rayne is a Gifted and there were hundreds of them that could do all these amazing things and…"

"Yes, but why do you know that, and I don't?"

Trista realised how it sounded as the words left her mouth but for some reason, she didn't attempt to take them back. She couldn't take them back now and the implication of what she had said hung between them like a bad smell. Dana straightened up with the book underneath her arm,

"What do you think I do all day every day while you're training, Trista?" Trista didn't reply and Dana scoffed,

"Why would you care about that? Well I read because Rayne thought it was a good idea for me to be able to help you when the time came. I might not be a Samaian, but I can still be useful, *Princess*." The last word sounded like an expletive as Dana marched angrily from the kitchen.

Trista stood feeling worse than she had in a long time, despite her training with Rayne.

She knew she had been unfair to Dana, but she didn't know how to apologise when she didn't even know why she'd said it. She'd wait until later and speak to Dana then. By then she would have calmed down and would be more likely to forgive her.

In the meantime, she needed some air and quickly left the house.

TO DO WHAT IS RIGHT

Since they had moved in with Rayne, Trista and Dana had acquired a much more practical wardrobe.

Gone were their long dresses and shawls and in their place, were trousers and fitted tunics. In Remora, they would have stuck out in what was considered manly attire, but here in the hustle of Dreston City; it was very much the norm.

There were women who chose to show a little more flesh especially those who worked in the taverns, but generally, the heat of the desert city allowed for loose fitting clothing for both genders.

In addition, Rayne had bought them both sturdy boots, as the roads in Dreston and beyond were a lot less forgiving then the well-maintained streets of Remora.

Trista left Rayne's house into the never-ending traffic of people and wagons and merged seamlessly into the flurry of the marketplace.

Vendors pushed their wares in her line of vision as she walked by, but she continued with no destination in mind; passing alehouses, whorehouses, regular houses and everything else in between.

There were bookstores, bakers, tailors and cobblers. Some were in buildings; some were just wooden stalls crammed together to accommodate all available space. City guards patrolled the streets on foot as well as horseback but none of them approached her. They looked especially intimidating in their steel armour and crimson cloaks with Dreston's crest embroidered on the back, trailing behind them.

Since her encounter with them in Joe's inn, Trista had had no reason to interact with the city guards, but she kept her distance. Their animosity towards the Samai was clear and she didn't want to draw any attention to herself.

Although the evening steadily closed in around them, the streets of Dreston were alive with an assortment of people and animals going about their lives.

Trista had grown to love the evenings here simply because there was so much action.

In Remora, it seemed the entire town went to sleep at the same time. The only activity that continued into the early hours would be in the tavern and her father would never allow to be there after dark.

She walked now, through the crowded streets, smiling politely at the faces that had now become so familiar. It felt good to be around other Samai and while she had yet to speak to one outside of a polite greeting, she felt it in their smiles and their gestures that she was accepted.

Trista continued to walk through the market until she stopped at a jewellery stall, eyeing the trinkets on display. There was a young Samaian girl behind the stall and she smiled at Trista warmly,

"Would you like something?"

"I'm looking for a gift...for a friend."

"Maybe some earrings or a nice bracelet perhaps?" the young girl motioned to the merchandise on the table in front of them and Trista had a look for what Dana might like. She spotted what looked like a necklace but when she picked it up, the girl explained that it went on your head,

"For parties or any special occasion," she said, taking it back to weave it delicately into her own hair.

"It's beautiful," Trista said running her fingers along the intricate silver metal work when the girl handed it back.

It had miniature roses woven into the framework.

"How much is it?" she looked up at the girl but was surprised to see that an older woman had now joined her. Although all Samai looked the same in terms of eye colour and hair, it was obvious that she was this girl's mother.

"It costs nothing for you, your highness."

"Excuse me?" Trista was momentarily taken back.

No one other than Rayne referred to her as royalty and even then, she was usually doing it to mock her in some way.

"No payment is needed Princess." The woman repeated as Trista continued to stare at her in disbelief.

"What did you say? How did you…?" the woman smiled warmly.

"I can feel it,"

"What do you mean?" the woman gave her a peculiar look.

"Your power, we can all feel each other; those of us who were born under it."

Trista had no clue what to say to this woman but did take notice of her long curly hair. She then noticed that her daughter's hair was as straight as Trista's had been meaning she had not yet Ascended.

Was this the price for not having the Everlasting?

Would this young girl never grow into her heritage?

"I have to go," Trista placed the headdress back on the table. "Thank you."

The woman nodded with a smile and warm eyes,

"Our thoughts and love are with you Princess. Soon, you will lead and know that we will follow."

Trista realised for the first time since leaving home that people genuinely saw her as something special and it terrified her.

She backed away from the woman and immediately bumped into someone behind her, this time an old Samaian man.

"Princess," he nodded his greeting to her. Trista took off down the street, crashing into more people but not stopping to apologise.

Trying desperately to get away from the fate she couldn't seem to escape, Trista barrelled head first into some type of commotion.

There was a large group of city guards yelling into a crowd who were fighting to get through them. More people were joining the uproar as the guards were violently pushing them back, shouting orders and threatening them with their weapons. Trista saw a few of the elderly keeping well out of the way and approached an old man standing wide eyed by a baker's stall,

"Excuse me sir but, what's going on?" the old man looked up at her and after a fleeting look of confusion he smiled at her though grimly,

"Another Gathering Princess," Trista ignored the title. "The third today."

"*Third*, why are they doing this?"

"They can, Princess, and so they do." Trista was immediately annoyed.

"Why does nobody stop this?"

"We are many, but we are weak. There are a few of us who remember what it was to have the power, but we live in turbulent times and we are not who we once were." Trista sighed, rolling her eyes.

"No one is saying we have to use our powers, why not just fight back; with brute strength. Why do you stand for this persecution?" the old man shrugged,

"Why do some choose to persecute? They do what is natural for them to do."

Trista was disgusted, was this truly how the Samai thought? That it was the way of the world for individuals to abuse others just because it had always been done?

"You say that as though it's *our* nature to be submissive. If it is, why have you been waiting for me? Just stay under Curian's rule and be done with it!"

The old man was obviously shocked by her outburst but had the decency to look ashamed. Trista stormed away and into the crowd but as she got deep within it, the most peculiar feeling came over her.

While she had been training with Rayne, she had begun to feel less nauseous when using her powers, but this feeling was all she could compare it to.

Rayne had taught her that her power was a physical thing that rested inside her. She could sense it inside her now, but it felt like her entire body were humming with power that had never been there before. As she looked into the faces of the people around her and saw that they were Samai she realised then that this was what they meant by *feeling* her.

She could physically sense the power around her from the Samai who of course had been born under the protection of the Everlasting. The ones who noticed her acknowledged her with a short bow of their head but were more occupied with the turmoil at the front of the crowd.

Decidedly, Trista pushed her way as far to the front as she could get and saw guards pushing young children into the back of caged carriages as their family members wailed and screamed for them to be released.

Trista watched in horror as a young girl of no more than ten, was ripped from her mother's grasp. The mother screamed and fell to the ground in despair before a violent guard kicked her in the chest away from him.

Trista was enraged and felt the familiar heat of her power begin to build inside. For a split second she composed herself; remembering her lessons with Rayne. She could use her power without Enflaming and still do something significant. She reared it in until the heat was gone but the power was still there, humming beneath her skin like something alive.

Trista pushed her way to the front of the crowd and as soon as she had the space to do so, she shot her arms out either side of her and yelled,

"Stop!"

Instantly, everything stopped.

Every person in the middle of the street came to an immediate stop as Trista concentrated on the ten or so guards that were causing this trouble. She turned herself so her right palm was facing the guards and her left palm was facing the crowds.

With a flick of her wrist, every civilian in the crowd was mobile again. Again, with a flick of her right wrist, Trista reanimated the Samai and other people in the cages.

"Quickly," she said, feeling the power draining from her ever so quickly. "Get your loved ones and get out of here!"

They didn't need to be told twice. Men, women and younger children rushed forward to help their friends and family out of the caged carriages. They quickly stole keys from the pocket of the guard who covered any locked wagon and quickly ushered their people out.

"Quickly!" Trista hissed at them. Her arms were shaking from the effort it took to keep her mind focused on keeping only the guards frozen. She took a deep breath to calm herself as people continued to escape.

"Hey!"

All eyes that were not focused on allowing someone to escape, turned to the sound of the voice who had yelled.

The Antonides Legacy I

"You're using magic! That's forbidden!"

The young human boy, no more than ten screamed down from the low rooftop of a rundown merchant's shop. He was an urchin, a probably orphaned street child who did spying for the high born for small amounts of coin. If he told anyone, it wouldn't end well.

"Get him!" someone from the crowd shouted back and with fear in his eyes, the little boy took off across the rooftops as a few men took off after him.

Trista didn't have the energy to worry about him and a young man who approached her seemed to know it,

"Hurry, she can't hold this much longer!" he called out to no one in particular.

Trista's arms shook, her head pulsed with an impending headache and just as the last few people were dragging their friends from opened cages, she collapsed and the guards were instantly reanimated.

"What the..." the confusion was clear as the guards looked at the now empty cages and the last few people trying to escape.

"Get away from him! Get back in there!" the Dreston guards drew their swords, choosing to fight instead of questioning how they had lost almost thirty detainees in a matter of minutes.

The guards slashed their weapons, forcing the crowd to step back to avoid being cut to shreds; leaving Trista exposed.

"You did this, you Samaian bitch!" a guard approached her, sword outstretched before Trista looked up and by narrowing her eyes at him, sent him flying back against a brick wall, knocking him unconscious. Again, she looked at the next guard closest to her and sent him against the same wall beside his comrade. His helmet dented as he hit the wall.

A sharp pain shot through her head as Trista scrambled back into the crowd to hide even has the remaining guards threatened to kill them all if they came any nearer to help her or the few people still stuck in the cages.

"Get away from here Princess, before they find you!" a woman hissed at her, but Trista shook her head,

"I can't, not now!"

"You have to! We thank you, but you have to be kept safe. Leave this place before that child comes back with more guards!" the woman was adamant that she leave; leaving Trista with no choice but to do so.

Even she could understand now just how important she was to the survival of her people and the salvation of the innocent people of Dreston and every other city and town like it, that she had yet to encounter.

HIDING IN PLAIN SIGHT

Trista awoke the next morning with a nosebleed and a severe headache.

She knew she couldn't tell Rayne what she had done at the market last night, so she lay in bed for a long time before getting ready to face her and the new lesson.

She arrived at the breakfast table ready to face up to her actions from last night, but Dana was nowhere to be seen. They had separate rooms now, so she hadn't had to face her last night.

Rayne was sat at the table when she got downstairs, drinking from a steaming cup and flipping through the thick pages of a large book Trista could see she wasn't reading. Trista took her seat quietly at the table and reached for a slice of toast from the bread rack. As she did so, a pot of tea emerged from the kitchen doorway and settled itself with a quiet thud by Trista's right hand.

"Thank you," she went to reach for an empty mug, but it slid across the table just out of her reach. Trista sighed, knowing this lesson. Rayne wanted her to strengthen her powers by doing what seemed mundane tasks. She wanted it to become second nature so that one day they would indeed be mundane and not require any concentration.

With a newfound determination, Trista brought the mug towards her. For added effect, she let the cup hover in the air then did the same with the teapot, allowing it to pour. As it poured, Rayne's mug slid from across the other side of the table towards Trista who pushed it back with her power, while continuing to pour the tea. As soon as she had pushed the mug back, it came back at her again, and then another flew towards her from the top shelf of a cupboard against the wall and another from the kitchen doorway.

Trista caught them all just in time, placing them onto the table or floor, whichever was easiest and continued to pour the tea. Various items were aimed at her, flying off the shelves and out from doorways and behind her and from above her. A few she intercepted, a few she didn't and instead had to send crashing against something.

Eventually, it became too much for her; her cup was nearly full and things wouldn't stop coming at her. She couldn't mentally control all this activity at once and so she lost her concentration,

"Stop it please!" the mug and teapot smashed against the table, sending the contents over the table and onto the floor and instantly the objects stopped attacking her.

Every book, cup, plate and flowerpot went back to its original place. Rayne closed the book that she had not looked up from, stood up and fixed her eyes on Trista; fierce with anger and disappointment.

"You might be the heir to our throne Trista but from what I can see you are not fit to hold that title."

"I..."

"Whether you are royalty or not, simple manners stop you from speaking to Dana the way you did last night."

"I only meant..."

"She knows exactly what you meant," Rayne stepped toward Trista who rose from her own seat to meet her. "As do I." Rayne sent the book she had been using back to its place on the shelf.

"Princess or not you have a lot to prove young lady before you can even attempt to be as ungrateful, conceited and outright rude as you were to Dana yesterday." Trista said nothing.

"She's in the garden." Rayne didn't bother to look at her before she stormed away.

Dana was crouched down amongst some long wooden poles with thin green vines growing up them. She was busy pushing them securely into the ground and tending to any that may have fallen a bit limp.

"Tomatoes," she said when Trista appeared by her side. "Am I allowed to learn about these without your permission?"

"I deserved that," Dana continued tending to the fruit. "Dana I'm sorry. I didn't mean what I said or at least I didn't mean how it sounded." Dana straightened up to look her in the face, wiping her hands on the gardeners apron she had tied around her tiny waist.

"Then explain to me, what did you mean?"

In all the years, they had known each other, Trista had never seen Dana so much as raise her voice. The anger and hurt that came from her now was intimidating.

"I meant...I meant that..."

What had she meant? Dana folded her arms across her chest,

"What you meant Trista is that you're more important than me so I shouldn't be partial to information that you aren't."

"No! I just didn't understand why Rayne would tell you things she hasn't told me if I'm supposed to be learning about my life from her!"

"Did you ever think that she did it for your own good?" Trista was confused and it showed on her face. "All you think about is how this all affects you, how unfair this all is for *you*, because of course everything is about you."

Dana was clearly on a roll,

"Did you ever think about what others have sacrificed for you! Trista, I may never see my family again. I gave them up for you."

"That's not fair, I told you to go back home!"

"Yes, and I chose not to because I thought you were my friend!"

"I *am* your friend!"

"Then act like it!" Dana screamed at her before seemingly realising how heated she had really become. She took a deep breath,

"All my life…I've been the quiet one, the boring one and now, now I finally have the chance to be something special…to be a part of something. I'm sorry if that offends you but I can't be on this journey with you and do nothing."

Trista felt terrible. She had truly hurt Dana's feelings and she would give anything to take that back,

"I never would have survived this long if it wasn't for you, I know that, and I never meant to hurt you Dana. Forgive me?"

"I know you didn't…and I do forgive you. It just hurt my feelings."

"I know and I'm sorry," Trista reached out for a hug that Dana gladly stepped into. They hugged each other tightly as Trista whispered into Dana's neck,

"You're my best friend."

Dana didn't say anything but just squeezed her tighter. When they finally let each other go, Trista knelt with her in the vegetable garden and helped with the tomatoes. She used her powers, to practice doing simple tasks and used the time to tell Dana about what happened the night before.

"Do you think the guards will recognise you or that child told anyone?"

"I don't know about the boy, whether he will remember me or not but the guard who tried to kill me definitely might." Dana was thoughtful for a moment as she pushed another wooden rod into the earth.

"We've only been here a short time and we've already seen how things work here. Everyone is out for themselves and a way to get in good with the Baron. If turning in a rebel who steals his slaves is the way to do it, do you think they will turn that opportunity down?"

***

A week later, Lyon sat in his audience chamber listening to another lengthy tale about why he should source another town with more money and supplies before their entire populous were wiped out.

He struggled to maintain looking interested as the emissary from Crol continued to plead his case. It struck Lyon as ironic that although he may not rule Mortania, he carried out all the duties of a king: listening to petitioners, deciding on taxes, liaising with foreign envoys and commanding an extensive military force to keep it all in line.

He raised his right index finger and a servant girl rushed to his side with a golden chalice on the matching tray. He gave her a fleeting glance before suddenly looking back at her, completely ignoring the representative from Crol.

"What are you still doing here?" the girl visibly trembled as her eyes darted quickly to his own then back again but said nothing. "I thought I told you to leave!" the representative had stopped speaking and an eerie hush had fallen over the crowded reception room.

His attendees, guards and of course other petitioners and representatives waiting their turn, said nothing though waited eagerly for the girl's response.

"Well?" he demanded of her.

"There was no one to replace me Lord. If I were not here, there would be no one to serve you."

The girl was meek and frail, one of the reasons he had wanted her dismissed in the first place. She had a nervous air about her that made him weary and it didn't please him.

"Nonsense, there are dozens of young women in my service," he almost laughed at her. He had his guards perform Gatherings frequently the past few days as his appetite for new girls had grown. There had to be enough girls to satisfy his attractions.

"There are no girls Lord," came a quiet but firm voice from behind him.

Lyon's eyes turned to rest on his Chief Attendant Aml. Aml had been his service since Lyon was a child and they had grown together although on completely different ends of the social spectrum.

Aml was an Agmantian who had moved to Mortania when he was four years old to live with his father who was employed by the Dreston family.

Aml's father Temyl, had been the Chief Attendant to Lyon's father and when the old Baron had died, Lyon was put into Temyl's care. As a companion for the young boy now in his care, Temyl had brought Aml to Dreston Castle when he was eight years old and Lyon seven.

When Temyl had finally retired, Aml took over his father's duties and was as such, the closest person to the Baron.

Aml stepped forward,

"Perhaps we could speak privately, Lord?" Lyon was confused but did not want to show this to the many eyes that were on him. He rose from his chair and followed Aml into his private rooms.

"What is it?" he demanded as Aml closed the door behind them and faced his friend and employer.

"There is a shortage in young women Lord. The guards have not been returning with the desired numbers for your entertainment."

"Why on earth not?" Lyon thundered. "I have ordered enough Gatherings, so, where are they?"

"We don't know Lord," was Aml's solemn response but as usually his expression was stoic and unwavering. He was a no-nonsense type of man who never showed his true feelings which Lyon liked about him.

Lyon began to pace with clear frustration.

What was going on in Dreston that this could happen right under his nose?

Were the people rebelling against him? No, there would have been news of fights and brawls if that were the case. Something much more sinister was taking place; he just needed to figure out what.

"Summon all the relevant guards to my study. I wish to get to the bottom of this."

"Yes, Lord."

Aml disappeared through the main door and Lyon followed soon after, making his way to his study, all thoughts of the emissaries forgotten.

A few minutes later, he was sat behind his large mahogany writing desk as four guards entered the room followed by Aml. He said nothing to them for a long time, waiting for one to make some sign that would incriminate them.

When no one said anything, Lyon stood up from behind the table and glared at them,

"Well?" the four men shifted nervously, clearly unsure of what was expected of them. "You have been brought here because my most trusted believes that you would know why my harvest of women has been somewhat lacking recently. Is this true?"

"These four men are the head guards for each quarter of the city Lord." Aml explained.

"Which quarter has been missing the most women Aml?"

"The First Quarter Lord."

Lyon nodded in understanding before moving from around the table to stand directly in front of the four armoured men.

"Could the leaders of quarters two, three and four leave us please?" the other three men rushed out immediately leaving one man trembling man behind.

When there were only the three men left in the room, Lyon stood in front of the man with his hands behind his back.

"What is your name?"

"Jethro, Lord."

"Jethro. Have you been in my employ long?"

"For the past four years Lord,"

"Hmm...then you understand that this turn of events is most vexing for me and that something needs to be done."

"Of course, Lord," Lyon nodded his head approvingly

"Could you also tell me how you have let Gatherings fail in the quarter that is meant to be the most protected? *My* quarter!" the last words could have taken Jethro's head off from the force at which they had come.

Dreston City was divided into four sections or quarters that began from the immediate vicinity of Dreston Castle.

The First Quarter was the most affluent, and as such should have been the most protected. That any defences could have been breached in the quarter that the Baron himself occupied was insulting.

Lyon started to pace the small space between himself and Jethro, anger seeping from his pores.

With a sharp movement, Lyon reached out and placed his thick hands around Jethro's throat. Aml instinctively stepped forward a fraction before thinking better of it and not saying a word. Jethro was clawing at the baron's hands, trying to loosen his grip but to no avail.

"Too. Many. Samai."

He choked out as he tried desperately to hold onto his last wisps of life.

Baron Dreston immediately let go of Jethro causing him to collapse on the ground as he tried desperately to catch his breath.

Lyon spun away from Jethro, his black robes fanning out behind him as he marched away in fury.

"Speak!" he demanded as he marched back again, clearly at odds with himself.

"They come up. All around. Always Samai," Jethro's words were splintered as he still struggled to breathe. Lyon was facing him now, his arms folded across his broad chest with his right arm up, two fingers in the shape of an L with his thumb supporting his chin and his index finger stroked his upper lip.

"Explain," Jethro struggled to stand again and spoke as best he could.

"At each Gathering, there was an unusual amount of Samaians. They fought back against us."

"How?" Lyon demanded, there had to be more to this. Jethro looked guilty,

"Magic…they used their powers against us somehow but…" Lyon's eyes that had been hooded in anger, now shot up to look Jethro right in the eye as he stepped towards him.

"But *what?*" he yelled at him,

"I…I…it was only one of them…a woman was there among them each time."

"So, what if there was a woman?" Lyon was getting impatient as he sneered at Jethro.

"They were protecting her, Lord."

The baron took a step back as the implication of Jethro's words finally became clear.

Lyon knew of the lost princess who was destined to reclaim her birth right but any sightings or talk of her had long stopped in the seventeen years since she'd last been seen.

Was the Samai princess in Dreston using her powers?

It seemed so as all Drestonians knew that to use the Everlasting magic was strictly forbidden and punishable by death.

Lyon knew that the Samai were a powerful people, they had to be to retain control of the country for as long as they had. If they were able to use their powers again, who could tell what they would do with it?

It was with indignation that Lyon had to admit they had only lost the Battle at The Wide because Curian's men – his men – had kept forces away from King Alexander so that Curian could kill him. They had determined rightly that the power would have a domino effect so that if Alexander lost his powers, the other Samai would too.

There was only one reason why the Dreston Samai population would risk lengthy imprisonment or death and that reason terrified him more than anything.

The baron turned his attention back to Jethro with Aml ever watchful in the background.

"You are fortunate Jethro that you have provided some rather valuable information, but your incompetence can not go unpunished. Aml, have this man arrested and placed in solitary confinement for a month then have a scribe sent here. I wish to write a letter to Princess Briseis."

THEA'S POINT

Lamya's arrival at Thea's Point could not have come a moment sooner.

Her time on the ship since Rick's death had been hard to bear not only because she knew he had not taken his own life but because she knew who had.

Having to share the same space as Juba had been unbearable as her own anger had steadily begun to consume her. Watching Juba walk around every day with another man's blood on his hands was more than even she could take. It hurt that she could no sooner condemn him for Rick's murder then she could bring him back to life. They would need proof other than her empathetic powers and she had none. For now, he would get away with it completely.

When the Mortanian shores had finally come into view, Lamya felt the relief wash over her like a warm ray of sunshine. She disembarked and waited at the end of the gangplank to say farewell to the Captain.

He had been welcome company through her days on his vessel and it was only right she show her gratitude. When she had said the appropriate goodbyes, her luggage had been collected and mounted on the escort she had flanked for this very purpose, she rode toward Main Street to find somewhere to stay.

As the main trading point for the country, there were countless inns but many were full to burst.

Lamya, with the help of her driver eventually found a decent enough establishment that had space for her and set up camp in one of their box rooms. She wouldn't be there long so there was no real need for excessive luxuries.

Once settled, she had something to eat in the bar downstairs then returned to her room to rest.

That had been three days ago and now she was in the bar again waiting for her breakfast. She sat at a small table in the centre of the room, it was always best to pick up conversation amid people and tuned into the hubbub around her until something significant caught her ear.

"…marched right past me, they did. That crow banner flying high like they own the place."

"They *do* own the place," came a chuckled response.

"You know what I mean. Bet they'll be heading over to Dreston from what Reyva tells me."

"Old wives' tales,"

"Don't put the wives aside. They talk to the right people, that's how they know things," the first man protested but his friend simply laughed.

Lamya went to stand and make her way to these men but the innkeeper, Dhiann arrived with her breakfast and a large smile. The older woman was tall with curly blond hair that she had gathered at the top of her head to seemingly keep out of her way, but tendrils of curl kept falling into her face anyway. She was gifted in the chest with a slim but tough body. She owned the inn with her brother who ran the bar. She took a seat beside Lamya as she placed the bowl of porridge and two slices of thick just baked bread in front of her.

"Thank you so much. It smells wonderful."

"Doesn't it though! My mother does make the best bread in the kingdom, ask anybody!"

"I'm sure I won't need to," Lamya assured her with a smile as she spooned some of the creamy porridge into her mouth and hummed appreciatively.

"So, do you plan to be here much longer?"

"Is that a discreet way to ask me to leave?" Dhiann covered her face as she realised how that must have sounded and her face flushed red.

"Of course not! We just don't have many people stay on too long here, mainly passing through to the capital or other cities. What are your plans while in Mortania?"

"To be honest, I have no concrete plans until I'm summoned by…some friends of mine. Once they send word for me to continue my travels, then I will."

Lamya hadn't heard from the Council since her arrival and it was starting to worry her. She had tried to connect with them a few times but with no luck so she just had to wait.

"Well, at least I'll have some female company for a while at least," Lamya smiled as she continued to eat. "You don't get many women travelling alone, are you sure it's safe?"

"Not always admittedly but I have a few tricks up my sleeve to keep safe. I must say Mortania is different than the last time I was here." Dhiann looked at her questionably.

"How do you figure?" Lamya chose her words carefully.

"Mortania is a lot more…unstable now and Thea's Point is definitely busier!"

Dhiann laughed though nodded her agreement. She shifted in her seat as she moved closer to Lamya and continued more quietly.

"Since they cut off connection to the rest of the kingdom, the Point has been busier but that isn't always a good thing. Sure, we get more trade but people are more violent now and have a lot more to fight for."

"Like what?" Lamya probed as she broke off some of the bread and dipped it into her bowl. Dhiann shrugged,

"No one can expect us to be stuck so close together like this without some kind of uproar. Dill thinks I'm being silly but something is brewing and it's not going to be pretty."

"What do you think is going to happen here? Surely Mortania is a peaceful place now that the king is ruling so justly."

From the look on her face, Lamya knew that Dhiann knew she meant this as a question rather than a statement of fact. Lamya watched as the woman became unsure of herself and whether or not she should continue to confide in her. Lamya sent her a positive smile but said nothing, knowing that Dhiann had to make any decisions to speak on her own.

"The king hasn't been ruling much if you ask me. We get more direction from the Sentry."

Since her arrival at the Point, Lamya had learnt of the castle enforcement team known as the Royal Sentry who patrolled the streets of the capital and beyond, seemingly on royal business but seemed to be involved in things a lot more underhanded.

She had seen them beat a young thief within an inch of his life in the street because he had stolen a bunch of grapes from a stall. No one had said anything and had left the boy on the ground to die. She had also learned that the Sentry took their orders from the princess, Briseis and not from the king.

The King's Guard were an entirely different entity whose sole purpose was to protect the king himself and not the kingdom. It made Lamya wonder, if the princess had so much power of the regulation of the city, what influence she had over the kingdom?

"Do you agree with their way of things?"

"It does not matter what I agree with or not. The princess runs the city and we all know it. It's only a matter of time before…" Dhiann trailed off as another thought took her elsewhere.

"Before what Dhiann?"

"Before…before we won't stand for it any longer."

"You are human, Man, what problems should you have with the crown?"

Dhiann sighed heavily as she stood up from the table, clearly finished with this part of the conversation.

"Man or not, doesn't stop us from starving and the weather being freezing in the middle of summer. No one is changing anything, especially not the king…I have to get back." she said sadly before disappearing back into the kitchen.

Lamya was left with her thoughts and she knew it was all connected to the discontent she had witnessed on the ship. Man were becoming increasingly dissatisfied with the way Mortania was being run and there was serious threat that something was going to be done about it.

There were Loyalists like Juba who would go to the extremes for their beliefs, but there were also men and women like Rick and Dhiann who were angry but suffering in silence. They were not the most radical of people but the fact the seed had been planted and they were having doubts was enough. It only took one person to choose to revolt against tyranny and other people would follow. Lamya knew who that one person had to be.

She finished her breakfast and made her way back to her room to collect some things before she left for the day.

As she had told Dhiann, there was not much she could do until she had further instruction from The Council, so she was biding her time. She collected some money, a few herbs and

The Antonides Legacy I

scrolls and made her way into the bustling streets of Thea's Point.

Thea's Point was essentially one long street facing the harbour lined with multiple inns and stalls all crammed together in a not seemingly obvious way.

The harbour was stacked with ships of various sizes, entering and exiting on various trade routes. There were the high and large guard posts that housed the harbour officials overlooking the ships, as well as the toll booths where captains and merchants and other traders paid for licences, trade fees and docking permits for however long they could afford.

In her emerald green short sleeved robe, Lamya stood out as a vision amongst the varying shades of brown and grey.

Sailors stopped to watch her, appreciative of her beautiful face and long flowy fiery locks of hair.

The salty air blew in briskly from the coast and Lamya acknowledged not for the first time that Mortania was distinctly colder than it should have been. It was the middle of the summer and yet many, including herself were wrapped up in warm cloaks and robes to keep out the icy winds. There was no snow as far as she could tell, but it didn't feel like it was far off.

As she walked leisurely down Main Street, observing the multitude of faces; Lamya felt the most peculiar sensation. It was warm, a heat that seemed to wash over her and settle in the centre of her chest. It felt familiar somehow and so she looked around earnestly to find the source. Her eyes led her straight to what looked like an apothecary and so she marched right over to it.

She went to open the door, but it was locked and as it resisted her, the feeling suddenly disappeared. She tried the door again and this time it opened instantly.

The bell above the door jingled in a merry way as Lamya closed the door behind her and went to stand in the middle of the shop floor.

The walls either side of her and the wall behind the counter directly in front of her were filled with varying colours and plants and herbs, some familiar and some less so.

Behind the counter stood a pair of twin girls, Samai twin girls with long curly black hair and polite smiles on their faces,

"Buying or selling?" one girl said

"Neither," Lamya said firmly as her eyes scanned their faces. There was something familiar about them too, "Who owns this establishment?"

"Our mother," the girls said together.

"...could I see or speak with..."

"Look who decided to come home," a rich and almost harmonious voice came from a door directly behind the two young girls.

A much older woman appeared from the back room with a serene but welcome smile on her face.

She was dressed in a long navy blue dress, tapered at the waist with a thick gold band. The sleeves were so large and long, you could not see her hands until she lifted her arms in Lamya's direction, ready to embrace her.

Her thick black hair was caught in a low ponytail that stopped at her waist. Her fiery green eyes gleamed as she looked at Lamya,

"Alexia!" Lamya rushed into her tight embrace while the two girls looked on in amusement. Lamya stepped back to look the older woman in the face even as they still held each other, tears brimming their eyes.

"It was you I felt outside," she said in amazement. "I thought your powers were forbidden here?" Alexia shrugged,

"They are but there are a few things we try to exercise now and then. I do not want my girls to forget their powers for when the time comes." Lamya nodded enthusiastically as Alexia still held her hands tightly, lovingly.

"How are you, how long has it been?"

"Too long," Lamya said quietly as Alexia turned to her daughters,

"Girls, please make us some tea and bring it upstairs."

Alexia led Lamya back through the way she had come that led to some stairs. They emerged onto the top level into the seating area of their living quarters. The two women sat down on two cushioned wooden chairs with a small table between them, smiling over at each other.

"Tell me everything," Lamya said instantly and Alexia just laughed. "How did you come to live here, in this place?"

"Where to begin?" Alexia sighed, her face suddenly stricken with sadness and Lamya was sorry she had caused it.

"When Alexander died, you know there was not much to live for even in Thelm where the fighting was considerably less." Lamya nodded. She remembered it like it was yesterday.

She had been living in Thelm, with The Lithania Council when the Samaian king had fallen. The world had changed that day as the power had shifted to Curian Greybold.

Even in the year that she had remained living in the North, the pain around her was too much to bare. Lamya made the choice to leave Mortania for her own sanity but she had left many friends behind, Alexia being one of them.

Lamya was been seventeen, had been on the Council for almost two years before the uprising but she had left as soon as she could.

"I was in Thelm for a long time even after you left," Alexia continued. "With the girls…waiting…but soon it became too much to be there and so we left."

Lamya knew what Alexia had been waiting for; news of her husband and all the other Samaian soldiers who had left for the capital to fight for their king and country.

"Were the Thelmians hostile?"

"Of course, I couldn't have my girls in that environment for too long and when I knew…when I accepted that Elijah would not be coming back, I made my plans to leave."

Alexia explained how she and other Samai had left Thelm together but were made to separate as Curian gave word that they were weaker this way.

"In the end we begun to use our powers just to survive and not to fight, but it drained us. After a few months in Drem we finally booked passage south and have been here ever since."

"But why come south, to where all the fighting was?"

To where Elijah was killed, were the unspoken words.

"I wanted to be close to the capital," Alexia explained as one of her daughters came in with a tray of tea and other small treats then exited the room with a polite nod. "Thank you Dawn. I wanted to be close to Tirnum when the time came."

Alexia didn't have to explain what time.

Lamya knew that all Samai were waiting for the lost princess to show themselves and take their place as ruler.

"Well you seem to have done well for yourself?" Lamya said with a smile as Alexia poured and handed her a small cup of tea. Lamya revelled at the expensive crockery that could only have been saved from Alexia's days as the Samaian Agricultural Ambassador. A time when she would have had position and power and of course wealth.

"There is a lot of business in sickness I'm afraid Lamya and many sailors come off those ships with a lot more, shall we say internal gifts."

The two women laughed, "I simply worked with what I had and made the best of it. I had to for my girls."

"I appreciate that, but I felt your power outside, how have you been hiding it for so long?"

"It hasn't been too hard, it took me a while to get back into using them again after feeling so drained, but Man aren't as opposed to us as they were before. We don't flaunt it in their faces in any case, but they know who and what we are, and they still come for healing and remedies."

"So, they tolerate you as long as you help them?" Lamya said with disgust but Alexia merely laughed.

"You must remember that the Point is where all different people come together and not all are as closed minded as Man. Most people have no grievances with us and those that do don't really come around here. They have bigger problems with someone a lot closer to home."

"The king."

Alexia said nothing for a while before leaning back in her chair and looking Lamya straight in the eye.

"There is a reason you are here Lamya and from the way you left, it can only be because the Council have summoned you. It has been a long time since I was an ambassador for the crown but there are things you don't forget. Is the Redeemer with us already?"

Lamya shook her head and hated to see the disappointment in Alexia's eyes. She knew there was a lot, namely their very existence riding on the Redeemer coming into their powers and the Samai needed it to happen now.

"I felt their Ascension, it was powerful enough for me to feel it in Agmantia but I have felt nothing substantial since then. I do not think they even know who they are or what they are destined to do."

"How can that be possible? Hasn't Avriel been preparing her?"

"It does not seem like it,"

"What has she been doing this entire time?"

Lamya had no response as Alexia was clearly angry with the way Avriel had handled the Redeemer's education.

"There has to be a reason why our princess has not been planning her own uprising since she was old enough to speak and why instead we are waiting for someone who might not even rise to the occasion!"

Alexia rose from her seat angrily and went to stand at the window that faced Main Street and the harbour beyond. Lamya said nothing for a while, desperate to find a way to make her old friend feel reassured but she knew there was no way. Her future and the future of her people rested in the hands of a young girl who might not know what was expected of her. Alexia would have found strength in the knowledge that this person was coming, to know that they may not would be a hard pill to swallow.

"I'm sure the princess knows what she must do Alexia,"

"I pray to the Mother she does or else there is no hope." Alexia turned back to face Lamya with her arms limply by her side as if defeated.

"We might not be able to survive as a race but Mortania will not survive if she doesn't do something soon. Even the Men are turning against their absent king who no longer attends meetings and hides away in his private chambers not bothering about the city or the rest of the country. Alexander would never have been this way...never!" Alexia's anger radiated from her like a heat but also an intense sorrow.

"They may have resented Alexander's rule but they will despise this king even more for turning his back on his own people. It is only a matter of time before they accept that their entire lives were better when my cousin was king and when they do, I pray with all that I am that our princess is able to take back what is rightfully hers."

Lamya nodded as she felt a calm come over Alexia. The elder woman had dealt with a lot in the uprising and the battle that followed but she remained strong.

Lamya understood more than ever that she needed to be with the Redeemer, to coach her and that needed to be sooner rather than later.

THE FINAL GATHERING

At Tirnum Castle later that evening, Princess Briseis was once again in the training yard but this time, with no opponent.

She was trying desperately to work off the anger steadily building inside of her.

For the past few days Briseis had been feeling the Redeemer.

She had felt her use her powers, but it hadn't been enough to pinpoint her location.

The first time it had felt like lightning had ripped through her body and charged her with energy so potent it was as though her mind were opened and she could see clearly for miles. She had known exactly where the Redeemer was but as instantly as she had this knowledge it had disappeared.

What further angered Briseis was that although she felt some remnants of the power, it was not as clear as before. The young woman had clearly learned to mask her powers somehow and therefore, made it harder for Briseis to locate her.

It was this notion that had Briseis pushing her body to the limit as she trained vigorously with a battle axe. Thrust after powerful thrust tore through the air as she familiarised herself with the weight and feel of the wood and steel between her fingers.

Briseis moved gracefully and purposefully around the open yard before she unexpectedly lost her balance and went crashing to the floor. Ever watchful guards rushed to her side, but one wave of her hand had them hurtling back from the magical force with which she pushed them.

The Antonides Legacy I

She clutched her hand to her chest as she tried desperately to regulate her breathing. The air felt thick and her throat desert dry as images raced through her head. Lurid images of people and animals all cluttered together and a distinct banner that had her heart racing with added excitement even as she still struggled to breathe.

Willing herself to stay calm, she waited for the pain in her chest to subside before lying flat on the ground. She lay there for a long while, staring into the evening sky before slowly searching her brain for a course of action.

She needed to get word to Baron Dreston to apprehend the Redeemer but although her location had been revealed, her face had not. Briseis decided then that every Samaian woman would need to be captured to find out who the Redeemer truly was.

Prying herself up from the floor, she called for one of her fallen guards,

"Help me to the library," she said hoarsely as the now terrified guard approached her on unsteady feet.

Both armoured bodies made their way unsteadily towards the library where Briseis gratefully took her usual seat behind the large oak desk that held her most precious possession.

The Samaian spell book, a tome left behind years ago had become as necessary to her existence as breathing.

Although she mainly used it now for the travelling spell, she knew there were various other spells and incantations that could be useful to her. The travelling spell took too much preparation and energy; she needed something more efficient to let Baron Dreston know to capture the Samai.

At that moment she despised the Samai and the knowledge that some of the more powerful ones could communicate with their minds.

Apparently, it took years of training and a group of more talented individuals named Gifted to achieve such abilities. She could use that ability now but instead had to find something else.

Removing her Phyn leather armour to rest in the chair just in her underclothes, Briseis went through the book, page by page, looking for something that could be of use to her. She was there for hours before something finally jumped out at her.

Eagerly she roamed the words and illustrations on the page, "Mind Messaging?"

According to the book, Mind Messaging was a primitive form of mind communication in which the person wishing to relay a message could effectively create a message that could be sent magically to a person.

"Once the incantation is complete," she read. "Repeat your intended message to lock it in, then send to the intended recipient."

This was exactly what she needed Briseis thought as she read the words of the incantation to familiarise herself with them.

She had only ever used her physical power, and of course the travelling spell. She had yet to really delve into the spells and potions that many Samai were privy to.

When she felt herself ready, Briseis repeated the words of the incantation and when she did, repeated her message to send to Baron Dreston.

An image of herself suddenly appeared in front of her and as clear as she had just said them, repeated her message back to her.

"To Baron Lyon Dreston in Dreston City," her voice ringing clear despite the excitement of having completed the spell.

Her image slowly shrunk into a tiny ball of bright light, that shot out of the window and into the night.

***

"How long has she been doing this?" Rayne demanded as she barged into Dana's room the following evening.

Dana said nothing as she sat upright in her bed.

"Thea help me, *speak* child!"

Dana bolted up out of her bed and rushed to answer the now raging older woman standing in front of her.

"She made me promise not to say anything, she didn't want you to try and stop her."

"Of *course*, I would have tried to stop her, she isn't ready! Not nearly as ready as she could have been had Avriel done her job correctly!" Rayne was clearly furious as she began to pace the small bedroom but Dana had to ask,

"What's happening?" Rayne, turned her angry eyes on Dana, pointing her finger at her accusingly.

"What's happening is that Trista is going to get herself *killed*! I can feel her getting up to something, but I can't stop it!" Dana was confused but said nothing,

"Where is she now?"

"I don't know,"

"I am not in the mood for games Dana!"

"I swear I don't know! She said she was going to The Swan and that she'd be back by dinner."

"Fine, I'll find her myself!"

Rayne marched from the room leaving the door wide open. Quickly, Dana rushed on some trousers, tunic and boots, and followed Rayne out of the door. She kept her short brown hair from her face with a tight band, her flush face exposed as she found Rayne in the middle of the foyer with her eyes closed and her arms outstretched. Dana watched her for a moment and realised that there was shield around her that seemed to pulsate like a faint humming.

Dana reached out to touch it and sure enough, the immediate space around Rayne rippled like the surface of a pond.

Suddenly Rayne opened her eyes and the field seemed to disappear.

"She's in the First Quarter," Rayne snapped with agitation and strode purposefully into her private rooms.

These specific rooms were where Dana and Rayne conducted their lessons, as this was where Rayne kept her most treasured and rare ingredients.

While learning the basics of healing, Dana had come across many exotic things that Rayne explained she would not have been allowed to handle even if she was a Samai. There were dangerous things in here that she had no business dealing with.

"Get in here and help me instead of lurking in doorways!" Dana stumbled into the room and stood by Rayne obediently,

"What can I do?"

"Whatever I tell you to. We need someone to realise what danger Trista has put us in!"

"Danger?"

"Yes Dana, danger."

Rayne stopped herself for a moment as though realising who she was speaking to. Her long white and black hair was as wild as her eyes but as she took a deep breath, Dana watched Rayne instantly calm down.

"Trista, in trying to become a hero has put herself, us and the Samai in Dreston in danger. When they catch her – and they will catch her – where does that leave us, where does it leave Mortania?" Rayne whirled around the room like a tornado as she took things from shelves both physically and magically and placed them on the table in front of Dana.

"Trista has made it necessary for you to leave here."

"Leave, and go where?"

"Priya, there you will find a man named Gorn. He was Captain of the Guard during Alexander's reign and led the Royal Army. He fought beside Alexander at the Battle at the Wide until he was injured. He will protect you and teach you how to fight when magic may fail you."

"Fight?"

"Will you *stop* repeating everything I say?" Rayne screamed at her.

Dana's mouth slammed shut as she looked away embarrassed.

Rayne took a deep breath and walked over to Dana and pulled her into a hug, before letting go to cup her face in her hands.

"I'm sorry Dana," Dana was too shocked by this unusual behaviour from Rayne who was always surly if not moody at the best of times. The older woman's hands were rough to the touch, but it was such a loving embrace, she didn't notice for too long.

"I don't mean to take my frustrations out on you but I'm so…" she trailed off before pulling Dana away from her to look into her eyes. She conjured a small smile,

"I just want Trista to be okay…will you help me?"

Dana nodded and walked with Rayne back to the table where an assortment of ingredients lay haphazardly on top of it.

"Trista is in the First Quarter and from what I could tell, she's in trouble." Dana's eyes widened,

"What kind of trouble?"

"Trouble that she won't be able to get out of on her own." Rayne gestured to the ingredients on the table. "We'll have to rescue her, but when we do; we'll need to get away from Dreston as quickly as possible…this potion will do that."

Dana looked down at the ingredients and saw a few she recognised: vervain, ginger root and fish scales to name a few.

"This spell usually takes a day or two, if you want it done right but we don't have the time so we're going to do something a little different…and Enflame."

"You said that was dangerous, that you hadn't done it in so long, it might hurt you."

"Do you have a better idea?" Dana sighed but shook her head. "Then let's begin."

***

"Get away from here your highness!"

"No, I will not leave you!"

Trista was caught up in the anarchy that was a brawl in the middle of the street between the Samai and the city guards.

Out of nowhere they had begun to capture young Samaian women and take them back to Dreston Castle.

What had started as liberating all people from being taken against their will, had turned into a search and rescue of all Samaian girls. Guards had rushed into house and stolen young women from their homes and Trista couldn't continue to let it happen.

There were hundreds of people now in the crowded streets; women screaming for their children and their men trying to hold them back from a futile fight. Once the guards had seen that the Samaian men were not fighting back, they started to mock them and make inappropriate gestures towards the young women whose fathers and brothers were among the crowds. Unwilling to step away from this blatant show of disrespect something had snapped in a young man who was made to watch a guard, take advantage of his sister. He had lunged after the guard and to protect him, others had joined in.

Now that retaliation had begun, it was slowly developing into an all-out war.

Trista had been in the First Quarter when she saw some girls being ushered away. Without thinking she had run into a guard and on connection used her power to knock him to the ground. The guard, bewildered for a few moments, had cursed at her before Trista had taken hold of the girls' hand and disappeared into the crowd before heading back for another.

"You need to get out of here your highness,"

"I can't just leave. This is my fault for taking her, what if someone else gets hurt because of me?"

"That is a chance we are all willing to take,"

"I won't let anyone get hurt because of what I did!"

"How do you plan to stop it?" the man had questioned reasonably. Trista hadn't had an answer but instead turned away from him and back into the crowd of people.

Straining against her instinct to use her power that would undoubtedly bring further attention to herself and of course, endanger other Samai, Trista took to more subtle means. She stunned guards with her powers; knocking them to the ground, hurtling them through small crowds, compelling them to forget what they were doing; anything that distracted them from fighting against her people.

On and on she went, plowing through guards with a few men that had chosen to stay by her side. When all the girls she had seen were safely hidden away, Trista and the four men heading in another direction towards another Gathering.

As they sped through the narrow city streets; a funny feeling bubbled inside of her and she looked directly up into the sky.

Directly overhead, a ball of light shot across the sky into the direction of Dreston Castle.

"We have to go princess! There are others near the Castle!"

Trista brought her attention back to earth; she had to get to the castle; to save more girls and find out what that light meant.

PRISONER

Her subtle use of power was slowly draining her as well as the physical exertion of fighting off fully-grown men.

More than once Trista had struggled to break free of the hold of a guard without the help of her powers and the other Samai. She was not sure if the other Samai were able to use their power or not and so was left to that on her own.

Trista and her currently unnamed companions barged through another crowd as three guards dragged a screaming woman from her home. Three small children watched from the door of the tiny house, the oldest one; a boy no older than eight held his baby sibling in his arms.

Trista's heart broke at the scene in front of her.

This could not be happening to her people and it wouldn't happen any longer, "STOP!"

Trista could not have stopped herself if she tried as the force of her words came out as physical power and pushed all the people in her immediate vicinity clear across the trampled street.

Where she'd not controlled her magic, the power almost recoiled into itself and knocked her to the ground as well; winding her

Trista was stunned as she lay on the ground, her vision blurry and for a second, she felt as though the ground was trembling beneath her. She struggled to get up, to at least check on the people around her but when she was finally level and her vision less blurry, the sight she was met with terrified her.

The ground *was* trembling; with the weight of hundreds of Dreston guards storming towards them on foot and horseback.

They crowded the small street,

"Desist this treason immediately!"

More and more guards flooded into the street and dragged everyone, women, men and children into approaching cages.

They were clearly reinforcement for the trouble erupting around the city. Everyone around was either too weak or to overpowered by Dreston guards to do anything including Trista. Her mind was still fuzzy as her heart rate increased while more soldiers stormed in.

Trista tried to scramble to her feet, but her head was screaming with pain as she got onto her hands and knees to crawl away. Strong metal covered arms grabbed hold of her,

"Let go of me!" she tried to fight but she had no more fight left as the guard threw her into the back of a cage with other men and women and locked the door behind her.

"To the castle!" the guard bellowed, and the wheeled prison took off for the hill.

***

The first thing Trista realised was that she was freezing.

To gain some feeling in her frozen fingers, she tried to move them but the pain that shot up her arm felt like prying open a rusty portcullis.

When that proved too much effort and pain, she tried to open her eyes and even that was a trial. Slowly, she lifted her eyelids as far as strength would allow and looked around.

Her vision was hazy but she made out the smoky shapes of other bodies huddled together. Whether to help warm themselves or from fear, she had no idea, but they did not seem to be moving.

Opening and closing her eyes in order to get some feeling in them, Trista finally realised that her vision wasn't obscure because of any effect on her but because it was dark.

Adjusting to the limited light, Trista finally noticed the single ray of faint light directed straight into the far corner of the room. Raising her head, she saw that it came from a tiny circular opening in the wall high above them. Too high for anyone to reach she could tell as it did not cast enough light into the room for her to see clearly. If she looked away, it disappeared.

Turning her head to the left, she finally noticed a large bolted metal door and knew what happened.

She was in a dungeon.

The events before she had woken suddenly came rushing back to her. The City Guard had captured her, but when and how long had she been here?

Desperately, Trista closed her eyes and tried to feel her power but that proved impossible.

She was completely drained.

She had not known it was possible; taking its presence for granted but it was depleted. A damning thought entered her head that if she couldn't feel it then, maybe Rayne wouldn't be able to and she would have no way of finding her.

She knew Rayne was powerful, but she had been restricted for many years. Did she still have the same breadth of power that she once did? There were many things she couldn't do anymore simply because the power wasn't capable in the hands of Man.

Trista was weak, physically and mentally and couldn't find her power to assist her. What could she do? She attempted to uncurl herself from the floor when her foot hit something,

"Sorry," she croaked, feeling as though she hadn't spoken in years.

Her throat burned with the effort it took to speak that one word.

"I have had worse," a deep voice said quietly. Trista tried to sit up, but her head immediately began to pound.

"Easy princess," the deep voice spoke again as large hands grasped her shoulders to steady her.

Now upright, he leant her back against the cold stonewall but kept his arm around her. Exhausted, Trista found herself leaning onto the shoulder of a man she couldn't see.

"Where are we?"

"The dungeons of Dreston Castle."

Shit!

"How long?"

"Just the night. They have been taking us one by one."

"Where?" The man was silent for a moment,

"We don't know. We hear cells open and then voices...a few screams, the cell closes and then.... nothing."

Trista tried to sit up in defiance, but the man stayed her with a firm but gentle hand.

"We have to get out!" she hissed at him

"How princess?" Regrettably she had no answer, "We are weak, now more than ever and not just the few of us that still have the power. Our people have been away from the Everlasting so long, it has even left some of us."

"That can happen?"

"It is how we are weakened and without constant use..."

"How can you just accept this?"

"What choice do we have until you are able to restore the power?"

That shut her up.

As much as these people may be willing to fight for themselves, they would always be at a disadvantage because of her.

Until she got to Tirnum and reclaimed the Everlasting, they would continue to deteriorate.

"Your return is what keeps us going.... most of us. The hope that one day…" he was cut off by a cacophonous bang that shook the dark cell.

Dust fell from the ceiling and clung to the thick putrid air that surrounded them and what sounded like a young woman or maybe a small child started to cry. Outside the cell, sounds of metal boots and dragging chains echoed through the walls and into their bones.

As the man had told her, Trista caught the screams and protests from men and women that were subsequently drowned out by the guards herding them.

Soon it was silent again and fear settled on them once more. Trista, without a word shuffled closer to the man who held her tightly against him.

***

The day drew on until the one ray of light that entered the dungeon was snuffed out and Trista knew it was night.

Their cell had been opened six more times throughout the day and each time people had been dragged away screaming, never to return. It was the unknown that scared them the most, even if the guard was not particularly violent; they screamed and protested. Were they being taken for execution; sold into slavery? It wasn't common or popular but not entirely unheard of.

The cell door closed again and was securely bolted, making the cell shake with the force of it. The air seemed to vibrate with the fear that hummed within it.

It was suffocating and gripped the prisoners like a vice. Baby cries from far away could no longer be heard, instilling a new sense of dread into everyone else.

It was this rigid fear that kept them silent, afraid that any sound would bring their seemingly certain demise closer to them.

"Where do you live Kemar?" Trista asked her new friend. She had grown accustomed to his deep voice, it calmed her even when she was so scared that she thought it might swallow her whole.

"I live in Mortansport on the coast. I'm a baker there with my wife and son…he's about your age," he chuckled. "I was here visiting my cousin and got caught up in the raid."

Trista felt guilty. All of this was her fault and innocent people like Kemar were suffering. Saying nothing she moved closer to him and he squeezed her tight, just as he did, each time she held him.

It was in this contemplative silence as Kemar ate his meal with one hand as he held her, that a thunderous explosion rattled their bones. Screams echoed all round as everyone tried to shield themselves from the scattered debris.

Moonlight covered them instantly, almost blinding them from the roof that had been ripped away, exposing them to the night sky and air. They scrambled over each other to get away from the falling stone, but some were not as lucky as others.

The gaping hole didn't register for a moment until men started charging through it. It was only when these same men began to try and lift people to their feet, did they realise that they were not guards.

"GET UP NOW, WE HAVENT MUCH TIME!"

Pandemonium ensued as adrenaline took over and got the prisoners into action. Determination got them to their feet, but urgency kept them moving when they heard the distinct sound of swords clashing.

This rescue attempt was going to cost more innocent lives, Trista thought as Kemar helped her to her feet and for the first time she looked up into the face of her protector.

Despite the chaos around them, Trista smiled at him. He had long black hair caught in a messy and dusty ponytail and an overgrown beard with piercing green eyes like all Samai.

"Come," he urged her with a kind smile as they attempted to join the exodus.

Trista could barely see or breathe but she kept going, relying on Kemar's strength to help her along.

"I can't," she wheezed but Kemar did not let her go,

"Yes, you can!" Kemar practically dragged her so she had to keep pushing.

As they ran with the developing crowd, she saw villagers helping others out of destroyed cells like her own.

The walls of the cells all seemed to open up to a central courtyard that was now littered with stone and bodies buried beneath them.

The sounds of clashing swords grew louder as they emerged into the centre of the courtyard and made to climb over a mountain of stone to the other side.

Another explosion rattled them with more screams and cries for help. Trista caught a glimpse of a man fighting a city guard with a pitchfork but couldn't afford to watch.

All around them people were running and fighting, either trying to make or prevent an escape. Flaming torches lit up the courtyard and the frightened faces making the whole affair look something out of a nightmare.

They kept running, past guards and men to preoccupied with fighting to stop everyone until they got to the pile of stone and began to climb over it.

Kemar helped her as ever, pulling her with him as she found her footing to climb over the rocks. As they scrambled with more ease down the other side, they saw a large arched doorway. It loomed high above them as the prisoners hurriedly made their way through, a few men on each side, holding the large solid oak doors open.

They were sweating with the force of holding it open against the mechanism that was trying to close it and Trista knew they were running out of time.

Once on the other side of the archway, Trista saw carriages of people being loaded to get away from the castle. Torches were everywhere like vicious stars as people were frantic to escape.

Kemar immediately made for one but someone grabbed Trista's arm and pulled her from his grip.

"KEMAR!"

"TRISTA!"

She heard him but within seconds she couldn't see him. With the little strength she had left, she tried to break free but the hand, held fast, pulling her along into the throng.

"KEMAR!"

"TRISTA!"

Again, she heard him, but it was faint and faded into the clamour of rushing escapees.

The person who pulled her, she could see now was hooded in a dark cloak and continued to pull her until they came upon a smaller cart with one horse strapped to it.

"Let go of me!"

"I'll do no such thing!" the person turned, and Trista saw Rayne's blazing green eyes glaring at her. Shocked, Trista lost herself and fell to the ground with relief and exhaustion.

The person pulled back their hood and Trista's eyes widened as she slumped to the ground,

"Get up girl, we don't have much time!" Rayne screamed at her but before she could respond, another pair of arms wrapped a blanket around her and led her towards the cart,

"Dana?"

"I'm here, quickly let's get you on the cart," she said soothingly, leading her to the back of the cart. Once Trista was safely on the back, Dana climbed in after her while Rayne jumped onto the driver's bench and whipped the horse into motion, riding off into the darkened surrounding lands of Dreston Castle.

They weren't riding long before they realised that the shouts and screams from the city were not fading but slowly catching up to them,

"We're being followed!" Dana called out to Rayne.

Armoured guard were in pursuit, intent on capture but Trista was no more capable to defend them, then she had been before being captured.

"Rayne!"

"I know Dana! Yah!"

Rayne pushed the horses as far as they would go, into the vast surrounding lands of the castle. Dreston Castle, though on a hill had many woods and farming land neighbouring it. Through these woods, one could get back into the city if they knew how. Rayne steered the horse as fast as it could go towards a small street that opened into the city. It was as close to the city walls as they had ever been, racing along the perimeter of the large city until they emerged into a main street in the First Quarter.

Rayne continued racing through the city streets are fast as space and people traffic would allow until they finally approached the fourth and final quarter of Dreston City.

Rayne held out her palm and the large city gates began to open. The guards in the watch towers above looked at the mechanism in shock before trying in vain to turn it back again.

They didn't need to be open for long as Rayne and the girls rushed through and Rayne disengaged her power from it, making the gate close again.

They sped into sparse lands around Dreston until Rayne reined the horse in until it came to a stop and she climbed down from the helm.

"Now Dana!" Rayne called out and Dana seemed to change right before Trista's eyes.

Gone was the panicky, quiet girl and in her place was a determined woman filled with purpose. Dana let go of Trista to shuffle to the edge of the cart and began to take small items out of a sack.

"Dana.... what are you doing?" Trista croaked,

"Helping," Dana replied as she began to arrange the small items she took from the sack.

Rayne was now at the open end, rolling her long sleeves up to her elbows, and outstretched her arms.

"Dana...I'm cold,"

"It's okay", Dana said from somewhere above her head. "It will be over soon.

Rayne was now with her back to them and her arms still wide. The girls watched as her long hair begun to billow all though there was no wind.

The Antonides Legacy I

The warm desert air was calm as still waters, the moonlight casting an ongoing light onto the plain wasteland that surrounded them.

The city could still be seen off in the distance, the towers of Dreston Castle, the clearest of all.

The dust around the cart suddenly began to writhe making the horse rear a little but was held firm by the fastenings on either side.

There was a quick flash of light and then what sounded like thunder before a strong wind picked up, surrounding the cart.

"Dana, what's happening?" Trista panicked but Dana just held her tighter,

"It will be okay just hold on Trista please."

The cart began to tremble with the force of the air around it, while in front of them, just outside of the vortex, Rayne still stood with her arms outstretched.

Trista watched as Rayne brought her arms in and she thought folded them, across her chest but she could not be sure. As she did so, the stones that Dana had taken out of her satchel suddenly began to glow. They shone a clear white light that grew clearer and brighter. They got so bright; the girls had to shield their eyes just before catching a glimpse of Rayne exploding into for fear of being blinded.

"Trista?"

Slowly Trista opened her eyes, trying to shield from the light but needing to look at Rayne. When she finally opened her eyes wide enough, Rayne was kneeling in front of her on the back of the cart and Dana was still by her side.

"Be safe little princess," Rayne murmured softly. "You have to leave me now but Gorn will protect you from now on. He is a good friend and a good man; he will tell you all that I was not able to share with you. Hopefully I will see you again and it will be in your rightful place as Queen."

It was only as Rayne began to disappear that Trista realised it was not the physical person in front of her.

"Rayne…Rayne!"

Rayne was gone but the lights from the stones were too bright once again.

Squinting to try and find Rayne, Trista caught a glimpse of her arms shooting out again and when they did, there was a clap of thunder and everything went black.

ALLIES

Lamya was worried. She had felt Trista's powers steadily fading and although it concerned her, it was terrifying now that it had simply disappeared.

Those not practised in the ways of magic or Empathy, as so few were, it was hard to explain what it was that she felt. The best way she had discovered to really explain the feeling was that it was a presence.

It was the knowledge that you could physically feel someone without them being near you. The type of feeling that some humans said they experienced, for example when a loved one had passed away.

When the individual in question was good-natured and harnessed the power they possessed for good, then this presence could be pleasant and even quite calming.

If, on the other hand the person used their powers for evil then that presence was completely dark. For someone not practised in the way of cloaking this presence, then that darkness could be very intrusive and drive people down dark paths. Over the years, Lamya had perfected her cloaking skills and knew how to push them away from her consciousness.

Now, there was no good or bad presence for Trista, just...nothing.

She had completely disappeared from her consciousness and although it scared her, she knew with no uncertainty that Trista was not dead.

That was something that she would be able to feel without question. The moment the Redeemer died would have a domino effect that would be undeniable; a shifting in the balance of magic.

Time was most definitely of the essence, and Lamya grew considerably frustrated with the fact that she had no real place in the order of things.

She was restless and after speaking with Alexia, she was anxious to get to Trista and assist her in the training that she was clearly lacking.

That was another worry for her: why Avriel had not trained Trista as she had been instructed to do?

Despite herself, the sinister notion that Avriel had intentionally neglected her responsibility to Trista wouldn't leave her.

What reason could Avriel have had for doing so?

She had been loyal to the crown while she had lived in Tirnum and for the years since her relocation to Remora.

It was unusual for a woman of Avriel's status to move to such a remote part of the country, but it was not unheard of. There had to be some explanation for why Avriel had abandoned her duty to the crown.

Lamya lay in her bed that evening looking at the tattered ceiling above her. The inn she occupied was a nice enough establishment but there was much to be desired in the way of maintenance.

While the hospitality, food and lodging was welcoming, tasteful and comfortable, it seemed they neglected the parts that were out of sight or reach. She sat staring at a particularly interesting cobweb in the corner of a rafter when she faintly heard her name.

In the split second that it took to realise the voice had not come from anywhere in the room but inside her head, Lamya closed her eyes and let herself drift into a meditative state. Taking deep and calming breaths, she soon reached a practiced state of complete awareness. She had studied and practiced this

The Antonides Legacy I

form of communication for many years at the Academy and so this was not as hard as it had once been.

Lamya concentrated and the voice in her head was as clear as if the person were sitting next to her.

"Lamya"

"I am here, Justice Lorien."

"Good, you can hear me clearly?"

"Of course," there was some murmuring before another presence entered her head making her smile but was then immediately weary, "Chief Justice Yeng?"

"Yes Lamya"

"I hope you are well?"

"I am fine, but there are a few urgent things we need to discuss," the older woman said before Lorien spoke again.

"Lamya, we are very pleased with your progress to Thea's Point, as well as your meeting with former Ambassador Alexia, but I am afraid there is no time for lengthy celebrations."

"What is wrong Justice Lorien?"

"You must leave Thea's Point as soon as possible and meet the Princess in Crol. You must be there waiting for her once she is on the move to Thelm…to us."

"How much time do I have before she arrives? Where is she now?"

There was a moment of silence before Lorien continued,

"We have lost sight of her momentarily, but we believe she will be in Priya to begin her training with former General Antos."

"You believe? Why don't you know?"

"I do not think it your place to…"

"Lorien stop," Yeng cut over him. "Lamya has every right to ask any questions of us. She is on this mission and as such should not be kept in the dark." There was no disagreement from Lorien, but he did not speak.

"Lamya," Yeng said to her. "We believe the princess is in trouble. She was last seen in Dreston but was very weak."

Lamya understood that by seeing, the Council might that they had felt her presence there. "Moments before we lost sight of her completely, her presence was...faint to say the least. We know the logical path of her training why we believe that she would go to Priya."

Lamya was frustrated but didn't say anything. Having just irritated a high-ranking member of the Council, she decided against asking any further questions.

"You must travel to Crol," Lorien re-entered the conversation. "Once there, we will contact you again."

"Yes, Justice Lorien."

Without another word, Lamya felt Lorien's presence move out of her mind but Yeng still waited behind.

"You have done well Lamya, very well."

"Thank you, Chief Justice,"

"He's gone now, Grandmother will do!"

"Well thank you Grandmother," Lamya laughed. "I have missed you, are you sure you are alright?"

"All the better for hearing your voice my dear but I must not stay long. Lorien is correct in that you must move quickly. The princess may be in danger and will need any help you can provide her."

"Yes Grandmother,"

"I regret that we cannot give you much more to work with but in these present times, our power and reach are limited."

"I understand, but Grandmother, something worries me."

"What is it?"

The Antonides Legacy I

"Avriel Remora, I assume you realise that she did not train Trista in her magic?"

"We do. We learned this once we established the connection with Trista's presence after she had Ascended." Lamya was instantly outraged,

"You've known for that long and did nothing?"

"Lamya, you have to understand that we have only recently be given the resource with which to know and understand how to observe Trista, and even then, we cannot interfere."

"Cannot or will not?"

"Cannot, we do not have the necessary power. Communicating amongst our kind and the other Council members is one thing but to enter the mind of a Samai; and especially one who is not aware of their potential is quite another. Only now we have been able to observe her and even that has been taxing. Her time in Remora was completely shielded from us and those who would help her."

"I see," Lamya sighed.

Although she was certain her Grandmother would not lie to her, it was still unsettling to accept that they had been unable to intervene until now.

"Why do you think Avriel neglected her duties?"

"That is something we will have to discuss further."

"Yes, Chief Justice."

Lamya knew the formality was back when her Grandmother did not correct her.

"As always, I will protect and watch over you as well I can but will never interfere."

"I know, and I am grateful for it."

She would never wish anyone to believe she had achieved anything because her Grandmother was the Head of the Council.

"And that is why you warm my heart. I must go; there is much to do here for the princess's arrival. We shall speak soon,"

"We will," Lamya felt her grandmother's love and warmth reach out to her before the presence moved from her mind and she instantly woke up.

"Let's find a ship shall we."

ENEMIES

The situation was becoming a lot more complicated than Briseis had originally thought. She was becoming more than a little irritated at the sudden turn of events.

On the wings of a swift raven, Baron Dreston had let her know that the Samaian Redeemer had yet to be apprehended. While he was doing all, he could by capturing the women, none had shown the power or sign that they were the heir.

Still, it didn't mean she wasn't still out there, mocking Briseis in her failure to capture her.

When she had completed the Mind Messaging spell and knew it had been delivered to the Baron, Briseis had felt the most potent and amazing power before it disappeared again.

There was a concentration of power in Dreston that was now nowhere to be found having reached a zenith that she had not felt before. The significance of this power was obvious as there was no other reason for that type of power to be present in Mortania.

Other than her father, herself and the small fighting force that Briseis was trying to create out of the newly empowered youth in the capital, no one had used the Everlasting for any significance in eighteen years.

Other than it being forbidden in many cities and towns, the Samai who had been able to wield it before the uprising could no longer do so. The power had been drained from them so spectacularly that as the years went by, most could not use it potently enough even if they wished to.

Briseis knew however that this was not an exhaustive rule.

The minute any Samai chose to regroup in any way, they could easily help each other grow in strength.

They could not create the same level of power that they would have from the Everlasting, but not all strength or power was physical. The slightest indication that one or more had control of the power and of course if the Everlasting were ever back in their possession, the Samai would be a force to once again be reckoned with.

Hope was as powerful a weapon as any sword or spell.

Briseis knew that this hope would drive Samaians out of hiding to follow their saviour. This woman was determined, she knew that at least because each time she felt the power, it was only getting closer. Undeterred by this, Briseis was determined not to be threatened was instead planning to be fully prepared.

She had to contact Baron Dreston again. She couldn't sit around waiting for the Redeemer to be captured or for them to arrive on the castle steps ready to take her crown.

Instead, she was going to be ready for that arrival.

Let the warrior come to her, and when they did, Briseis would have an army waiting for them.

Still, that army needed to be assembled and so, later that night she sent another Mind Message to Baron Dreston told him that he should send men to Tirnum in preparation for another civil war. In return, he would receive a handsome amount in gold, extended lands across Mortania and a place on the Royal Council for his efforts in this and the previous war.

She would have to wait for his response but there was no question on what it would be. He was a greedy and selfish man from what she had briefly heard of him and gold was the language he spoke.

With that done, Briseis called for Endora.

Endora entered the chamber promptly and bowed, "Yes your Highness?"

"Bring a palace scribe to my study, I wish to write a formal declaration."

"Yes your Highness," Endora hurried off and returned a few moments later with a palace scribe. He was one of the younger ones she had seen and so had a nervous look about him but bowed as was required.

"I wish the following to be sent to all Barons and Lords in the kingdom along with an edited, more succinct version posted around the country for the lowborn. I want this news on everyone's lips by the morning."

"Yes your Highness,"

"Good, you may begin with," she paused for a moment as she sat in a lounger against the wall and peered out of a small window.

"I, Princess Briseis Myrenda of Mortania, Duchess of Dyam and Lady of the Imperial Lands; heir to the House Greybold, summon you to our country's aid. The one many have named the Redeemer of the Samai has threatened our kingdom and I have accepted their declaration of war."

She thought about her next words before continuing,

"To defeat this threat to our homes and families and lands, I request you supply ten per cent of your defences to the Royal Army. While the Royal Army is fit to defend our walls and lands closest to the capital, where you will eventually be needed, we will need the reach of the capital to spread throughout Mortania."

She stood up then and paced the room for a moment,

"Send aid to the capital as soon as possible while enough are to remain who will defend your home territories against these savage invaders. Do this for your king and country and be rewarded in the knowledge of your impending victory as well as riches and station."

Briseis paused for a moment and looked around the study. She needed the aid of trained military men, but she also needed the help of the low people who ultimately made up more of the population. They would not accept this war as readily as the people, who would benefit from it,

"Close with my usual inscriptions and I will sign and seal the relevant copies. On the posters for the small folk, add the following. All men and women aged sixteen to forty-five must report to the capital for conscription into the Royal Army."

The scribe briefly looked at her in disbelief before turning back to his work. For once Briseis did not rise to the occasion and continued,

"Any who do not adhere to this summons will be sent to the city cells to await hanging."

The scribe had the sense not to look up this time and Briseis smiled. She was not a fool to believe that the kingdom loved or respected her but that did not matter.

If they did what they were required to do, she had no need for their love, just their obedience.

The following morning Briseis sat in the Great Hall having breakfast when the large door crashed open and Curian marched in. He reached where she sat at the far end of the table and smashed his fists onto the surface sending the cutlery, crockery and food spinning across the table.

"YOU HAVE DECLARED WAR?"

"I see you have heard the morning news," she said reaching out for the slice of bread that had been on her plate and proceeded to butter it.

"Are you insane, what authority do you have to do this?" Briseis looked at him but said nothing. "Do you live to shame me, why would you make such a bold move as this?" Briseis chuckled,

"This is no game Briseis! To what end do you do this?"

"To what end, are you serious? I have declared war to stop this idiocy of the so-called Redeemer from continuing. I have felt their presence father and they are coming to take this throne!"

"They cannot win,"

"The words of a fool!" she spat at him. "I have managed to stay alert with my power and as such have felt their presence getting closer to Tirnum, to us and this crown. If you refuse to acknowledge the significance of this then I pity you. I pity you for the poor excuse of a man that you have become and the even worse example of a king."

Curian leaned back from the table from where he had been leaning down into Briseis' face. Her beautiful angelic face, so like her mother's that only knew how to spit fire and venom; poisonous words that only brought pain.

He felt the familiar heat of anger rise in his blood as he clenched his fist together and watched as the black flame grouped there then subsided.

"You will end this debacle Briseis and I will do my job as king, *not* you. Until the moment I take my last breath, you will never rule this kingdom. Never."

Briseis said nothing but had the decency to look away before Curian stepped away from her,

"As tradition states, you will retract this declaration of war as you were the one who declared it. You will do this immediately!"

Before Briseis could respond, a horn sounded indicating a messenger just before the green robed man entered. He bowed low to the two as they exchanged intense looks at one another but was reluctant to speak,

"Well, what is it?" Briseis barked at him, the first to break eye contact with her father.

"I-I have news your highness, news from Lord Weilyn of Thea's Point."

"What is it?"

"He would like you to know that his tithe will be in the capital at your disposal within a week. He would like to express that he will be at hand to aid you in this coming war against the Samaian threat."

Briseis turned to her father,

"Does he now?"

If it were not for the current situation, Curian would have been happy at the radiant smile that erupted onto Briseis' face. She stood up from her seat,

"Let Lord Weilyn know that the crown thanks him for his contribution, and we will call on him when he is needed again."

The messenger hurried away and Briseis once again turned to her father,

"You were saying?"

"This changes nothing, stop this now. You do not know what you're doing!"

"I know exactly what I'm doing. I'm stopping a threat from rising up and taking this throne directly from under us!"

"Maybe that would be best, the Gods know you do not deserve it!"

There was an eerie silence as his words penetrated the air and the implication of her father's words registered on Briseis's face.

"Then I guess I know whose side you're on now, Father."

Briseis walked away leaving Curian in her wake wondering what he had unleashed into the world.

The Antonides Legacy I

***

Baron Dreston had been entertaining the plain but gracious Geneiva Thelm for the past few days.

She had been less than responsive to the news of his practice of Gatherings and the outbreak the night before. It ceased to matter when he needed her for her father's cooperation and not her opinion.

In the few short days that he had spent in the young woman's company, he could see that his attention would not be held and would only grace her bed to perform his marital duties and produce the heir he needed to solidify his claim to the throne.

She sat across from him and her father that morning at breakfast, a picture of serenity and grace as he and Erik talked of the news that had just arrived,

"What army does she propose to fight?" Erik asked, throwing the declaration onto the tabletop.

"As of yet, I do not know. I have assisted her in the apprehension of Samaians that she deemed a threat, but I can only determine that these are no longer of consequence if they have declared war on us."

"We have heard nothing from the other Lords in the way of disruption. Do you think she's mad?" Dreston laughed,

"No, I do not think she is mad...just highly prepared as any good leader should be." Thelm looked unsure,

"You believe her to be a great leader?"

"I believe her to be better than her father at playing a strong hand and following through." Thelm nodded.

He had received the unusual message from the princess the night before and had already sent his promise of aid before the message had arrived this morning. He explained as much to Erik.

"What are you talking about? Why are you helping her, how will that further our own ends?"

"You wish me to decline the summons and bring the Princess's suspicions to our city steps?"

Dreston took a sip of his warm ale and reclined in his chair. "It is best we act from as close to the capital as we can Erik so we can know who we are up against."

"We know who we are up against, you just said so yourself!" Dreston chuckled,

"You worry yourself old man, we must play this smart if we are to get what we want."

"And playing smart is helping our enemies?"

"Playing smart is knowing the moves of your enemies before they do. The men we will send to Tirnum will be the same men who help defeat the Samai and then turn on the Royal Army in order to secure the throne when I arrive."

Dreston turned to Geneiva, who was sat beside him,

"What do you say to that my dear, how about a journey to our fair capital to test how our thrones will feel?"

"It will make me happy to do whatever you wish of me my Lord."

"Perfect. Ready the ships," he shouted to no one in particular. "We make way for Tirnum…our new home."

FINAL DESTINATION

If she was not dead, then death had to be better than this.

She was laying on the ground with her eyes shut and her head was pounding wondering how long she could continue to take head injuries like this.

When she could finally concentrate on something other than the pain shooting through her head, she noticed a multitude of sounds and smells that were at once unfamiliar.

Although she knew she was laying down, there was still an unnerving feeling of weightlessness and she could not determine if she was on her back, her side or on her front. Her head continued to scream at her with an ache that simultaneously seemed to pierce into her brain and behind her eyeballs.

Dana?

She knew she hadn't spoken the words aloud, but she heard them. She didn't care to find out what had happened right now, but she had to find out where Dana was.

Where's Dana?

Nothing else mattered for the moment but finding her friend but nothing seemed to be cooperating.

All she could do was think outward, but no movement was registering to her limbs. Trista tried to open her eyes but the sliver of light that entered was so excruciatingly painful, she clamped them shut again.

Dana, where are you?
Trista? Is that you?
Dana?
Yes!
What's happening?
I don't know…I don't know anything.

Dana's voice disappeared from her mind and she almost screamed with the fear that it wouldn't return,

Dana…Dana!

There was nothing but her own voice until she distinctly felt herself rise off the ground. She tried to fight but her limbs were completely immobile,

"I've got you,"

Who are you?

"Robin! Get help quickly"

The person was practically screaming at her and the pain was unbearable.

Too loud, you're just too loud

"Oh my Gods…what has happened?"

"I don't know, let's get them home. Quickly!"

No, not home. Who are you? Leave me alone, where is Dana? We need to see Gorn, Rayne said to meet Gorn. Go away!

"She's trying to say something; I can't make it out. Robin leave the other one, she's stable. Get help!"

Get Gorn, he must be here. Where are you taking us! Bring me to Gorn!

"We need to get her to a healer now or she won't make it, there's too much blood."

Blood? No, please…

"GORN!" Trista's eyes shot open with the strength it took her to scream that one word and as the word left her lips, she slumped back into oblivion.

The Antonides Legacy I

Pronunciation Guide

ANTONIDES - An-Toe-Nee-Deez
AVRIEL - Av-Re-El
BRISEIS - Brih-Say-Uss
CURIAN - Kerr-Ry-Yun
DRESTON - Dress-Tun
LAMYA - Lah-My-Ah
LYON - Lee-On
MORTANIA - Mor-Tan-Ya
PHYN - Fin
THEA - Thay-Yah
TIRNUM - Ter-Num

Printed in Great Britain
by Amazon